BRONZE AND BROKENNESS

- MIDIANITES -

LIGHT OF NATIONS
BOOK FOUR

CHRISTINE DILLON

LINKS IN THE CHAIN PRESS

In memory of my mother, Judy (1939—2024).
I am so thankful for your prayers, training, discipline, hugs, and many, many letters.
What a legacy you left in my life.
Thank you most of all for leading me to Jesus. That has made all the difference.

I will make you as a light for the nations,
that my salvation may reach to the ends of the earth.

Isaiah 49:6b (ESV)

Let them give thanks to the Lord for his unfailing love
and his wonderful deeds for mankind,
for he breaks down gates of bronze
and cuts through bars of iron.

Psalm 107:15-16 (NIV)

LIST OF CHARACTER AND PLACE NAMES

FICTIONAL **C**HARACTERS

Reuel — Midianite coppersmith from a long line of smiths tracing their ancestry back to Heber and Jael (Judges 4), Hobab and Jethro.

Jael — Reuel's wife.

Reba and Hanok — Reuel and Jael's two young sons.

Zura — Jael's elder sister. She is a member of their household because she is blind and unmarried. Zura also does the final polishing of all copper and bronze objects.

Abida — Reuel's father. A widower who has mostly retired from being a coppersmith.

Ephah — Reuel's elder brother. He lives with his father in Ramoth Gilead.

Zipporah — Ephah's wife.

Naftali — a wealthy customer and patron of Reuel's.

Dedan — a survivor of the battle with Gideon.

Dinah and Asher — a couple who show hospitality to Reuel.

BIBLICAL **C**HARACTERS (found in the book of Judges 4–8)

I have chosen to use more Hebraic-anglicized versions of the familiar names. This helps us approach the story with different eyes and hopefully makes the biblical parts, feel less familiar.

Gideon — from the tribe of Manasseh. Yahveh commissions him to fight against the Midianite/Amalekite coalition.

Purah — Gideon's servant.

There are many mentions of earlier historical characters — Avraham, Job, Hagar…

<u>**PLACE NAMES**</u>

Most of the action for this book takes place in the lands of Manasseh on the eastern side of the Jordan River. The cities of **Ramoth Gilead** and **Jabesh Gilead** are mentioned in particular.

PROLOGUE

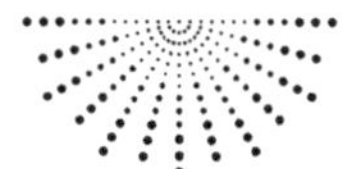

Near Heshbon, east of the Jordan River
Period of Judges, pre-1050 BC

"Aren't you ever going to get married?" Jael asked her elder sister, Zura, as they played in the shade under a gnarled oak tree.

There was a long pause as Jael looked up at her sister who was sitting motionless. A single tear welled up in Zura's eye. Jael took Zura's hand and stroked it. She hadn't meant to make her big sister sad.

"I doubt I'll ever marry," Zura said, her voice low.

"Why not? You're wonderful! Everyone loves you and the stories you tell."

Zura squeezed Jael's hand. "The problem is that parents want their sons to marry someone whole."

Jael pursed her lips. "Whole? I don't understand."

"My beloved sister, you look at me with the eyes of a girl and you see someone who plays with you and loves you. But other people don't have the same kind of eyes as you."

Jael frowned. "Their eyes look the same to me."

Zura sighed. "You see with the eyes of love. You don't see my blemishes."

"What's blem-lishes?"

Zura sighed. "When I was your age, I could see the blue of the sky, and the blush of pink that came on the apricots as they ripened. That all changed when …" Zura touched her face.

Jael winced as she remembered what Zura had told her about the boiling water and the pain. "When the lady made it so you can't see any more?"

Zura nodded. "No one wants a blind woman to marry their son. No one is willing to accept someone …" She hugged her arms around her middle. "Someone so scarred."

Jael hadn't thought about it. To her, Zura was simply her sister. A sister who cared, who never told Jael she didn't have the time for her. Jael looked at the doll in her lap. Zura had made it out of a small piece of sheepskin and fitted a wooden head on it. She'd even attached fine wool for hair. She'd told Jael how to mark on the eyes and mouth and nose. Jael took this doll everywhere. Before bed, she nestled it into a little cradle Zura had made. First thing in the morning, Jael reached out to stroke the doll's hair. Last thing at night, she whispered her good nights, just as Zura did for her.

Zura drew Jael into a hug. "But you will probably get married, my joyful one."

"I hope so," Jael mumbled as her face warmed. She was glad Zura couldn't see her blush. Jael might be young, but there was one boy she might want to marry. Reuel was tall with an unruly mop of curly dark hair. Already he was apprenticed to his father as a coppersmith. Their people had been wandering coppersmiths for generations. Zura's eyes might not be able to see but her hands were skillful when it came to copper. Jael had not forgotten how Reuel's father's eyes had opened wide when he had seen a sample of Zura's work. He'd immediately employed her to do all the finishing work which made their finished copper products shine.

Jael had first seen Reuel while visiting Zura at work. She might not have paid any attention to Reuel if he hadn't smiled at her, a smile that ensured she would remember him and want to see him again. Now she used any excuse to visit her sister's workplace, both guiding Zura to work and home again, and taking her food for her rest break. Some days Reuel noticed Jael, and some days he took no notice of her at all.

Zura pushed back a tendril of hair and straightened her back. "Time to help Ima with the meal."

Jael loved it when the three of them cooked together because Zura was often too busy nowadays with her work. When Father had been alive, Jael would have been given some small task to help, or she'd play on the floor with her doll and listen to the hum of conversation between her mother and sister. A gloom settled on Jael. Things had changed the day her father had died. When they heard him cry out in pain, Ima had rushed toward his workshop with Jael trying to keep up, but Father had stopped breathing before they could even reach him. As they had no brothers to carry on the smithing, Zura had gone to work for Reuel's family.

Jael helped Zura to her feet and packed away her doll, tucking it under one arm, and using her free arm to guide Zura home. Not that they had far to go. Being coppersmiths, they'd always lived in a tent and traveled wherever their work led them.

"Ima is making sure you're ready for marriage," Zura said. "You're doing well with your cooking. If you'd only concentrate, you'd keep things neat and tidy too."

Jael's face heated again. She had been dreaming rather than tidying yesterday, and Zura had tripped over a bowl that shouldn't have been in the middle of the doorway.

"Once you are betrothed you will leave us," Zura said.

Jael kissed her sister's hand. "I will never leave you. I need you."

"That's not how it works," Zura said. "A woman leaves her family and joins her husband's household."

Other people might leave, but Jael had no intention of abandoning her sister. It made sense if Zura was going to a home of her own, but if Zura couldn't marry, Jael wouldn't leave her behind. Ima said that life was hard for widows or unmarried women. Jael had heard Ima telling Reuel's father how grateful they were that he'd given Zura work. Especially now that they were in the middle of a drought. A drought that Zura said was because Israel had abandoned their worship of Yahveh, but that didn't make sense to Jael. Wasn't Baal the lord of these lands?

CHAPTER ONE

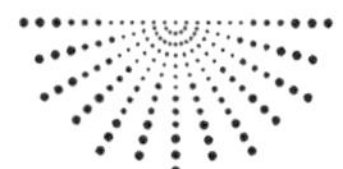

"Jael, how many times have I told you to tie that tighter?" Reuel said. "My mother—"

Jael blocked out the next few words. She was sick of hearing about Reuel's perfect mother. She barely remembered the woman, as Reuel's mother had died well before their marriage. Yet the dead woman had stalked her from the first morning after their wedding. Jael's cooking, Jael's housekeeping, Jael's mothering, and now even her camel loading was compared to Reuel's mother, and always came out in second place. According to Reuel, his mother had been perfect in every way. Apparently she had anticipated Reuel's every need. The woman couldn't possibly have been as perfect as Reuel remembered, but her death had elevated her above anything Jael could hope to achieve.

"Here, like this." Reuel pushed Jael aside and tied the leather straps.

Reuel didn't seem to understand that Jael wasn't as strong as him. Jael rubbed her hands together where the leather ties had cut into her hands. They were on the move again, and she'd been up since well before dawn cooking the food they needed along the way. They weren't moving far, just south through Manasseh's eastern territory to the city of Jabesh Gilead.

"Are the mirrors packed carefully?" Reuel asked.

Jael bit back a retort at his lack of trust in her. "They are wrapped in the softest of the clothing and buried deep in our packs." She'd even stitched a sackcloth bag around them.

Jael would never risk damaging the beautiful mirrors. The richest man in Jabesh had wanted something special for his only daughter's wedding, something no one else in the land had, something beautiful and not merely practical. He had mentioned to Reuel that he'd often seen his daughter trying to view her face in a pool of water and wondered if metal could be burnished to provide a viewing surface. Reuel had never been asked to make something so luxurious, but his father had once made a crude mirror at his mother's request, so he'd known the basic idea.

With such an important commission, Reuel had not risked making a single mirror, so he'd made two. One round, circled by a festoon of fruit, and one oval, surrounded by flowers. Each stood on a stand. Pride in her husband's craftsmanship had filled Jael's heart. Anyone who received such a mirror would be the envy of all the women around her. Jael stifled a sigh. Would Reuel ever make such a gift for her?

Reuel looked around their campsite, scanning the ground for anything that might have escaped their notice. Jael tried not to feel hurt, for he was redoing the task he'd already asked her to do. She had paced the ground, sharp-eyed, to spot any tool or tent peg they might have missed.

Reuel took a swig of water from the skin hanging off the lead donkey. "Are the boys ready?"

"I'll call them."

Jael walked toward the boys' favorite tree. "Reba and Hanok, we're about to leave."

"Do we have to?" Reba, the elder, whined. "We like this place."

So did Jael. This was one of the places she'd liked to have lingered. "We'll be back, but the mirrors have to be delivered, and there will be pots and pans waiting for us to repair."

There was a groan above Jael, and the branches shook as the boys began to climb down. Jael looked around as Zura came from behind the bushes and walked toward where the camels were snatching some last mouthfuls of dry grass. Moving camp was hardest on Zura because she couldn't see to help her adjust to a new campsite. Over the years, they'd learned to set up the tents in the same configuration each time, and they kept to the same circuit of towns: Jabesh Gilead, Ramoth Gilead, Mahanaim, Heshbon, and all the little places in between. They only went as far as Heshbon because Jael's mother had lived there until her death, and they still had customers there.

Other coppersmiths had their own circuits to travel, and Reuel made sure his family didn't stray into their areas.

The boys hung off the bottom branch and dropped to the ground. Jael brushed the leaves and bits of bark from their hair and took them by the hand to walk them toward their camel. They were often mistaken for twins although there were nearly two barley harvests between them.

Reuel coaxed the camel to sit. Zura found the wooden pommel and swung her leg over the saddle. Jael helped her smooth her skirt.

"Comfortable?" Jael squeezed her sister's hand, then picked up Reba and placed him in the special seat Reuel had fashioned.

Zura wriggled to find the best spot then reached to the side to tousle Reba's head. "We're off on adventures again. Back to the high country."

"I wish we didn't have to leave the river," Reba said as Jael placed Hanok in his matching seat on the other side of Zura. The boys sat with their backs to the camel and their eyes to the passing scenery. It worked well on long trips, as they always had something to look at and Zura enjoyed talking to them.

"Being beside a bigger river was good, wasn't it?" Zura said. "I'll miss it too, but we might find some streams where we're going."

"But they won't have pools because there hasn't been enough rain," Hanok muttered.

This year and last there had only been enough rain to settle the dust. The last time Jael had been inside an Israelite town there'd been murmurs the drought was because Baal had cursed these lands. The Israelites burned much incense and made many sacrifices to Baal, but nothing had worked.

Reuel came over to check that the boys were secure in their seats, then took the camel's lead rope and commanded it to rise.

"Yippee!" The boys enjoyed the sensation of being thrown forward then backward as the camel straightened its front legs to stand fully upright.

Reuel went to the first of their string of four donkeys, took up the lead and started off on foot. Jael followed. Three donkeys carried their tools and ores, and one carried their belongings, including extra clothing and cookware.

The two cooking pots were Jael's pride and joy and were stuffed with sackcloth to prevent them clanking.

Jael adjusted her head covering. It was going to be another scorching hot day. Already the cicadas were falling silent as the temperature rose. The hills ahead shimmered in the heat. It looked unlikely that things would be any cooler on the heights.

Zura still persisted in believing the drought was because the Israelites had abandoned Yahveh. Well, the Israelites were certainly not worshiping Yahveh nowadays. On the far side of the donkeys was a pile of stones and an old fig tree with a stone altar underneath. The flowers in front of the altar were fresh. Even from here, Jael could smell the drying blood from a recent sacrifice. Sourness rose in her throat. Blood sacrifice had always revolted her. One of the things she'd found attractive about Reuel was that he didn't bother with religion. He said a man should trust his own strength, not the stupid superstitions passed down from the elders.

Zura had warned Jael not to rush into marriage with someone lacking religion. Zura had wanted Jael to wait until she found someone who followed Yahveh, but Jael had as little time for Yahveh as she had for Baal, Asherah, and Astarte. They all demanded effort and hard-earned resources, and she didn't have the excess energy to bother. Baal hadn't brought rain despite the blood poured upon his altars, just as Yahveh hadn't healed Zura despite her faithful worship.

Once Reuel and Jael were married, Zura had never repeated her reservations about the marriage, but Jael knew Zura prayed for them every day. It irritated her, but she couldn't prevent Zura from praying, so Jael pretended she didn't know.

They passed another stone altar buzzing with flies. Ahead of them, the track began to zigzag up a hill. Reuel took the lead, and Jael plodded on in the rear. Reuel insisted the children be in the center for safety. For the past seven years, there had been increasing animosity against their people. Jael understood it, as her people, the Midianites, had joined with the Amalekites and were seizing their chance to gain the upper hand while the Israelites were weak.

Why couldn't people just live in peace? Why did men always want power and refuse to be content with the way things were? Reuel wasn't any better. He delighted in the current rise to power of their own people. Yet, as far as Jael could see, such struggles only made life more dangerous for ordinary folk. Struggles sowed distrust, and distrust impacted their livelihood.

CHAPTER TWO

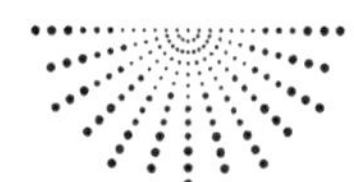

As they approached the city of Jabesh Gilead, Reuel felt the pulse pounding in his neck. Nowadays he never knew what the situation would be in a city. Would they be welcomed or turned away? More importantly, was there danger for his family? He'd heard of Midianites being spat upon or beaten. In former times, they could walk safely into any Israelite city and be welcomed. Welcomed because people wanted their wares, whether knives for ceremonial or practical use, bells for their livestock, or plainer items for daily use. People used to only cook on a hot stone, but now wealthier folk wanted a bronze pan.

It hadn't mattered that Reuel was an outsider. A Kenite, one of the many tribes of Midianites. The Kenites were related to Mosheh, the man who had rescued his people from Egypt and brought them to the boundaries of the land promised to Avraham centuries before. His successor, Yehoshua had been a great leader too. He'd led the conquest of the peoples of Canaan. But the greatness of Mosheh and Yehoshua was long gone. The Israelite culture and beliefs had weakened as they lived among a mix of peoples, adapting and taking on many of their customs, their ways of life, and even their gods.

And into the gap left by such weakness, Reuel's people had seized the chance to take all they could. The Israelites would never have been happy about being raided, but the fact that Reuel's people allied themselves with the Amalekites—that had really stirred things up. Now the Israelites locked themselves in their towns and hid their crops rather than allow them to be taken.

If his customers hadn't liked and trusted Zura and Jael, Reuel doubted he would be able to sell anything at all. Reuel stopped the donkeys, reached into a pack, and pulled out a bronze gong. Standing well out of the arrow-range of the walls of Jabesh Gilead, he set the gong on a rock and struck it once, then twice more. The bong-bong-bong reverberated off the city walls.

"Abba, can I hit it?" Reba asked from his seat atop the camel.

"Later, son. I'm hoping the buyer of the mirror hears our signal." The signal that had been Jael's idea. As animosity towards them had grown more tense, she'd made the sensible suggestion that whenever they arrived at a town, they should sound the gong to alert potential customers of their arrival. It was certainly much easier than pounding on heavy wooden gates and risking something being dropped on them from above.

Reuel waited. Seeing no reaction from anyone in the town, he struck the gong a few more times.

Still no response.

Reuel spat into the dust. He'd be angry if the mirror he'd spent so long crafting was no longer wanted. It was the most expensive item he'd ever made. Although his customer, Naftali, was wealthy, the man had had plenty of time to change his mind. It was even possible the wedding might have been called off. It wasn't unusual for one of the parties to die before a wedding day. Accidents or illness so often snatched life away.

With a creak, the city gate opened a little and a small group emerged. One carried a rolled-up carpet. Others in the group were laden with various skins or containers. Reuel straightened as he recognized Naftali, the father of the bride.

If only the children would stay quiet. Reba had once ruined a sale by commenting loudly about a wart on a man's nose. If Reuel remembered correctly, Naftali had a similar blemish. Reuel glanced toward the camel and his shoulders relaxed. Zura was playing some sort of game with the boys and keeping them occupied. Good woman.

"Jael, can you get the mirrors ready to display?" Reuel asked in a voice that wouldn't carry to the approaching men.

His wife nodded and moved toward the donkey carrying the mirrors.

Reuel watched the approaching group until they were close enough to speak and be heard.

"Greetings, Reuel, greetings," Naftali said.

Reuel inclined his head and bowed. From the early days of his apprenticeship, his father had impressed on him the need to always make the customer feel superior.

"Sorry for the delay in welcoming you." Naftali shrugged and spread out his hands. "But nothing is as it used to be. Our chieftain no longer permits us to leave the city gates open during the day." His tone suggested he didn't agree with his chieftain's policy. "It is disastrous for the sales of any goods. We are now cut off from most news, so I didn't know you were due today."

In the past, a man such as Naftali would have had many people eager to tell him about the movements of people through the area.

"We have brought the item you requested," Reuel bowed. "In fact, I have made two so that you can choose your favorite."

Two of the men who'd accompanied their master had unrolled the carpet, set up a covering to give some shade, and poured drinks and laid out dried figs and pistachios. Naftali gestured toward the carpet and led Reuel into the little patch of shade cast by the covering. Behind them, Jael came forward, now fully veiled and carrying the two sackcloth-bound mirrors. Tucked under her arm was a soft polishing cloth.

She handed Reuel the first package, and he pulled the fastenings and unwrapped the round mirror. Taking the offered cloth, he buffed the mirror and placed it carefully on the carpet. One of the servants gasped, receiving a swift look from his master who had also blinked but had quickly covered his surprise.

Reuel unwrapped the second mirror, buffed it, and placed it near the first. His breath caught in his throat, but he forced himself to relax. He knew the worth of the objects. A price had been agreed on beforehand, as long as the mirror pleased the man.

Naftali took his time. He picked up the first mirror and examined it closely, leaving fingerprints all over the lustrous surface, fingerprints Reuel tried to ignore.

"You've done well," Naftali said. "Exceedingly well. I know we agreed on a price--"

Reuel swallowed.

"But in this case, I will increase the price. I'll take both mirrors, for my wife will almost certainly wish for one as well when she sees the one I have for our daughter."

Reuel had trained himself to keep his smile just right. Neither too broad, as though the sale had been in doubt, nor too narrow, as though he was displeased. Naftali was clever. By buying both mirrors, he had ensured no other family in the area would have such an object. He must know that once others saw the gift, anyone who could afford such a piece would be nagged by their womenfolk to purchase one. Reuel had already bought more copper ore in anticipation of such a demand. He'd also asked Jael to sketch an outline of the mirrors onto clay tablets, to show potential customers.

Jael might irritate him sometimes, but she'd proven extremely canny. Reuel's father had been an excellent coppersmith, but he had undervalued his work. Reuel intended to be the best coppersmith in the land. He would provide his family with a life his father could not imagine with his limited dreams.

"Try a fig," Naftali said. He gestured to his servants. "Make sure that Reuel's sons and wives are also served."

Reuel didn't bother to tell him that Zura wasn't his wife. A man's status was often measured by how many wives and children he had.

Reuel reached for the offered fig and accepted some of the goat's milk. Its coolness slid down easily, and he relaxed. He had questions, but they must wait. Questions about whether he could stay here and for how long. Reuel needed Naftali's protection. Without it, the Israelites would think nothing of cheating him if they could. Small signs of rebellion from a people who were too weak and too divided to fight back against their oppressors.

Reuel had been waiting for the Midianites to be on the ascent all his life. He could still remember the bitterness in his father's voice whenever an Israelite had insulted or cheated their family. His father had nursed old grievances, especially the one about how the Midianites were also descendants of Avraham, yet all the blessings went to the descendants of Yitzchak, the second son. No other nation did such a thing. The inheritance should go to the eldest son or be divided evenly: Midian, the fourth son of Keturah should have been included, yet that had not been the case. Tension radiated across Reuel's broad shoulders as he considered this old grudge.

"Are you feeling well?" Naftali asked.

"Very well." Reuel forced his lips into an appropriate smile.

"Good, for I wish for you to be my guest at my daughter's wedding. Many people will want to meet the maker of her mirror."

"I would be honored," Reuel said. And he would. If Naftali promoted Reuel's work, he might gain many more customers. His father would have to acknowledge his skills were greater than his older brother's, and Reba and Hanok would be proud to be known as his sons.

"Is it safe for us to set up our tents out here?" Reuel asked.

"It is safe enough. Raiders come, but they shouldn't bother you," Naftali said.

He was probably right. The Midianites recognized their own, and Reuel would make certain of it by displaying the coppersmith's flag on the top of his work tent. As the master craftsman of the family, Father's flag should have come to Reuel, but of course it had gone to his elder brother, Ephah. Ephah, who only played around with smithing, preferring a more settled existence on the outskirts of Ramoth Gilead with their father. Seeing Reuel's hurt, Jael had made him a flag. She'd been so proud of it, and with good reason. It was much finer than the original, even if it didn't have the same symbolism.

"I will send a messenger to bring you to the wedding in two days' time," Naftali said. "First, I will bring you what I owe." He stood and gestured toward the city wall.

Almost immediately a pair of servants came out of the city gate, carrying a sack between them. Reuel had requested payment in copper. It was less of a temptation for thieves, and he could use it to make more objects. When the servants arrived, Reuel took the ingots out of the sack and weighed and tested each. All was as it should have been.

With much mutual bowing, Naftali and his servants left for home with the carefully wrapped mirrors. Once the city gates closed, Reuel unloaded the camels and the donkeys and led them to water. Then he called to Jael and together they began the process of setting up their living and working areas, in the same configuration as usual for Zura's sake.

Now that the main business was done, the townsfolk should start bringing out any metal items that needed repair or requesting new items. The next few days should be busy and if the mirrors did their work, they'd soon be using the new copper.

CHAPTER THREE

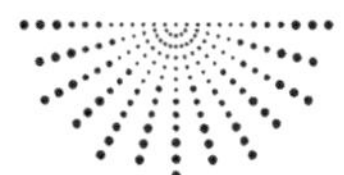

"Jael, you've got to keep the boys under control. I can't focus on my work with them running around."

The criticism stung, and Jael bit her lip to keep back the retort that rose in her throat. She supposed his mother had been a perfect parent, too, although somehow she doubted that Reuel had been quiet and sedate.

"I'll take them away from your work tent," she said.

"Good!" Reuel said.

She should have known Reuel would be more easily angered today. The first customer had arrived soon after dawn, aiming to miss the day's heat. Jael's job was to sort out the arrivals so that similar repair jobs were grouped together—cracked pans, broken handles, metal becoming too thin and brittle and needing to be strengthened. It was easier for Reuel to do similar tasks one after another.

Once she'd grouped the customers, Jael had spent most of the day keeping Reba and Hanok out of mischief, but the boys had the energy of summer fleas. And, like summer fleas, they were hard to catch. From the moment they had woken in the morning she'd been keeping them from annoying Reuel, and it was exhausting. Why couldn't children sit quietly or whisper? Their words exploded into the quiet spaces between conversations. This morning, they'd loudly asked about the white streak running through the dark hair of one of their customers, then embarrassed Jael further by going closer to look and exclaim. Jael, face burning, had scurried to take the children as far as possible away from the customers squatting on their haunches in any shade they could find.

"Boys, your mother is going to take you to the stream," Reuel said.

Reba groaned and Hanok copied his elder brother. Jael shooed them in front of her, but not before she'd seen Zura pause in her polishing and turn her face toward Jael. Long ago, Zura had mastered an expression that signaled to Jael that Zura understood and they'd talk later. Jael was sometimes glad Zura had never married, or she'd have been alone. It would be nice if they could sometimes talk about normal topics instead of continually discussing Reuel's treatment of her. He didn't mean to be unkind, but how Jael longed for kindness and consideration. For kindness that acknowledged her part in running this household. It didn't run itself, no matter what her husband seemed to think. He took his meals and the tidiness of the area as if it was his due as the man of the family, but never thanked her for producing them. It was all so different from the days when she'd longed to be married to Reuel.

"Ima, the stream isn't fun anymore," Reba said.

Jael ruffled his sweaty hair. "I know. There hasn't been enough rain. If you help me dig, we should be able to give you enough water to sit in."

She led them toward a large tree that hung over the stream. Even the tree looked thirsty with its leaves dusty and drooping.

Jael found a sluggish trickle of water. Standing in the tepid water, she demonstrated how to scoop the sand to one side to form a backrest. Then she dug a bottom-and-legs-sized hole and let the cleaner water wash out the water muddied by her digging.

"This one's yours," she said to Hanok. "Now, Reba, where do you think we should dig?"

Seeing Hanok contentedly settled, Reba helped her dig another hole and found a stick to dig under rocks while they waited for the dirty water to be washed downstream and the shallow hole to fill up before he seated himself in it.

"Splash some of the cleaner water over your head." Jael cupped her hand to scoop water over a rock so it would be cool enough for her to sit on. She'd bring Zura here later. It was cooler here than under the trees where they'd pitched their tents.

Zura had to work with Reuel nearly every day, but Reuel was seldom annoyed at her. She said it would make someone feel pretty low to be angry at a blind person. There were times that Jael wished she were blind, so she could be treated with the same respect.

"Ima, can you set up a target for us?" Reba asked.

Jael looked for a suitable flat rock and stepped toward it. "Is this far enough?"

Reba narrowed his eyes. "Probably. It's far enough away for Hanok anyway."

Jael added smaller rocks until they formed a lopsided tower. Then she took a few steps back to her rock. Hanok was already searching for fist-size rocks to throw.

"Me first, Ima," Reba said.

Jael shook her head. "No, Hanok can go first."

Hanok peered at the target. Frowning, he launched his first rock. It fell short.

"Have another try," Jael said.

"But it's my turn," Reba said.

"Let Hanok have another turn first. Then you can have two turns," Jael said.

Reba stuck out his lip but kept silent. Hanok's second throw was closer to the target. Reba's first shot also missed, but his second took a chip out of the rock close to the pile of stones.

"If you stand up, you might find it easier," Jael said.

Hanok stood up, water streaming down his legs. His third attempt sailed over the target. His fourth hit the top stone and it fell off with a clunk.

"Well done, Hanok," Jael said. "Now, Reba, you try."

Reba's two throws demolished half the tower, and Hanok wailed. "I want to do it."

"You need to learn to play together," Jael said. "There's still half the tower standing. Keep your eyes on the tower, not the stone in your hand."

The next stone hit the tower.

"Throw the stone a little harder," Jael said.

Hanok took a deep breath and launched his stone. It hit the bottom of the tower with a thud and scattered the remaining stones in all directions.

Hanok cheered and barely paused before saying, "Build me another. I want my own tower to knock down."

Finally, she'd found something that might keep Hanok occupied. There was not a suitable tree nearby for his short legs to climb.

"Reba, do you want your own as well?"

He nodded.

She'd build a few more towers and then teach them, or at least Reba, to build their own. Sometime soon, Reuel would start to teach Reba the basics of his craft. Both the boys enjoyed watching their father. What boy wouldn't enjoy watching the flow of molten metal and the noise and excitement of forming metal into different shapes? Jael had loved to watch her father when she was little, but he'd died before she'd had the chance to learn any of his skills. Would Reuel have appreciated her more if she'd been able to work alongside him?

* * *

*T*he late afternoon sun was casting an orange glow over the hills. Jael and Zura had grabbed a few moments to wash some clothes. Jael settled Zura on a stable, flat rock.

Zura placed her bare feet in the water. "Is there anyone around?"

Jael checked. "No."

"Good," Zura said. "I am dying to rinse out my hair." She pulled off the veil. Beneath it, her hair was damp with sweat. Reuel insisted Jael and Zura were veiled among the customers, but the veils on top of their long hair made their heads so hot.

"I brought a scoop," Zura said. "Would you pour water over my head?"

Usually, Zura did this task herself, but not when the water levels were so low. She wanted clear water over her head, not mud and pebbles.

Jael took the scoop and filled it with the cleanest water she could find. Then she poured a few scoopfuls over her sister's head. There were now a few strands of grey among the dark hair that hung to Zura's waist. Jael never knew if she pitied Zura for her childless life or envied her freedom from such responsibilities.

"That's much better," Zura said. "Hand me the boys' dirty tunics."

Jael picked up the tunics and peered at them. The cloth was wearing thin. She'd have to weave some more soon. Both boys were growing like young trees. What with climbing trees, fighting with sticks, and scrambling over rocks, they were not gentle on their clothes.

They scrubbed in silence until Zura spoke. "Jael, I don't think he means to be unkind."

"Don't you stand up for him," Jael said. "He is often unkind. I keep hoping that he'll change, and he never does."

"People seldom change much on their own. They need strength beyond their own," Zura said.

Ugh. Zura always managed to bring Yahveh into the conversation. Zura would say only Yahveh could change people's hearts. Maybe she was right, because Zura was continually changing. The longer she'd followed Yahveh, the more at peace she became with her lot in life. She seemed to accept her unmarried state and not being able to see the results of her labors.

Jael's emotions were so mixed up. Sometimes she envied Zura for her part in Reuel's life, and sometimes she pitied her sister. Jael's emotions went up and down depending on how Reuel had treated her that day or how well the boys had behaved. Up and down. Up and down. As though she was molten metal, easily bent to any shape while she wanted to be hard and resistant to hurt.

"You always were a dreamer. I fear you have unrealistic expectations of Reuel," Zura said.

It irritated Jael, like a stone caught between her toes, that Zura seemed to be excusing Reuel. After all that Jael had done for Zura, couldn't Jael at least have her sister's unqualified support?

"I don't see how respect, kindness, and love and not having to do all the boring or dirty tasks are high expectations," Jael snapped.

"Maybe not," Zura said. "But sometimes we have to lower our expectations. I've had to do that in my situation. Most people can't be bothered to talk to me directly about my blindness and how they can help. Instead, they talk about my blindness as though I'm not there."

Jael was always telling people not to talk to her about Zura but to ask Zura herself. Jael wrung out the tunic she'd just washed and laid it on a hot rock to dry. "I don't see why men get to tickle the children or climb trees with them but hand them back the minute they throw up or start crying. It's not fair!"

"As I've often told you, life isn't fair," Zura said.

Jael sighed. "That doesn't help me." Why was she expected to do the changing? Shouldn't Reuel also have to change?

"It's amazing how we keep hoping and expecting life to be fair. It doesn't help me to wish that woman hadn't tripped with the pan of boiling water or to wish I hadn't been in the way and hadn't ended up blind." Zura rinsed out the tunic Jael had scrubbed then passed to her. "It doesn't help me to focus on all I can't do and can't have. Instead, I focus on what I can change and can do."

Zura was much better at being content than Jael. Jael wasn't going to comment, because she knew what Zura would say. "I'm not naturally more contented than you, but Yahveh has changed me."

Jael didn't want to hear about Yahveh. She already had enough trouble with one man in her life.

She didn't need another man telling her what to do.

CHAPTER FOUR

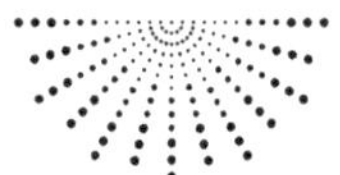

"*bba*, the servant has come to take you to the wedding!"

Reba's urgent summons broke into Reuel's daydream about how today would be the day he became famous. Well, perhaps not famous, but at least well known for his craft, thus increasing the demand for his wares. The more he sold, the more he could provide for his family.

Reuel went to the entrance of his tent where the servant bowed and held out a new tunic draped across his arms. A new tunic! What would be the cost of all these favors? Surely a coppersmith couldn't have much to offer to such a man. If there was a cost, Reuel hoped it wouldn't be too high to pay.

The servant waited while Reuel changed.

"You look handsome," Jael said as she combed his hair and beard.

"Don't fuss. I've already done that." Reuel brushed her away.

Jael tightened her lips and turned. She was so easily hurt, and it annoyed him to have to smooth things over. He didn't have time to stop now, not when Naftali's servant was waiting. Reuel left the tent and followed the servant toward the city gates. In the old days, such a large wedding would have been held outside the city with pavilions set up for days. In these times, having a wedding outside the city would be inviting trouble. Once inside the gates, they pushed on into the center of town. The crowds increased as they got closer to the central square, and their progress became slower and slower.

There were pavilions at the entrance of the main city streets which led into the main square. The entire square would be taken over. Everyone would be inconvenienced a little, but it was a small price to pay for such an event.

The sound of horns and drums swirled around them, and Reuel's nose twitched with delight at the smell of roasting lamb. They'd slowed to almost a standstill as they reached a bottleneck. Everyone was dressed in their best, for no one would turn down an invitation from the richest man in the area.

Reuel's stomach was churning as they pushed through the most crowded section and came out into the square. Would today change his life? Being sent a tunic was a good sign, but he'd know for sure what Naftali thought of him when he was led to his seat. The closer he was seated to the bride and groom and Naftali and his wife, would show the extent of the esteem in which Naftali held Reuel.

"This way," the servant said. He led Reuel halfway down the status stakes. Naftali was shrewd. He'd placed Reuel neither too high nor too low. He was placed among the other artisans, but Reuel was pleased to see he was the only one in a tunic supplied by the host.

Reuel found himself a space on the carpet, under the shade offered by the canopy. The servant brought him a beaker of goat's milk. The container was cold to the touch. The milk must have been cooled by standing it in water in an underground chamber.

Reuel took a swallow and looked around. Already half the mats were occupied by guests, with more arriving all the time. Neighbors greeted each other by touching their hearts and clasping hands. Some of Reuel's customers recognized him and nodded politely. No one would want to be overly friendly with a Midianite. Reuel stifled a sigh and prepared himself for a long, hot day. Reuel might be secretly pleased that the Midianites were on the rise at last, but he wasn't going to say that out loud. Saying something out loud would only lose him customers. Once their rule was established over these lands, things might be different. Meanwhile, he intended to increase his wealth from anyone who would pay him.

Reuel's stomach rumbled. The man next to him said, "Naftali won't keep us waiting. Look, here comes the bread."

Every baker in the town must have been hard at work for days. Each basket required two men to carry it as they handed various kinds of flatbreads to each group of guests. The last of the guests scurried toward their places.

There was a blare of trumpets. Naftali, covered by a canopy, led his wife by her arm toward the raised platform. He looked like what he was, a rich man adorned in the best garments who always had plenty to eat. He waved and nodded to all he passed as they wended their way through the clumps of guests to the center. When they had reached their places, he helped his wife take her seat on the carpet and solicitously placed a heavy cushion behind her. Once she was comfortable, Naftali came and stood in front of them all.

"Welcome, friends and family, to the wedding feast of my daughter and her new husband."

It was likely that Naftali's son-in-law was the son of another wealthy merchant. The negotiations would have been conducted when his daughter had survived infanthood.

There was another trumpet blast. Reuel and all those around him scrambled to their feet. From the entry of a home in the square, a troop of dancers emerged dressed in colored garments. As they twirled, they scattered grains for fertility before the couple. The bride was so heavily veiled that her groom had to lead her slowly over the grains and toward the central dais.

Once she was standing near her father, Naftali said. "Let us pray." He raised his hands. "Great creator god, we thank you for the glorious day. Not only are we bathed in sunlight, but we celebrate the marriage of this precious daughter and our new son. May their union be fruitful."

Naftali would be hoping his daughter would be more fruitful than his wife had been. Maybe that was the reason for the fertility grains, a custom beloved by followers of Baal. Like many Hebrews, Naftali seemed not to notice that he was mixing religious customs. Perhaps he believed the more gods, the better. Certainly his prayer seemed directed to Yahveh, although no name had been mentioned. Perhaps he was referring to another creator. It made no difference to Reuel. He didn't bother exercising his mind thinking about where this world had come from. He had more than enough things to think about: keeping up supplies of copper and the tin which turned it into the more workable bronze, as well as how to survive the drought. A drought that was in little evidence today as servers brought out steaming platters of sliced meat, yogurt with added herbs, onions, and more bread. No one here would go hungry.

The oldest man on the mat tore the bread into big pieces and handed them to those around him. Reuel placed fragrant meat, cucumber, and a covering of yogurt in his bread and took a hungry bite. Juice oozed down his chin, and he used the bread to dab it up. Delicious. The boys would be excited to eat some of the leftovers.

Glancing over to the women's area, Reuel could see some of the women already placing meat and bread aside for their families. He didn't think they needed to worry. Naftali knew the family members at home would be waiting for their share as a sign of their host's joy and generosity.

No one talked to Reuel. Maybe his ancestry was branded on his head. Sometimes he felt like yelling, "I'm a descendant of Avraham as well. Aren't we just as entitled to his promises?" Reuel's ancestors had had to eke out an existence in much harsher places than

Canaan. The Israelites talked about Avraham like he was some sort of god, a hero for all time, but Reuel felt disappointment and anger every time he thought of the man. He wished he could forget Avraham, but every time Reuel saw one of Yitzchaq's descendants, the anger rekindled in his gut. It might have been better for his health if he'd gone back to their ancestral desert lands south of Canaan, but he loved the hills here. Hills that were as familiar as Reba and Hanok's bright-eyed faces. If Reuel could make his name as a craftsman, Reba and Hanok would have a fine start to their smithing.

More food was served. Course after course, with music and dancers in between. The highlight had been a singer who'd accompanied herself on the harp.

"Look! What's happening?" the man at the far end of their pavilion said.

Reuel was startled out of his food-induced doze. He straightened to watch two men carrying a low table covered with an exquisite length of cloth. Could this be what he'd been waiting for? His stomach churned.

The men proceeded up to the dais, and every pair of eyes followed their progress. They placed the table in front of Naftali and the bride and groom.

Naftali stood up. "As you know, Deborah is my only child. I asked myself what gift I could possibly give to her to show my love for her. I wanted something special, something unique. Something no one else had." Naftali looked out at his listeners, carefully avoiding looking at Reuel. Reuel's heartbeat pounded in his ears. Would the people of this town recognize the worth of all his work? Or would they simply say, "What's the fuss over something with only one use and that only for women?"

"I wanted to give something beautiful, something that would last. Something that could be passed down from generation to generation." Naftali lifted the cloth so only his daughter could see the object through the slits of her veil. She stood and gave her father a fierce hug. Pride welled within Reuel's chest. The mirror had passed another critical test.

Naftali whipped off the remaining cloth. "Behold. A bronze mirror."

There was a gasp from the women's corner and some excited squeals. The mirror had been buffed to perfection with the special soft cloth Reuel had wrapped it in. It glowed in the late afternoon light. It was the best object Reuel had ever created, and it made him want to throw out his chest and crow. If only he'd been able to show his father. His father had always been absorbed in Reuel's elder brother, Ephah, named after Midian's eldest son. No matter what Reuel did with metal, it never deflected the glory from his brother.

"What did he say it was?" asked one of the men nearby.

"A mirror. I've never seen one," another man said. "But by the keen interest from my wife, I'm going to be hearing a lot about mirrors."

Reuel nearly cheered.

"Reuel, my friend." Naftali's voice boomed across the crowd. "What are you doing down there? Come here and show the mirror to the other guests."

Would he have simply ignored Reuel if the guests had not been so impressed? Perhaps, but Reuel wasn't going to miss the opportunity to take credit. The servant who'd accompanied him into the city was at his side and led him to the front. Naftali picked up the mirror and a polishing cloth and accompanied Reuel across to where the ladies were waiting.

As they approached the women, the chatter died down. Each one looked at the flowers shaped in the metal. One lady reached out a tentative hand and stroked the smooth surface. She'd leave marks on the bronze, but they could easily be polished off. When each group had looked their fill, they moved on to the next. Reuel felt as if he was floating as person after person exclaimed at the workmanship. When he reached the corner where he'd been seated, someone asked, "How long did it take to make?"

Reuel frowned. "Longer than anything else I've ever made." What else could he say? For the work itself was not the hardest part. The hardest part was the design, then trialing new techniques to get it to look the way he'd imagined it.

There'd been many failures along the way when he'd had to abandon all his work, put the metal back in the furnace, and start again. There'd been times he'd cursed Naftali and his request. Now, looking at the awe on the men's faces in front of him, he felt it had been worth it.

Naftali slapped him on the back. "Good job. My daughter loved it."

If the looks on people's faces were any indication, she was not the only one. Reuel would be getting a lot of new customers. To think that his mirror was the center of attention in this extravagant celebration. Yet Reuel's stomach still churned. Naftali had given him these opportunities. What would such a man want in return?

CHAPTER FIVE

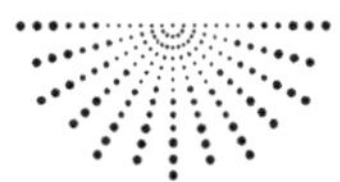

"**J**ael, I want you to go and fetch water from the well in the middle of town," Reuel said.

Jael rubbed her already aching back. She'd been busy since before dawn trying to get things done in the cool of the day. "The other well is much closer."

Reuel frowned. "My mother always assumed I had a good reason for any requests."

It was a good thing Reuel's mother was long dead, or Jael would have wanted to punch her and ask why she had spoiled her son. Reuel's snappiness was always laid at Jael's feet. He implied that if she'd just imitate his mother and learn what he needed, she wouldn't have to put up with his moods. His moods were as unpredictable as the weather, and the tension of keeping him happy wore her out.

"I want to know whether all the compliments about the mirror will lead to more commissions," Reuel said.

"Why don't you go? I can only speak with the women, but it is the men whose arms must be bent to request a commission. Take the boys. A long walk will do them good." And Jael would love a long rest with a chance to soak her dusty feet in the trickle that was all that was left of a once-rushing stream.

"People will recognize me from the wedding yesterday. You'll be able to hear people's real opinions. Take Hanok with you. He's been driving me crazy."

Reuel didn't seem to care that Hanok might drive her crazy. Reuel had already turned back to mending a pan. He couldn't imagine that she'd ever disobey him, and he was right. No matter how hot and tired she felt, she'd drag her body to do his bidding. Perhaps bringing back good news would change his mood. Perhaps he'd turn his charm back on to warm her heart as he'd done before they were married and at the birth of the boys. Perhaps.

Jael went to put on her veil, so she'd draw less attention and be able to eavesdrop with ease. Hanok skipped along beside her with his own tiny version of a waterskin looped around his shoulders. If only she had his energy.

"I like going with you, Ima," he said, tripping over a small rock.

"Careful." She held out her hand to steady him. "I like going with you too." Even as she said the words, her spirits lifted. The boys sometimes exhausted her so much she couldn't wait for dark when she could go to sleep. But they also made her laugh and gave her a reason to live and hope things might change with Reuel. She'd longed for his attention as a child. Now that she had it, she longed for less of it—or at least a more kindly form of attention. The kind of attention Reuel gave to Zura or even the livestock. Sometimes she wished she was just a donkey, content with life. Long days of simply eating and resting wouldn't hurt either.

"Ima, why are we not getting water from that well there?" Hanok pointed to the well they were passing.

"Abba wants water from the well in the center of town. He likes it better." It wasn't true. Jael knew Reuel was just as likely to complain the water didn't taste nice. She wouldn't dare tell him he was the one who had insisted she walk the further distance. She didn't dare to say many of the things that were often on the tip of her tongue. The last thing she wanted was her situation to get worse. Men had divorced wives for lesser things. Without Reuel, she'd have no means to support herself and Zura. In a divorce, menfolk often took their sons, so she'd never see her children again. Her throat tightened at the thought.

As Reuel had hoped, the central well was crowded with women waiting in line to collect water. Children ran in and out of the row or drew figures in the dust.

"Can I draw?" Hanok asked.

Jael nodded. It would keep him quiet and allow her to listen in on the conversations. Conversations that so far were not about mirrors.

"My mother-in-law has insisted she cook sometimes, and the children tell me I'm not as good a cook as she is." The lady wiped perspiration from her brow.

So Jael wasn't the only one to have mother-in-law problems. They seemed to make problems whether they were alive or dead. Reuel had told her after the first meal she'd cooked that his mother was a much better cook. Of course she was. His mother had been cooking for years. Jael had always helped her mother cook, like other girls did, but she'd never had to cook a full meal until she'd married. Her long-dead rival probably hadn't been able to cook when she'd first been married either.

"We're still eating leftovers from the wedding yesterday," a young mother with two children holding her skirts said.

"Naftali is the most popular man in Jabesh Gilead today," the first woman said. "I haven't eaten lamb like that since before the drought. Our sheep are so bony they wouldn't be worth eating."

Several women nodded.

"Don't you wish we could just order servants to do all the work?" one woman asked.

"And that we had so much money that we could afford a mirror like what Naftali gave his daughter."

Jael turned her head to hear better. Hanok was still happily occupied drawing with his stick at her feet.

"But would what we saw in the mirror be anything like what she sees?" laughed another.

"Maybe not, but there are times I'd love to check if I have flour on my cheek or that my hair isn't a mess." The speaker was a young girl wearing the attire of a maiden.

"Not all of us still need to catch a man's attention." The perspiring woman fanned herself with a large leaf.

The girl flushed. "Well, I wish my father would give me a mirror for a gift."

"You'd be better to ask for a pan. It would be more useful."

"I know," the girl said. "But sometimes I'd like a gift that was just for me, not something useful."

What woman didn't long for gifts that communicated love rather than those that benefited the whole family? Reuel would gather wildflowers for Jael before they were married. Once they married, he seemed to have forgotten the pleasure they'd given her. Perhaps he'd never cared about her pleasure, only attracting a wife to spend a lifetime cooking his food, bearing his children, and obeying his commands.

"Most men could not afford a mirror like that. You saw the intricate decoration," the young mother said.

"People might be able to afford a simpler design." Jael hoped no one would want to know who she was.

Reuel had told her not to talk, but these women were about to give up on the whole idea of owning a mirror. This wasn't what Reuel wanted. He wanted mirrors to be the dreamed-for item for new brides and himself as the exclusive craftsman of such wonders.

"Simpler? I wonder if I could convince my father," the young girl said.

"First you'll have to have a wedding," one of the matrons said with a giggle.

The girl flushed. "My parents already have a young man in mind."

The woman fanned herself vigorously. "You can try to convince your father, but I still say a pan is much more useful."

"But not nearly as beautiful." The girl moved along as the people in the line moved forward.

Hanok darted off toward a tree, and Jael seized the chance to go after him. It would be better if she rejoined the line at another point and listened in to more conversations. Hanok found some more sticks and allowed himself to be led back into the line.

The next group of ladies was also discussing mirrors.

"Naftali didn't just give a mirror to his daughter. He also gave one to his wife. I hear it was even more elaborate," a grandmother said, awe in her voice. "Now every woman is going to be hoping their husband gives them such a token of esteem."

Reuel was going to be delighted with what Jael was hearing. Maybe he'd even consent to rub her aching back. Although then she'd have to consent to what he wanted after.

Another woman leaned forward. "What was the second mirror like?"

"I think I can draw it for you," the older woman said. "Little boy, can I use one of your sticks?"

Hanok looked up at Jael.

Jael picked up one of Hanok's carefully selected collection of sticks. "The lady will give it back when she's finished."

Hanok nodded and went back to his own drawing.

"It was much rounder than the wedding mirror." The lady used the stick to illustrate. "And festooned around with grapes, figs, and pomegranates."

"I think I preferred the wedding one with the flowers. More

elegant," said one of the women. "Do you think the coppersmith can only do those two designs?"

"I'm sure he would let you choose the shape and decorations," Jael said.

The woman peered at her. "And who are you?"

"My father was a metalworker. He loved to try different things. It gave him a chance to show off his skills."

"And what man doesn't like to do that," the woman said with a snort. "It wouldn't hurt to go and ask how much it would cost for a design. My daughter is getting married soon, and she came home babbling about the mirror."

The line moved forward. By the time that Jael had filled their two waterskins, she'd heard three more conversations about mirrors and planted the idea of cheaper, simpler designs each time. She smiled to herself. Naftali hadn't forbidden Reuel from making any more mirrors, but he would be pleased if none surpassed the ones he owned.

Jael had already sketched some simpler designs in both the round and oval versions. She'd see if she could find time tomorrow to come up with another six or seven designs. The more she had to show people, the more Reuel would appreciate her efforts. Sometimes she felt left out of the coppersmithing side of things, but this would give her a role, an important role. Maybe it would fill some of the emptiness she felt when she longed to be valued for who she was and all she contributed.

Reuel's success was not his alone. She and Zura were a part of the team.

CHAPTER SIX

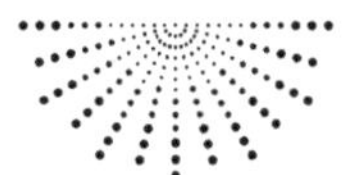

euel sighed and stretched up to the sky, attempting to ease the crick in his neck and the stiffness in his hands. It had been a great couple of days. They'd been here long enough to complete all the mundane fixing of metal objects, and now he could concentrate on making some more mirrors.

Jael had reported all the conversations at the well and proved his point about why he'd asked her to walk into town. She'd come up with some stunning designs that would be much easier to make, simply a polished disk with a single stalk of wheat or flower on each side of the mirror. If this demand went on, he'd have to go down to the port and buy more tin ingots. The best tin came from Cyprus or Persia to the Far East. Naftali had paid for his mirror in copper, so Reuel still had plenty of that to use.

"I'm going to take the boys and walk into town." Reuel had promised Reba that he'd spend some time with him, and he meant to keep the promise. Besides which, he needed a break from leaning over molten metal.

He turned to Jael. "Is there any water?"

"Only enough for drinking. We've dug a hole in the stream bed and use that for everything else," she said.

He sighed. "It will have to do. What we need is rain."

"Everyone is wishing for rain. I've seen more and more people going to the high places and making offerings to Baal and Astarte."

"Yahveh won't be happy about that," Reuel said with a snort.

"I guess not, but he hasn't provided rain either," Jael said.

He peered at her. He didn't think she cared about Yahveh or any of the gods any more than he did. Maybe Zura had been talking to Jael about Yahveh. He'd have to speak to Zura about it. He didn't want her influencing Jael or the boys. The last thing he wanted was a wife wasting their grain by making offerings. She was repressed enough as it was, never welcoming his attentions. He wished he had someone to ask about how to make his wife more welcoming, but he hadn't seen his elder brother or father for a long time. Not that he'd talk to them anyway.

Reuel stood and went to get his second tunic. He'd wash in his work clothes and try to get rid of the pungent odor of his sweat. Then he'd put on the new tunic and go and buy something different to eat. Some fresh vegetables or fruit. Pomegranates were in season, and nothing beat their tartness for taking the taste of smoke out of his mouth.

The stream was as inadequate as he'd expected, but he managed to rinse out his work tunic. By waiting patiently—something he was not good at—the mud settled, and he was able to wash himself off. He even rinsed his hair and combed it back. He placed a few bronze and copper bells in his pocket to exchange for anything that took his fancy. He made them by the hundred, as he had several different-sized molds that he used. People liked to add bells to the hems of their best clothes or to dangle from their window frames. The sound was supposed to frighten away any ghosts and keep them safe. They sold in large quantities, so who was he to argue?

He collected the boys and set off, with the boys trotting beside him.

"Abba, slow down. Hanok can't keep up," Reba said.

Reuel stopped and waited for Hanok to catch up. "Want to ride on my shoulders?"

Hanok held up his arms, and Reuel swung him up.

Once Hanok felt secure, they set off again and after a short delay to enter the gates they walked to the central square. There was a motley collection of stalls, with goats wandering freely among people's feet. The air was pungent with the smell of fresh meat and too many sweaty bodies close together.

Hanok clung to Reuel's head, and Reba held on to the edge of his tunic. Reba had once lost hold in a crowded market and ever since he'd been super careful to hold on tight.

"Little masters, come and look at my stall," an old woman cried. "My fruit is juicy and sweet."

Reba looked at the display of fruit. By Canaan's standards, it looked shrunken and dry. The drought had impacted every growing thing. They had to be satisfied with anything they could get, even if it was double the price it used to be. Reuel allowed each boy to choose something. Pomegranates for Reba and figs for Hanok. The woman was willing to accept a small bell in payment. Reuel added another to get leeks, garlic, and onions for Jael. They'd add flavor to a lentil stew.

Off to the side, there was a series of thuds usually used to gain attention. Reuel glanced sideways and saw a grey-bearded man in a dusty robe clambering up onto the dais Naftali had used for his speeches at the wedding.

The man turned around. "This is what the God of Israel says, 'I brought you up out of Egypt, out of the land of slavery,'" the man called in a ringing voice.

A man with sinewy muscles spat on the ground. "Not another crazy prophet."

A prophet? Reuel had heard of such people, like Mosheh of old, but he had never seen one.

"For the Lord says, 'I rescued you from the hand of the Egyptians and I delivered you from the hand of all your oppressors.'"

Some in the crowd were nodding, but many shuffled their feet and avoided looking at the old man.

Hanok leaned toward the man, pushing Reuel's head forward. "What does he mean, Abba?"

Reuel reached up his hand. "Shh. Let me listen."

"'I drove out the Canaanites before you and gave you their land. I said to you, "I am the Lord your God, do not worship the gods of the Amorites—"'"

A muttering started toward the back of the crowd and spread.

"Tell Yahveh we want rain," shouted a man in the middle of the crowd.

"Yes!" one voice yelled and was quickly supported by others.

Heart rate escalating, Reuel shuffled toward the edge of the crowd. The boys were too little to be here if things turned ugly.

"That's right!" yelled others.

"Give us rain," chanted one.

Soon the crowd was joining in. "Rain! Rain! We want rain!"

"Silence," the prophet yelled. "You have not listened to Yahveh." He paused and took another deep breath. "You have worshiped the gods of Canaan."

The crowd was silent now, the tension in the air was like that before a hailstorm.

"Reject the Baals and Asherah, and worship Yahveh alone. Then the land will have plenty again, and you will not be oppressed by other peoples."

Someone looked at Reuel and must have recognized him. "Down with the Midianites," he yelled.

"Quick," said the fruit seller at Reuel's side. "Take the children through that door and climb out the window at the far side."

Reuel flashed the woman a tight smile and swung Hanok down to the ground before grasping both boys by their hands and going through the door. Something splattered on the closed door behind him. Peering into the dim room he searched for the exit. There!

"I'm scared, Abba," Hanok whimpered.

"Keep moving. We're getting out of here." Reuel hoped they could leave Jabesh Gilead before the crowd got carried away and remembered that the Midianites had been hassling them for seven years. He might never have been part of raids on people's crops at harvest, but many Midianites had. A mob didn't stop to ask questions.

They went through a second room, and Reuel kept moving toward where the back of the narrow home would be. It wouldn't be safe to go out the main city gate. They'd have to try one of the side gates.

Jael! She and Zura were camping outside, completely unprotected should the mob take their grievances outside. They went through a third room.

"Abba, it's brighter ahead," Reba said.

Light meant the promised window. He moved forward. Reaching the window, he peered outside. It was only a short drop to the alley behind.

"Reba, you first. Show Hanok how easy it is."

Reuel lowered Reba a full arm's length then let go. Reba dropped to the ground and stood looking up at them. "It's easy, Hanok. Come on."

Once Hanok was on the ground, Reuel followed and they headed along the alley. There was a side gate somewhere in this direction, one Reuel had never used but one that would keep them well away from the center of town.

Reuel strained his ears but couldn't hear anything but the usual sounds—a baby crying in a courtyard, a goat bleating, someone pounding barley. He reached down and took Reba's and Hanok's hands. They couldn't run, for that would attract unwanted attention.

It didn't take long to leave the city and walk around the wall. Rounding the last corner of the city wall, they saw their tents. Reuel blew out a breath. There was no sign anyone had been near their home.

"Come on, boys." He swung Hanok on his back. "Hold on, let's get home."

He set off at a steady trot with Reba running alongside.

They were almost home when he heard the city gates creak open and then slam shut. A voice from the wall yelled. "Don't come back! You are not welcome."

Reuel stopped and looked back. The prophet, disheveled and covered in what was probably a mixture of manure and mud, drew himself up straight.

"Listen," the prophet called back toward the city. "Listen and live. Don't let further ruin strike you."

The only answer was a clod of manure thrown from the wall. It splattered at the prophet's feet. He stepped back and turned away.

Hanok pounded on Reuel's back. "Where will he go, Abba?"

"I don't know, son. Maybe he will go to another town."

"But why, when no one wants to listen?" Reba asked.

"I guess he believes Yahveh has spoken to him, so he must keep warning people even if they refuse to listen."

"I wouldn't like to do that," Reba said.

Who would? But now it looked like they'd have to move on toward Ramoth Gilead for they couldn't risk staying here. Reuel would need to return with the mirrors he'd been commissioned to make on another visit.

CHAPTER SEVEN

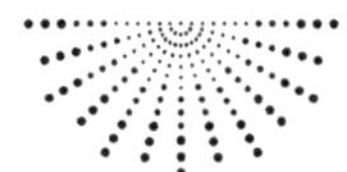

*J*ael walked beside the camel carrying Zura, Reba, and Hanok.

"Boys, who will be the first to see the city gates?"

"Me, me." Hanok raised his hand. "I want to be first."

"Then you'll have to pay attention. You should see it when we reach the highest point of the road," Jael said.

"And then we'll nearly be at Grandpa and Uncle Ephah's," Reba said.

Jael stifled a sigh. She didn't much like visiting Ramoth Gilead. Being around Reuel's father and brother always brought out the worst in her husband.

Reuel and the donkeys he was leading scrambled up the last rise. He moved to the side of the path to wait for Jael with the camel and the other donkeys. Jael wiped sweat from her face, glad she'd covered everyone's head from the relentless sun. Just ahead of her, the camel's feet raised small clouds of dust with every step.

"There! I see it, Ima," Reba said.

"I wanted to see it first," Hanok wailed.

"It's alright," Zura soothed. "There will be other things to see. Are there any eagles soaring?"

"Yes, I see one." Hanok pointed upward as though his aunt could see the magnificent bird.

Zura turned her face upwards. "Tell me about it."

"It's huge, bigger than me. Look! There's a second one."

Jael joined them in watching. Up in the pale blue sky, the eagles were free. It would be easy to pretend they were free of responsibilities, but they also had to provide for their young. As she did.

A breeze ruffled her hair. The cooler temperatures on the heights were one of the main reasons that Abida, Reuel's father, had decided to settle here after he ceased being a traveling smith.

Ramoth Gilead was one of the biggest cities in Manasseh's eastern lands. It would be good to see Ephah's wife. She had children of similar ages to Reba and Hanok. She and Jael and Zura got along much better than the men of the family.

They rested for a brief while, and Jael made sure the boys had a good drink before they moved on to their usual campsite.

"Let's unload the animals and get the boys down for a run," Reuel said. "Then we can send a message to invite everyone for a meal."

Jael's shoulders slumped. She should have known there would be no rest for her. For her it would be long, hot hours of preparing food and trying to keep the boys from annoying the men.

* * *

"More wine, Jael, more wine." Reuel thumped his empty beaker on the mat the men were sitting on.

Jael had been trying to slow down their consumption of wine, but it still slid down the men's throats almost as fast as she could pour it. Jael brought the wineskin and filled the men's beakers.

"Your arrival is well-timed," Abida said.

"How so?" Reuel said with a lift of his eyebrows.

"You're just in time to go raiding," Abida said.

Jael saw Reuel's jaw clench. Why, oh why, were the men going early? Reuel had wanted to come to Ramoth Gilead at this time so he wouldn't come under pressure to go raiding.

Reuel would lose the trust he'd built among the Israelites if they found he was raiding their people on the western side of the Jordan. She knew Reuel wanted to make a name for himself as a craftsman, not a fighter. Yet there was always the sting to Reuel's pride because their people were not accepted and respected.

If Reuel joined the raiders, Jael would be forced to stay with Reuel's father as they'd have no other protector.

Reuel signaled for another refill. Jael wanted to tell him to stop drinking. Reuel only ever drank with his father and brother, and it never led to anything good. Zura said the drinking was an escape, but what did Reuel need to escape from? No one ordered him around. He'd built a life where all his needs were met. She couldn't see that drinking helped anything anyway. But it was no use saying anything because Reuel wouldn't listen to her. He never listened to her. He had a strong belief in the rightness of his own opinions.

"Why raid so early?" Reuel said, his words already beginning to slur.

"The Amalekites are impatient." Ephah picked his teeth with a twig. "They'd like to possess the land instead of merely raiding it during harvest."

"Do you trust the Amalekites?" Reuel asked.

Ephah spat on the ground. "No, but we are not strong enough to raid on our own."

"The problem with the Amalekites is they don't know when to stop. They strip every grain and fruit and olive. They round up all the animals. Is it any wonder that the Israelites hide in the clefts of the rock and put their harvests in caves?"

Tell them, Reuel. Convince them not to go.

Abida thumped his knee. "That's why the raids must be now. Before the Israelites have had time to gather and hide their harvests."

Reuel finished his mouthful of bread. "Who looks after the coppersmithing if Ephah goes raiding?"

"Raiding has been far more lucrative than coppersmithing. Where do you think the lamb you're eating came from?" Ephah said.

Jael had wondered when her sister-in-law had turned up with roast lamb to add to the meal. The boys had certainly enjoyed it and were now climbing a half-grown tree while Zura sat at the base in the shade.

Reuel burped. "And what about your customers? Do they notice you're missing?"

Abida laughed. "I just tell them Ephah hankers after the traveling life. He sets off with his pack animals and fills the packs with leaves and rocks to make them seem full."

"I doubt it will fool them forever. Sooner or later, someone will work out that he only disappears during the raiding season."

"And your point?" Ephah asked.

"My customers trust me," Reuel said. "If I lose that trust, I will lose customers. Raiding is only going to be for a season. Smithing is for a lifetime."

"Which is why I am going to seize the opportunity while I have it," Ephah said.

Ephah's wife, Zipporah, avoided Jael's gaze. What did she think of Ephah's words? Jael doubted that she approved of her husband's actions, but Ephah had always been a bit wild. He'd led his younger brother into lots of danger when they were children. Ephah was the sort of boy who always climbed higher, jumped further, and generally showed off his abilities for all to see. While Reuel had tried, he'd never been able to match Ephah in their father's eyes.

"Listen to your excuses," Abida growled. "Makes me think you're a coward."

"I'm no coward," Reuel answered.

Abida shook his head. "A coward," he murmured. "To think that a son of mine is a coward."

There was a tightness across Jael's chest. *Don't listen to him, Reuel. Don't listen.* But already the fear was rising in her.

"I am no coward," Reuel said, but less confidently than the first time.

The fear worked its way up Jael's throat.

"Then prove it!" Abida's gaze stabbed at Reuel, pinning him to where he was seated.

Oh Reuel, you don't have to listen to him. But she knew her unspoken pleas were no use. He'd never stand against his father's taunts. Which was, of course, why Abida was using his words as weapons. He knew how to manipulate Reuel.

Reuel took another large swig of wine. A swig that gained him time but would further cloud his thinking. *Fight, Reuel. Fight for your dreams, not your father's whims.*

"You won't believe me, whatever I say." Reuel avoided looking at her, for he knew Jael's opinion on the matter. "I will go." He sighed. "I hope I don't regret it."

Abida nodded and silently raised his beaker.

Jael clenched her fists. It wouldn't just be Reuel who regretted his decision. She would, too, for all the days he was away. Days in which she'd have to work with her father-in-law. He could no longer produce the fancier items, but he'd make the daily use items for Zura to polish. Meanwhile, she and Zipporah would make sure the household kept functioning and the children didn't cause too much chaos. *Curse the foolishness of men and their pride!*

CHAPTER EIGHT

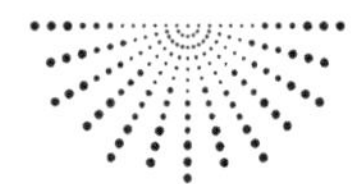

Jael stood outside the tent with the boys on either side of her and waved Reuel off. Her lips were curled up in a dutiful smile, but her heart was seething. Since making his decision, Reuel had been laughing and joking with his brother and father. Jael blew out a breath. Reuel was so thrilled at his father's rare approval that he didn't stop to think it was only because Abida had got his own way. Abida could now boast that two of his sons were loyal Midianites. Of course, he wouldn't remain happy if they weren't successful.

"Ima, why is Abba going away?" Reba asked, tugging at her arm.

Jael hated that she had to cover up for Reuel. "He's going to help Uncle Ephah."

"Help him with what?" Reba asked.

"To bring back some animals," Jael said. And he'd better come back with a good-sized flock or Reba would have more questions.

Reuel and Ephah were both riding camels. Camels they could ill afford to lose if anything should go wrong. The two men had each taken a flap of their tent to wrap themselves in at night and provisions for a week. After that, they'd live off what they took from Israelites.

"Ima, do we have to move in with Grandpa?" Hanok looked up at her. "I like living here better."

She did too. "With Abba gone, there is no one to protect us out here."

"We'd protect you." Reba stood up straight and puffed out his meager chest.

Jael placed her hand on Reba's head. "You're a good boy."

They'd be much safer inside the walled city. So far, the raiding had all taken place on the far side of the Jordan River, but trouble always had a way of spreading. She'd heard the stories of what happened to women and children caught in the path of raiding parties.

Jael and the boys watched their father and uncle and their camels until they disappeared into the hot haze in the direction of the river.

"Come on, boys. You'll have to be my helpers today," Jael said. They'd have to be her helpers for many, many days to come. Why, oh why, hadn't Reuel stuck to his principles? Now it would be many moons until they were selling their wares again. Meanwhile, they'd have to live with Abida, who really didn't want them around.

* * *

"*Z*ura, do you think Abida would be willing to start teaching the boys how to work with copper?" Jael asked.

Zura reached her hand down and brushed it across the leaves of the herb they were gathering for the evening meal. She put her hand up to her nose and sniffed. Once she'd confirmed she'd found the right herb, she reached down and picked it. "Don't you think Reuel might want that privilege?"

"Maybe, but he hasn't shown any inclination to teach the boys so far. Reba should have started a year ago," Jael said. A coppersmith didn't happen by accident. Their skill was the result of years of training.

"It might give Abida something to do," Zura said.

And giving Abida something to do might decrease his anxiety about his sons. Especially his eldest son. His anxiety had already broken out in snapping at the children. The boys loved playing with their cousins, but Abida found the noise hard to handle in an enclosed space.

"Can you hold all the herbs?" Jael passed them to her sister. "I'm going to collect some grass for the donkeys."

Using a sickle, she leaned down and grasped clumps of grass and cut through the stems. She tied each bundle with a long grass stem. If Abida taught the boys, she might have time to bring the livestock out to graze.

Once back inside the encircling walls of the town, Jael led her sister back into Abida's home then went out to his old work shed to find Abida. He was holding one of his tools and staring at the furnace.

"Father," Jael said.

He jumped and turned to face her.

"Would you start to teach the boys?" Jael indicated the furnace.

"I was thinking the same thing. They're bored. Perhaps I am too. I'm used to working alongside Ephah and with him not here—" He shrugged. "We'll start with polishing, then pour some simple bells."

Jael smiled broadly. Generations of coppersmiths had made the same start.

* * *

*J*ael found Abida on the city wall, looking toward the west and murmuring his prayers. He came up here every day.

Zura prayed to the Israelites' god, but who did Abida pray to? Did he even know, or were they random words tossed out into the breeze which he hoped would reach the right ears?

"Who are you praying to?" Jael asked.

"Kothar-wa-Khasis," he said.

It was a name she'd not heard before. Besides the main gods, there were many minor ones.

"He's a special god for craftsmen. I know the boys don't worship any of the gods, but I gave Ephah an amulet before he left. He promised to wear it."

Jael hoped Reuel didn't see it. He might not worship any gods, but he would be upset at one more sign of his father's favor toward Ephah.

"It is so hard waiting for Eph–them to return," he said.

She wasn't going to let the correction bother her. Abida wasn't the only one praying. Zura would be praying all the time. She said it mattered which god a person prayed to, for those who followed a god became like that god. Jael shuddered. She had no desire to be like the cruel blood-hungry gods of Canaan.

Abida turned around to search the distance for anyone returning. It looked like he'd finished his prayers. Jael wished she could demand an answer for why Abida favored Ephah, but she couldn't. Maybe she could work it out if she knew more about the family.

"How did you meet your wife?" Jael asked.

Abida looked at her for a long moment before replying. "I didn't meet her until our wedding day." He leaned on the parapet of the wall. "She was a distant cousin, but my father approached her family to see if they'd agree to a betrothal."

"And they obviously did," Jael said.

"They did." Abida paused. "She was beautiful, but she had no background in coppersmithing and that was hard. Once the boys came, she devoted her life to them."

Them? Or mainly Reuel? When had the favoritism started? Had Abida been jealous of her focus?

Jael began to see why Reuel might be so enamored of his mother. Not only had she catered to his every need, but she had been beautiful. Jael couldn't possibly compete. By the end of the day, Jael was so exhausted from cooking, cleaning, and keeping the boys out of trouble, she doubted she looked beautiful at all.

CHAPTER NINE

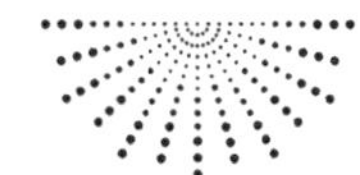

"What's that?" Reuel asked Ephah.

Crossing the Jordan had been easy because the water levels were low. Now the vast group of Midianite raiders approached the first town along with their Amalekite allies. All around the river side of the fields, rows of branches had been driven into the ground and covered with thorn bushes.

"This first town is the most vulnerable to our raids. They put up the fence to prevent us seeing when the wheat and barley is ripe." Ephah grinned. "It's a sort of game to see if they can harvest the grain before we discover it's ripe and cross the river."

The Israelites' plan had partially worked, for the field was already half harvested.

"We're not really interested in the grain," Ephah explained. "It's too heavy to carry at this stage, but we will leave behind a group to cut, dry, and pack it onto carts and take it straight across the river. We're after other things."

"Such as?" Reuel asked.

"Such as almonds, pistachios, and livestock. But the Israelites have become skilled at hiding them. Keep your eyes open for caves."

"Caves can be more easily defended," Reuel said.

"They could, but so far these raids have been like taking food from a baby."

"That's because the Israelites are not united." Reuel's camel strode toward the higher ground. "They've always seen themselves as twelve separate tribes. If they learned to work together, they might have the strength to resist us."

Ephah guffawed. "Have you seen any signs of unity? We've barely seen any people since we crossed the river. They're all hiding in their holes. Too afraid to come out."

Reuel looked toward the town. Its gates were shut tight against them and nothing moved. No people on the walls, no soldiers on the gate, no animals wandering in or out. The silence was eerie. At harvest, the fields should be filled with teams of people working together with much laughter and teasing. Harvest had always been Reuel's favorite time of year. A time when he laid down his tools and the whole family worked together for a wage of grain. A change from the heat of the furnace and the demands of his craft.

One of the Amalekites pointed at the town walls. Reuel let his gaze follow the pointing finger. There! Something—or, rather, someone—moved. It made sense. Old people and children couldn't easily hide out in the caves with the Israelite men and the stores they'd hidden away. Instead, the remaining people watched the Midianite horde descend on their fields and trusted their city walls to protect them. Not a bad assumption when it was obvious the Midianites and Amalekites were intent on raiding rather than conquest.

"That's what we're looking for." Ephah pointed to the trees nearby.

Already eager men surrounded the grove of almond trees. With a sharp command to their camels, Reuel and Ephah descended and shook out sections of their tent and laid them on the ground under a tree so the nuts could be more easily collected.

"Help me shake the first branch," Ephah said.

Reuel reached up and grabbed the branch, pushing off the ground with his legs to make the branch shake violently. The almonds rained down onto the waiting cloth until it was covered.

"I'll hold the mouth of the sack open if you lift the corners of the cloth and funnel the nuts into the sack." Ephah said. "Tonight, we'll take off the outer skins to make them lighter to transport."

All around them, men were doing the same. Stripping the trees and leaving only the still unripe or deformed nuts. The sour taste of shame filled Reuel's mouth, but he tamped it down. He was here because his father had manipulated him into coming. He'd also hoped this trip would allow him to get to know his older brother away from the clinging favor of their father, but they'd barely had time to talk. Ephah had many friends among the raiders and preferred to spend his time drinking and jesting with them.

By late afternoon they'd stripped the trees bare and cut the grain, leaving it to dry under the watchful eyes of a chosen group of raiders. With the sun setting over to their left, they moved toward the next town.

* * *

They'd been moving steadily north, raiding town after town. Ephah said there had been more resistance to their raids in the first years, but the raiders were so much stronger now that the Israelites avoided confrontation and simply worked to hide any early harvest. The raiders were now accompanied by baaing flocks of sheep and goats, strings of donkeys, and the occasional camel. Not that the Midianites dared take the camels, for the Amalekites were always quick to lay a claim. They prized the camels for their desert existence.

"We'll have to head home soon." Ephah gestured toward the flocks and herds. "We've become too large a group to move quickly.

The more produce we load up and the more animals we find, the slower we become. And the slower we become the easier it would be to attack us." He slapped his thigh. "Lightning speed is what is needed."

Lightning speed was no longer possible.

The first few nights, Reuel had joined in with the heavy drinking, but the appeal had soon palled. Besides which, there had been too much work to do. All the outer husks of the almonds had to be removed to lighten the weight of the plunder and to enable greater speed.

The camels were also loaded with pistachios. With all their sacks full, the raiding party's attention had turned to sheep and goats. Livestock were the way to riches. They could be milked, shorn, and eaten, and they were easy to sell or exchange.

"How much longer until we head back to Ramoth Gilead?" Reuel asked.

"Not much longer now. Next year we'll cross at a different place and raid a different part of the country," Ephah said. "There'll be better pickings elsewhere."

Reuel didn't intend to join the raids again. He would prefer to rely on his craft to build up his wealth, rather than rely on raids. There was no honor in raiding people too frightened to resist.

* * *

They were camped for the night near a small river. Reuel had taken the camels to drink their fill, but his camel bawled as he tried to encourage it out of the water.

Reuel used a long, supple willow branch to switch the camel's behind and pulled on its halter.

The camel jerked its head in protest and spat. Reuel stepped back to avoid the slimy stream of saliva and tripped over a rock. He heard the crack as he fell. Pain pierced his left ankle, and he sat down hard with a groan.

"What are you doing down there?" Ephah asked from his superior perch on his camel.

"My leg," Reuel said through clenched teeth.

"You'd better not have broken anything." Ephah swung his leg over his camel's neck and dropped to the ground. "You're no use to us lame."

Reuel wouldn't just be useless. He'd be a liability. He would have to somehow get back across the river, and there would be little mercy directed his way if he was unlucky enough to meet an Israelite.

Ephah came over and looked at Reuel's leg which was already changing color. Ephah cursed.

"You won't be able to come into the valley with us. You'll have to stay up here. We'll collect you on our way back." He shook his head. "We'd better get that leg splinted first." He looked around and then took his knife out of its sheath on the camel's shoulder and stomped toward the nearest tree. Ephah squinted at various branches then broke off four, quickly removing any side twigs and leaves so he had four straight sticks. Then he went back to the camel and rifled through his pack, pulling out several strips of leather.

"I'll get two of the other men to help me," Ephah said. "This is going to hurt."

Reuel grimaced and thought of Jael. She'd have been gentle. He had no such hopes of the raiders. They had been drinking most nights since crossing the river, so there'd be no steady hands.

Ephah laid down the branches and leather and went off to get some help, probably wishing their father hadn't pressured Reuel to come now that he was proving so useless. Reuel groaned. He was going to be a burden. Burdens ended up being resented by everyone.

Ephah returned accompanied by three raiders, expressions grim and obviously longing to be elsewhere for they didn't look Reuel in the eye.

Ephah ran his hand along Reuel's leg, and Reuel almost screamed.

Ephah grunted. "Could be worse. It doesn't feel displaced."

Maybe not, but already the leg throbbed and Reuel's ankle and foot were swelling rapidly.

"Bite on that." Ephah handed Reuel a piece of leather.

Reuel put it between his teeth. He wouldn't shame his brother by making a sound. The four men held a quick discussion.

"It'll be easier if we stand him up and let the leg dangle," one of them said.

Reuel allowed them to discuss him as if he was an injured sheep. He didn't trust his voice not to betray how much pain he felt.

Two of the men braced themselves to help him stand. Reuel clamped down on the leather as he was hauled to his feet. Sweat broke out all over his body. He could feel his good leg trembling as wave after wave of pain rolled up his broken leg.

Ephah put the four branches around Reuel's leg. "Now use those big hands of yours and hold these while I tie the splint together," he said to the fourth man.

Reuel concentrated on breathing, in and out, in and out. His jaw ached from biting down on the leather, but he didn't let a sound pass his lips. Ephah didn't mess around, and he bound the splint firmly. "Lower him carefully onto the ground."

It was a relief to lie flat while the men discussed what to do with him.

"We need a cave." Ephah sent two men to find one.

Reuel closed his eyes. The sound of a broken twig woke him, and he squinted through half closed eyes. The men returned and picked Reuel up as if he was a sheaf of barley. Once again, he clenched his jaw shut as each of their steps caused shafts of pain to shoot up and down his leg. They carried him over the crest of the hill to a cave partially hidden in a tumble of rocks.

"We'll leave you enough food until we return," Ephah said as they entered the cave. "But we'll need to take your camel. You can't look after it, and it would give away your position."

The men dumped Reuel beside the cave wall. The pain of the fall ravaged his senses, blurring his vision. When this wave of torment had passed, he noticed Ephah laying his pack of supplies beside him and two waterskins. Would it be enough? How long would he be alone?

The other men returned to their camp, but Ephah lingered. He found a heavy stick Reuel could use as a cudgel and placed it beside the provisions. "I'm sorry to leave you, but there's one last raid down in the valley. When I return, we'll work out how to get you home."

Ephah touched him on the shoulder, a gesture that shocked Reuel in its tenderness. "Wish us luck. Sorry you're missing this raid. I'll bring you back something."

Ephah left the cave. Reuel heard the crunch of his footsteps and the slide of small stones as he climbed the ridge. He took a shaky breath. His leg burned as if it was on fire. He felt as weak as a baby lamb and as vulnerable as one too. If a man or animal came into this cave, Reuel could do nothing. He glanced at the cudgel Ephah had left him, doubting he could even wield it.

Hurry back, brother.

CHAPTER TEN

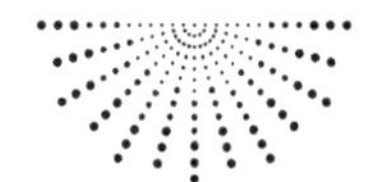

Five days later, Reuel lay under the lip of his cave, protected from the heat of the late afternoon sun. Below him, the valley was filled with hordes of Midianite and Amalekite raiders. Dust rose as the raiders corralled their new livestock behind temporary thorn fences. Livestock had been streaming into the camp all afternoon. The raid had clearly been successful. Would Ephah come soon to end Reuel's isolation?

Reuel shifted his position and grunted as the searing pain shot up his leg again. If an Israelite came across him, they could deal with him as easily as he'd deal with a mosquito. The pain was still bad enough that he only moved when his limbs became numb from the previous position. He reached into his pack and drew out a tiny handful of pistachios, then took a sip of water. The main thing was to rest so he'd be as strong as possible to get on his camel. Not that it was easy to sleep, for he woke every time he knocked his leg.

As the shadows lengthened, Reuel ate and drank and dozed. Dozed and sipped and nibbled his diminishing supplies. Ephah had to come soon or he'd run out of food and water. A bird came close.

He watched as it pecked the stalks of grass, hoping for some seeds. It didn't see him and, finding little food, it flew off. If only it had stayed to keep him company. But he mustn't get sentimental. If Ephah didn't come tomorrow, he'd need to think how to devise a trap.

The men below were setting up tents and lighting fires. They would slaughter some of the stock and make bread to eat with their meat. They didn't fear attack, for they were strong. Stronger than a people who skulked in caves and holes in the hills.

The orange blaze of the sun dropped lower, silhouetting the trees below and burnishing their tops with bronze. Reuel would give a lot to be back, traveling with his family and using his metalwork skills. How long would his leg take to heal?

A mosquito buzzed in his ear. He reached up to try and squash it without jerking his leg. A fire would have helped to keep them away, but it would also announce his presence to any wandering Israelites, if they had dared to wander in these times.

The sun sank lower and disappeared out of sight, leaving only the golden memory of its passing. Reuel pulled his cloak across his body and drifted off to sleep.

* * *

A screech woke Reuel. It was pitch dark without any moonlight, and even the stars were dim. He shivered and began the laborious task of turning over without hurting his leg. Midway through the maneuver he froze. What was that?

A rattle of pebbles had been dislodged somewhere below him. Was it an animal? Or a human? And if human, why would men be moving around with the dangerous host in the valley below?

Reuel slowly raised his head and peered below. There! The merest shadow gliding across the paleness of a slab of rock. Men.

Two men. Their silence and stealth meant they must be Israelites, and they were young and strong. Spies! If he'd been able, Reuel would have warned the camp below, but then again, a couple of spies were not much danger to the camp below. They would see the strength of the Midianites and Amalekites and return trembling to their caves and holes.

But they were a danger to Reuel. He rubbed his eyes. He must keep watch.

Reuel waited until he could no longer hear the men, then carefully shifted his position, trying to find whatever part of his body ached the least from five days lying on the hard ground. Reuel's eyelids grew heavy. He was on the edge of sleep when the two men ghosted up the hill again. If they were spies, they now knew that attacking the host below would be suicidal.

Seeing no more danger, Reuel allowed himself to drift back into the sleep his body craved.

Later—it must have been much later—he woke with a start for the second time that night. What was it this time? He seemed to do nothing but sleep yet remained nothing but tired.

He peered through heavy-lidded eyes down the slope of the hill. Out of the corner of his right eye he caught furtive movement. Men! And far more than a mere two.

Reuel tried to make his breaths slow and shallow. He must not move while these unknown men were near. He still wasn't sure if they were soldiers. Each carried some sort of large object from which a faint glow was occasionally seen. They were soldiers for the faint flickers of light gleamed on swords and something else. Something curved. Were they a threat to the camp below? How could he raise a warning?

Like the passing of the two men earlier, the men were easiest to see as they flitted across the slab of pale rock. Reuel focused, counting the men like he had counted sheep in the past. There were not many more than a large flock. He let out a breath and his shoulders relaxed. These men were no threat to the men below, whose camels were as many as the grains of sand along the banks of the Jordan.

Below the pale rock, he could see a figure waving his arm to direct the men. The men split into three groups. Reuel scanned the hills around for any more telltale glows but could see nothing. He wiped the beads of sweat from his forehead and prepared to settle back into a more comfortable position. Whoever these men were, surely the lookouts at the camp would soon see their lights.

He'd stay awake, for even a small raid on the camp could indicate that the Israelites were beginning to retaliate. The last thing anyone wanted was the different tribes uniting behind a single leader. Leaders like King Zebah or Zalmunna who had reigned over different groups of Midianites yet had been able to work together and unite all their raiders behind them. Seeing the vast array of their camels as they'd crossed the Jordan, Reuel hadn't been able to control the swell of pride that he was one of them. That at long last, they were taking some of their rightful inheritance. The inheritance of Avraham's favored son, Yitzchak.

An owl hooted, passing by with barely a whisper of its wings. Moments later Reuel heard the squeak of its dying prey. Where were the men he'd seen? Reuel narrowed his eyes and scanned the valley below. A tiny glow of light was momentarily visible on the far side of the camp. He clenched his jaw. The men seemed to be surrounding the camp. But what did they hope to prove? Maybe they planned a swift in-and-out raid to scare the Midianites. To see if they could scare them back over the river and give the Israelites time to gather an army to resist the raids the next year. It was a risky tactic but perhaps one worth trying. A test of the unity and purpose of the Amalekites and Midianites.

A breeze blew up the hill toward Reuel and brought the pungent smell of camel. Reuel's camel always gave fair warning when strangers approached. The camels would be aware of the men waiting on the hillside just above the camp, but was any Midianite guard alert enough to pay attention? The camp looked silent and asleep. Not as alert as Reuel had hoped.

There was a sudden blare of horns from the near side of the camp. Reuel jumped, and his leg collided with a small rock, sending a jolt of pain up his body so sharp he bit his tongue. Now he knew what the unknown objects he'd seen were. More horns blared from other sides of the valley. There was a smashing sound like the breaking of many earthenware vessels. Flickering lights sprang up all around the Midianite camp as if every man in this small horde had lit a flaming torch. A great shout went up, but the words were unclear. Then the lights raced down the hill toward the Midianite tents like tongues of fire burning dry grass.

Reuel thumped his fist on the ground. How he wished he was down there with his brother and his people. By now they would be out of their tents, grabbing their bows and swords. The Israelites were about to get a rude shock as they discovered how many men they had aroused. The Israelites would be lucky to escape with their lives. Excitement surged in his belly. Maybe this would be the start of a conquest of the Israelites, and his people would finally rise in power. Their kings would rule these broad lands. Then there would be more than enough money to make. His mirrors might earn him both fame and fortune.

The wind had picked up and brought the sound of swords clashing and people screaming. He'd expected the Israelites to be fleeing by now. Perhaps they'd brought more men from a different direction, because the fighting was taking longer than he had anticipated. The Israelites would be learning a lesson that should keep them subjugated for another few harvests. If the Israelites were soundly beaten, perhaps it might be worthwhile for Reuel to come raiding again. Next year he'd be more careful. No more injuries.

The wind changed direction, and Reuel could no longer hear more than an occasional scream. He might as well sleep. Ephah would likely come tomorrow. They could return home laden with plunder. If he was lucky, Ephah might bring him an Israelite sword. No point leaving the Israelites with weapons to plot another attack.

CHAPTER ELEVEN

"What are you doing, Zura?" Jael asked.

Zura was standing under a tree in the courtyard, rocking gently back and forth.

"I'm praying for the men to return safely," Zura said.

Jael's throat tightened. "So, you think they might be in danger?"

"There is always danger when men go raiding," Zura said. "But I am not worried yet. It has only been one moon since they left."

Jael was not eager for the men to return. Once Abida had started to teach the boys his trade, he'd been less short-tempered and she'd had more time for herself. She was now glad Reuel had gone raiding despite her earlier anger at his decision. Now she had time to work with Zipporah and Zura and do tasks that she seldom had time to do. Today they were going to make new tunics with the cloth they'd woven.

"Ephah said there's never been much danger," Jael said.

"Not all danger comes from war. Sometimes danger comes from your friends," Zura said. "But don't worry. That's why I pray. I ask Yahveh to care for them."

Jael stepped closer to her sister. "It's alright to mention Yahveh with me, but don't let the others hear you. They will be angry. Until Reuel returns, we have nowhere else to stay."

When Zura had first met Abida, she had spoken of her trust in the god of the Israelites. Abida had told her he didn't permit traitors in his family. Zura had bowed her head and kept quiet.

"Dear sister, I learned that lesson long ago, but your father-in-law can't prevent me praying for him."

Jael snorted. "None of us can prevent it, but don't waste your prayers on us."

"I never waste my prayers," Zura said quietly.

Jael sighed. She loved her sister, but her loyalty to Yahveh was puzzling. If Yahveh had healed her sister she could understand her fervor, but worshiping Yahveh never seemed to be of any benefit to Zura. Not that Jael ever asked her questions. She didn't want to open up a conversation she had no interest in continuing.

"Are we going to work on the tunics today?" Zura asked.

"We are."

Until the men returned, they would work hard to repair tents, weave cloth, and prepare for the travel ahead. Zipporah had told them when the men returned, a messenger would arrive instructing her to take the cart to the prearranged meeting place. She'd also help Ephah to bring in any of the sheep, goats, donkeys, or camels they'd rounded up. If the Manassites they lived among knew Ephah went raiding, it would endanger them and give the locals an easy excuse to throw them out of the town. Or worse.

Zura turned toward Jael, and Jael took her hand to guide her to the stairs that led to the rooftop. The light up there would be better for Jael and Zipporah as they sewed, and they would catch any breeze that blew.

Coppersmithing was hard on clothes, and many of Reuel's work clothes were ripped where the material had grown thin or caught on sharp objects. If the men stayed away a bit longer, Jael might have a chance to make him more than one new tunic. New clothes would be important if Reuel's dreams for increased sales of mirrors were fulfilled.

"The boys seem to be making progress," Zipporah said as she handed the first tunic to Jael.

"Yes, Reba takes pride in the little bells he's making, but Hanok is getting tired of polishing them." Jael chuckled. "He can't wait to play with the furnace."

"Boys always want to play with fire, but Father is wise enough to know he is not ready yet," Zipporah said.

Jael had gone to watch the boys once, but was worried her anxiety would distract Reba from taking the care that was necessary to avoid being burned. Abida had made it abundantly clear that she was a nuisance and she'd best leave it to him to get on with supervising the boys.

Jael used her needle to weave back and forth through the material she'd folded around the neck of Reuel's new tunic.

"Zura, since the men aren't here," Zipporah said, "why don't you tell us a story?"

When Jael had been a child, she'd liked nothing better than hearing stories of their ancestors. Zura would put her arm around Jael, and Jael would snuggle into her side and listen and try to imagine those long-ago people.

"Which story do you want to hear?" Zura asked, cutting another length of thread.

"How about the stories of our namesakes?" Zipporah handed Jael the cut cloth for Reba's tunic.

"I'd prefer to hear yours," Jael said quickly. She'd loved to hear the story of Jael when she was a child until Reuel had laughed and told her she'd been misnamed.

Zura carefully laid aside the knife and the ball of thread she'd been cutting lengths from. "Once long, long ago, Midian was born to our great ancestor Avraham. Avraham was rich and famous in all the lands on the other side of the Jordan. Adonai had blessed him, so his flocks and herds were more than any other man in the land."

Jael wished her sister would leave Yahveh and his many names out of her stories, but it seemed not. Jael just ignored that bit and enjoyed the rest of the tale.

"Avraham was already old, older than anyone else in Canaan, when his wife, Sara, died. In his loneliness he turned to our ancestor, Keturah, and she bore him six sons: Zimran, Jokshan, Medan, Midian, Ishbak, and Shuah."

The names rolled off Zura's tongue from long years of practice.

"Of course Midian was the greatest, even though he was the fourth son," Zipporah said.

"Of course," Jael murmured. She was sure each of the descendants thought their ancestor was the greatest.

"When Avraham gave each of his sons their inheritance, they spread out into the great deserts of the south. Midian roamed far and found those who could teach him to wield fire and mold copper to his will. That skill has been passed down from father to son, right down to Ephah and Reuel and is now being passed on to Reba and Hanok."

Reuel was bitter that Avraham had not treated his eight sons more equally. He believed they should all have been allowed to stay with Avraham in Canaan and not have to battle the sandstorms of the deserts and the burning sun. Yet, if they had remained in Canaan, would they have become coppersmiths, the craft Reuel was so proud of? Life was too short for bitterness. It made more sense to Jael to be thankful for what they had rather than longing for mirages they might never find. She was thankful her family had come to Canaan and left the harshness of the desert. She'd met some of the desert Midianites as a child. They looked much older than their years, their skin weathered and leathery. Women in the desert died young, worn out by the hard life they lived there. She preferred the hills and plains and rivers of Canaan to what she'd heard of the desert.

"Midian had sons, and their sons had sons for generation after generation," Zura continued. "Until one of his descendants, Jethro, was born. He grew up to be a leader among men and a priest, and he had six daughters and one precious son. His daughters were shepherds for their father's flocks."

"And Zipporah was the most beautiful of all," Zipporah said.

"Well, she certainly stood out from among her sisters," Zura said with a smile. "Do you want to tell the story?"

"No, you're better at it," Zipporah said. "Do you need a drink?"

Zura held out her hand. Zipporah unstoppered the water bag before taking a few mouthfuls herself and passing the bag on to Zura. From below and across the courtyard they heard the sound of metal being struck as Abida demonstrated something to the boys.

"Now, where were we?" Zura asked.

"Zipporah and her sisters were shepherds," Jael said.

"The girls watched their father's flocks every day, and every evening they had to go to the well to water them, but the other shepherds were stronger and more aggressive. They would push in and water their animals first, and Zipporah and her sisters would have to wait. Every day they were the last ones home because the men thought they deserved to be first."

"And?" Jael said leaning forward as though she was hearing this story for the first and not the hundredth time.

"And one day they arrived home much earlier than usual. Their father, Jethro, said to them, 'Girls, why are you home so early tonight?' The girls said to their father, 'An Egyptian was at the well, and he drove off the shepherds who always push in ahead of us. He filled the troughs for our animals and made sure they were watered first.' Their father looked at them. 'Girls, where is the man? You can't leave him sitting at the well. You must bring him home for a meal.'"

Jethro was a wise man, and he had six daughters to marry off. Like any father, he would want the best match for each daughter, and here was a man who had already proved himself by fighting the injustice his daughters experienced every day at the well. At the very least, he must have wanted to meet the mysterious Egyptian and find out why he was so far from home.

"Over that first meal Jethro must have asked Mosheh his story." Zura laughed. "I wonder how much Mosheh told him. I doubt he said anything about fleeing because he'd killed a man or being brought up in a palace. Anyway, Jethro must have seen something he liked because Mosheh ended up shepherding Jethro's sheep."

"What do you think the girls thought about that? Were they glad to have another helper, or did it mean they didn't have to shepherd anymore?" Zipporah asked.

"Maybe they worked together at the beginning," Zura said. "But eventually it seems that Mosheh looked after the sheep on his own, for he was alone when Yahveh spoke to him on the mountain."

"The stories never tell us anything of Mosheh and Zipporah and how long it was until they married," Jael said. "I'd love to know all the details."

"We do want a good love story, don't we? But look at us. Most of our marriages are arranged and love only comes later." Zipporah blushed.

Was what Jael felt for Reuel love? She didn't think so. She'd wanted to marry him when she was a child and he'd noticed her, but had she fooled herself? Once they were married, his unkind words often pierced her defenses. Defenses she was trying to build up to protect herself from his frequent snide remarks.

"I think Jethro—or Reuel, as he was also called—probably arranged for Mosheh to become his son-in-law as quickly as possible. Certainly, it wasn't long until the birth of Gershom, which means?" Zura prompted.

"I have become a stranger in a foreign land," Jael said.

"You've listened well over the years," Zura said.

Listening to stories had been Jael's escape from life after their father's death. Once the sun went down, Jael would curl up and listen to her sister's voice in the dark.

"Mosheh lived with Zipporah for forty years in the desert where Jethro made his home. Mosheh was no longer a prince of Egypt, but a humble shepherd. A man who spent much time on his own protecting his sheep. He didn't know he would end up caring for a far greater flock, a flock that would be even more difficult to move together in one direction."

Zipporah laughed. "He probably looked back on herding sheep as the easy years. The Israelites were much more difficult than Jethro's flocks."

"At least sheep can't voice their complaints and are content as long as they have food in their bellies and enough water," Jael said.

"Do you want me to continue?" Zura asked.

"Yes," Zipporah said before Jael had had time to consider the question. As a child she'd naively loved the stories, but her belief in the promise of blessings had waned after her marriage. This god was not for her. He didn't care about Midianite women, and, as far as she could see, he no longer cared for his own people either. They were not blessed in any way that was apparent to her, but instead they were cursed with drought and raided harvests.

"One day, when Mosheh was eighty, he was herding the sheep on the side of Mount Horeb. Suddenly he saw something strange, a bush that seemed to be on fire, yet it didn't burn up. When he approached the fiery bush, he heard Yahveh say to him, 'Mosheh, don't come any closer. Take off your sandals, for the place where you are standing is holy ground.' Then Yahveh said, 'I am the God of your father and the God of Avraham, Yitzchak, and Yaacov. I have seen the misery of my people in Egypt and I have come down to rescue them and bring them into the land I promised, a land flowing with milk and honey. Now, go and speak to Pharaoh for I am sending you to bring the people out of Egypt.'"

Zura's voice had them all mesmerized. She continued to tell them about Mosheh's four objections to obeying Yahveh until finally Yahveh said, "Enough. Go and I'll send your brother as a helper to you." And amazingly Mosheh went, and Yahveh did many miracles through him until finally the people of Israel left Egypt.

Jael took the last of the tunics and pushed the wooden needle through the cloth one stitch at a time. She added blue-dyed wool to the neckline to make it special. Reuel could wear it when he met with potential buyers for the mirrors.

"After Mosheh and the Israelites crossed the Red Sea, they met up with Jethro, Zipporah, and Mosheh's two sons in the desert. Mosheh told Jethro about all the wonders Yahveh had performed and how Yahveh had rescued them from every hardship. Jethro said, 'Praise be to Yahveh, who rescued you from the hand of the Egyptians and of Pharaoh. Now I know that Yahveh is greater than all other gods, for he did this to those who had treated Israel arrogantly.'"

"I'd forgotten this part of the story," Zipporah said. "Many of our people still worship the old gods, the gods of tree and rock, and fear the spirits, but Jethro seemed to have come to worship Yahveh."

Zura nodded. "He brought sacrifices and offerings to Yahveh. He also acted as an advisor to Mosheh and said, 'The work is too heavy for you, and you can't handle it alone. Appoint officials over thousands, hundreds, fifties, and tens. Have them serve as judges and only bring you the most difficult cases.'"

"It was wise advice," Jael said. "And Mosheh was wise enough to listen to Jethro." If only her husband was as wise as his namesake. Maybe such wisdom only came with age.

Zura stretched her back. "That is enough for today. It is getting hot, and it is time to eat and rest. Maybe the men will soon be home."

Maybe, but Jael wasn't sure if she would welcome Reuel's return or not. Would he be kinder to her when he came home? She doubted it. It was more likely that he'd return more resentful of Midian's unimportance in the lands and more determined to right old wrongs. And she would suffer for his bitterness.

CHAPTER TWELVE

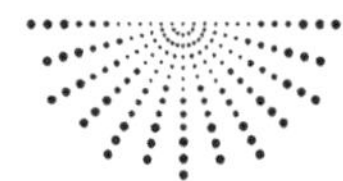

*S*omewhere nearby a bird burst into a trill of song. Reuel had found it difficult to get to sleep the night before. It must be late, for already the sun's heat was radiating off the rocks at the entrance to the cave.

He turned over and looked down into the valley below, then looked again. It seemed too silent. There should have been movement everywhere by now. He looked across the whole camp then raised his gaze and stiffened. Birds of prey circled the camp. Even as he watched, the first landed with an awkward hop, then, moving forward it landed on what looked like a pile of clothing. No, not a pile of clothes, but a body. Nausea surged in Reuel's throat. More birds landed. Now he saw that what he'd overlooked as camp detritus were in fact bodies. Many, many bodies. Bodies that might have been thrown here and there by some giant or god in a fit of anger.

Where was Ephah?

Reuel's gaze followed the trail of destruction to the south. More bodies lay under the burning sun, and the vultures were now descending like dark leaves. Vomit rose into Reuel's mouth, and he spat onto the ground. The sour taste remained because he had no water to waste on rinsing out his mouth.

What could possibly explain the silence and destruction below? Where had the raiders disappeared to? Were they off somewhere, chasing the Israelites? But if so, why were there so many bodies below? His eyes found the shape of several dead camels, now stripped of their gold chains.

A cold shiver went up Reuel's spine. The Amalekites loved their camels. Had the few Israelites he'd seen pass the cave managed to kill some of the raiders?

There was no sign of anyone alive in the camp. Where was Ephah? Had the battle moved south?

Ephah was strong from years of metalwork and had made his own sword which he regularly practiced with. He'd be fine, but where was he? Would he return soon, bringing Reuel the camel that was essential to return home?

Reuel had only a few handfuls of nuts and mouthfuls of water remaining. His leg remained useless. But if Ephah didn't return, Reuel would need to work out a way to move or he would soon be food for the carrion birds himself. The call of a hawk echoed across the empty silence of the valley. He remembered how Ephah had rested his hand on his shoulder for comfort before he had departed. This gesture had given Reuel hope for a renewed relationship after this raid, beyond his jealousy over his father's favor. But then Reuel's eyes took in the scattered thorn fencing within the camp now devoid of livestock, and his stomach ached. Where was Ephah?

* * *

*L*ast night, Reuel had finished the final handful of the pistachios and followed it with the last drop of water. He'd slept knowing he must move or die. His life now depended on guessing correctly which way to crawl toward water.

Yesterday he'd managed to drag himself to the nearest thicket and had found two sturdy sticks. Even crawling the short distance to the trees had convinced him that crawling wasn't a long-term option. He would have to use the sticks to help him hop, and each hop would cause him more pain.

The light of dawn was still dim and Reuel knew he must move before the heat of the day. He stood, using the rock wall for support, and placed the waterskin with its leather loops in the small of his back. He used the leather around his waist to tie the empty sack to himself. He couldn't afford to leave anything that might be useful behind.

He took a deep breath and braced himself on the two sticks before taking his first tentative hop. There was a dull ache in his leg, but the swelling had decreased markedly and he'd had to tighten the leather straps around the splint last night. He gritted his teeth and hopped across the flat ground. When he reached the slope, he lowered himself to the ground. Dragging the sticks behind him, he inched his way upwards.

Above him there was an extended bubbling grunt. Reuel stopped. Was there someone up ahead? It couldn't have been Ephah or his friends, for they would have come down to the cave where they'd left him. Any person must now be presumed to be the enemy, because there had been no sign of a single Midianite or Amalekite. It was as though they had disappeared off the face of the earth. Reuel assumed they must have gone back across the river. Surely they couldn't still be pursuing the enemy?

There'd been no sound above for a long moment, so Reuel began his laborious ascent. He'd tied extra leather around his knees to protect them from any thorns or rough ground. He shuffled forward a few handbreadths, and then he listened. Nothing. Perhaps whatever had made the sound was gone. He repeated his crawling.

Sweat trickled between his shoulder blades. He was close to the top now. He crawled forward and then looked over the top, scanning side to side. No one was visible, but someone could be hiding in the trees or behind the pile of rocks. He strained his ears and listened. Somewhere, over in the trees, he could hear water. He swallowed, his parched throat anticipating cool relief. Reuel crawled to the nearest rock and used it to help himself stand, then he hopped, awkward step by awkward step, toward the trees.

The closer he got to the trees, the louder the sound of water. It wasn't going to be a river, but it would be more than enough to fill his waterskin. He'd look for some sort of fruit or edible plants too.

A small spring fed into a rock pool. He knelt as quickly as he could manage with his useless leg and scooped up the cold water into his parched mouth. Oh, that was good. He dipped in his waterskins and filled them.

Behind him there was a crack of a twig. Heart racing, he swiveled and then let out his breath with a whoosh. His camel was looking down at Reuel as though she'd never left his side.

"Good girl," he said, a crack to his voice. "Am I ever glad to see you."

Using his walking stick, Reuel hauled himself to his feet and picked up his waterskin to put it on his back. Then he left one stick on the ground while holding out his hand and hopped toward the camel. She shied from his reach.

"Good girl. Don't be scared. It's just me. You know me."

The halter was dangling almost within reach.

"Good girl." He kept his voice low and steady. "No need to fear."

Finally, he took the halter and stroked the camel's side. She didn't appear to have any injuries. Using the stick, Reuel led the camel to the spring, but she refused to drink.

"You've already drunk your fill, have you girl? That's good."

He commanded the camel to sit. Taking both sticks, he attached them to the side of the saddle before grabbing the longer hair on the camel's neck and clambering on.

The camel snorted.

"Yes, girl, I know. I am not my usual agile self."

The main thing was that she remained seated while he got himself as comfortable as possible.

"Up, girl, up."

The camel straightened its back legs, throwing him forward. He gritted his teeth at the stab of pain in his leg. The camel straightened its front legs and took the strain off his back and legs.

He patted the camel's neck. "We must look for clues to what has happened first."

The camel snorted but didn't resist as they headed for the deserted camp. Once there, the air was heavy with the smell of decomposing bodies. The camel balked at going past the outskirts of the camp. Stomach heaving, Reuel allowed the camel to walk around the boundary.

He'd come expecting dead Israelites, but so far he hadn't seen a single one. The dead were Amalekites, easily recognizable by their clothing, and Midianites.

Reuel kept the camel's head toward the camp because it wanted to flee. Reuel pulled his scarf across his nose and mouth. It didn't make any difference. The smell of rotting flesh and feces was choking anyway. Reuel scanned the bodies for the one he didn't want to see. He couldn't see all the bodies because he couldn't risk getting down off his mount. She'd run if he gave her the chance, and he couldn't blame her. The same desire welled up in him.

They'd completed half the circuit when he heard voices. Reuel swiveled his neck, looking for where the sounds came from. Cupping his hand around his ear, he guessed there were men coming from behind the hillock to the south. Tension gripped his shoulders. He'd have to go. He was in no state to risk an encounter with Israelites or angry raiders. Neither would be in the mood for asking questions.

The fighters had gone south, so he would head north. North to the crossings he was familiar with and into territory where he and the family had only recently traveled.

Reuel kicked the camel's side with his good leg. It took no more urging to head away from the camp. The voices grew louder.

Reuel bent low. He must reach the shelter of the trees before he was seen. The camel sped up the hill. Once in the shelter of the trees, Reuel turned to check whether they'd been seen. The first of a group of men, most likely Israelites, was in sight. Even as Reuel watched, a man got off his mount and used his foot to turn a body over. Reuel swallowed the sourness in his stomach and turned away. Away to the north and a crossing that he hoped would be unobserved.

Now he'd have to be alert. Alert to finding food along the way and alert to any signs of Israelites. He hadn't planned to be away this long. Jael and the family would be worrying. He must get home before the news of the battle reached them.

Was Ephah alive? The question made Reuel's gut churn. Without Ephah, he would have to support Zipporah and her children and his father, as well as his own family. The weight of the possibilities settled on him like a load of ingots. He must not think of Ephah now. First he must reach home. Through enemy territory. Alone. And with a useless leg.

CHAPTER THIRTEEN

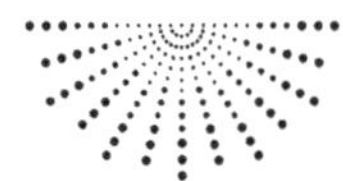

Jael and Zura were outside the city walls, playing in the stream with the children. Jael couldn't bear to be inside the city walls much longer. She hadn't realized how much she preferred the open road and their itinerant lifestyle. Out here she could also keep an eye on the road for Reuel and Ephah's return. For they must return soon. Abida said they were usually only away for one moon, and it was far longer than that now.

Jael had enjoyed the time with Zipporah, but now she was beginning to worry. What if something had happened to Reuel? There were times she wished he'd never return, but he must, for they needed him to provide for them all. Yet surely they would know if something had happened, wouldn't they? Reuel and Ephah weren't the only men to have left Ramoth Gilead, but no one else had returned either.

"Ima, come and help us dam up the water," Reba said, already shin-deep in the stream.

Jael stepped into the water. Maybe being out here with the boys would stop her worrying.

"Hanok, put bigger stones here first." Jael pointed to the gap between two rocks. "We'll add smaller stones and sand later."

"I can't, Ima," Hanok said, straining to pull out a bigger stone.

"Let me do it then," she said.

Zura had gone a little further upstream and was washing clothes.

Jael stacked up a series of bigger stones. As the water started to back up behind them, she showed Hanok and Reba how to find smaller stones to place in the gaps and crevices.

"Someone's coming," Zura called.

Jael stood up straight and looked down to where she'd last seen Reuel when he left. A man stumbled up the hill. Was he drunk, or ill, or just weary?

"Help me, Ima," Hanok said, pulling on her arm.

Jael returned to the dam building, but something bothered her. What if that man had been one of the raiders? She'd go and check that he wasn't a Midianite, that he wasn't carrying news.

"Zura, will you be alright here if I go back and get something?" Jael didn't want to alarm her sister although her own stomach was unaccountably churning.

"If you'll get us settled under the big tree, we'll be fine. Won't we, boys?" Zura said.

Jael helped Zura scramble up the riverbank and get comfortable, then headed back to the town. She hurried through the gate and had barely turned toward their home when she heard a moaning scream.

"No! No, no, no!" Abida wailed.

Her gut had been right. Jael lifted up her tunic and ran. *Please not Reuel. Please not Reuel,* her feet seemed to pound out.

Something dreadful must have happened, but was it to Ephah or Reuel or both? Were they injured? Or worse?

The wailing continued. Jael grasped her side, with a stitch jabbing into her at every stride. Pushing in through the courtyard gate, she found Abida rocking back and forth and moaning. Zipporah was white and tearless. The man she'd seen walking up the hill had collapsed on the ground with his head lowered.

"Oh, Ephah, my son, my beloved son, how could you leave me?" Abida moaned.

Ephah? What about Reuel? Was he alright, and if so, where was he?

"Water," gasped the man on the ground.

Jael went over to a bucket, took off the cover, and filled a dipper which she carried to the man. He drank, spilling half of it in his haste.

"More," he said.

She filled the dipper. "Slowly, or you'll be sick."

He ignored her and drank until he had drunk his fill. It was all she could do not to shake him and demand answers. What had happened to Ephah?

Jael squatted down next to the man. "Now tell me."

"Ask them." He jerked his head in the direction of Zipporah and Abida.

"They are beyond being able to tell me anything," Jael said.

"Gideon wiped us out," the man said.

"Gideon? Who's he?" Jael asked.

"A mighty warrior of Yahveh. He led the Israelites and attacked during the night. We panicked and attacked each other before flee-ing," the man said. "I was knocked out and when I came to." He shuddered. "Piles of dead. There were no signs of Israelites. I walked until I found a cave. I stayed there for days and days. Didn't eat, barely slept." He looked up at Jael with glazed eyes. "Too afraid to move."

Jael could hear her own heartbeat pounding in her ears. *Piles of dead...* "How do you know Ephah is dead?" she asked, voice lowered. Abida and Zipporah didn't need to hear the news once again.

"Ephah was lying with many others," he said.

"Are you sure it was Ephah?" Jael could barely force out these words.

"I have drunk many times with Ephah, and I brought this for his wife." His voice was flat, unemotional. He pulled a band of copper out of his pocket.

Jael's throat constricted. It was the ring every coppersmith worked as one of their early pieces. She put her body between the messenger and Zipporah and took the ring. She'd give it to Zipporah when the first pangs of grief were over.

Jael swallowed. "What about Reuel?"

"Reuel?" he asked, forehead wrinkled and confusion clouding his eyes.

"Reuel, my husband. Ephah's brother."

"He was not there," he said.

"What do you mean not there?"

"He broke his leg," the man said.

"In the battle?" Jael asked. Once again, she wanted to shake him. Could he not offer information instead of her having to drag it out of him?

"No, before." He rubbed his head. "He wasn't in the battle."

"So where was he? Is he?"

"I don't know. Ephah took him somewhere and left him."

"Where did he leave him?" she said, voice rising.

He raised his hands as though to protect himself. "No need to yell."

"Sorry," she said. "I am just trying to find out if my husband is alive."

"I don't know. They will kill anyone they find."

Piles of bodies... If Reuel was miraculously alive and had missed the battle, he was still deep inside enemy territory and with a broken leg. How could he possibly get home?

CHAPTER FOURTEEN

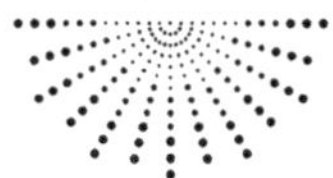

"Get up!" The gruff voice was accompanied by a hard kick.

Reuel groaned and squinted into the sun to find five silhouetted figures surrounding him. Dread settled deep in his belly. He should have known not to risk a quick rest.

"I told you to get up," the man said again. "Let's get a look at you."

Arms trembling, Reuel pushed himself up into a sitting position, grateful the man had kicked his good leg and not the bad.

"We almost missed you," the spokesman said. "But your camel gave you away."

Riding a camel had always been a risk. Reuel had successfully avoided all people up to this point by traveling in the hotter times of the day when people would normally be content to doze in the shade. But today had been so hot, even he had sought shade.

"He looks like an uncircumcised fellow to me," the shortest man said.

That was one accusation they couldn't make. "All descendants of Avraham are circumcised," Reuel said.

"But you're not an Israelite?" the man persisted.

Reuel said nothing. Were these men looking for fugitives or were they merely curious?

"Are you an Israelite?" The man peered at Reuel. "And have you got the stomach to admit it if you aren't?"

Reuel clenched his jaw. If these men intended to kill him, then he'd rather die as a Midianite. He lifted his chin. "I am a Midianite, a descendant of Keturah, and Jethro, father-in-law of Mosheh, and Jethro's son, Hobab, and also a descendant of Jael the heroine."

"A worthy lineage indeed," a third man said. "But a dangerous one these days. We are just returning from fighting Midianite raiders."

Reuel licked his dry lips, wishing he had access to a god, any god, who could offer him an escape. "I was not with the raiders."

"And why not? Are you a traitor to your own people? Or simply too afraid to fight? Whatever you are, you are surely in the wrong place at the wrong time."

Reuel pointed at his broken leg. "I couldn't have fought."

"And how do we know that you have not put the splint on your-self? A good disguise if you ask me," the main spokesman said. He pointed his chin at the man standing closest to Reuel. Before Reuel could protect himself, the man kicked Reuel's broken leg.

Reuel screamed. Fire ran up his leg. He braced his arms on the ground and sucked in a sharp breath and then another.

"Your mother would be proud of such a scream." The man guffawed.

"I don't think he faked it," said another of the men, one whose beard was streaked with silver. "Look. His whole forehead is covered in sweat."

Reuel raised a shaky hand and wiped off the sweat and shook it onto the ground.

"How did you break it?" the main spokesman said.

"My camel spat at me—" It was an effort to speak, and Reuel took a deeper breath. "I stepped back and fell over a rock."

"That rock might have saved your life," the short man said, taking a step back. There was a look in his eyes Reuel struggled to identify. Sadness? Pity? Mercy? That seemed impossible. Reuel struggled to keep his breathing steady, the pain of his leg still returning in sharp waves.

"Not so hasty," the leader said.

Reuel's heart hammered in his chest.

"If he is on this side of the Jordan, he was one of the raiders, and the raiders deserve to die." The man spat on the ground. "We have lived like rats in caves these last seven seasons."

Reuel forced himself to meet the man's eyes. He'd not die cowering.

"He's right," said another man. "Our people and families have suffered." He jabbed a finger at Reuel. "You say you are a descendant of Avraham? Well, you have not remembered mercy."

Zura spoke of mercy on occasion, but Reuel had ignored her. Instead, he had been more intent on revenge for generations of put-downs. Been glad and more than willing to humiliate those who'd humiliated the Midianites.

"I am not willing to kill a wounded man," the silver-bearded man said. "I have had enough of killing."

"Then walk away," the leader said. "I have no such qualms."

Reuel focused on breathing steadily, drawing in what could be the last breaths he would take as these men discussed who would put him to death.

"I will not kill a man who is defenseless," a man with a squint said. "There is no honor in that."

"Pah, honor!" The leader spat on the ground. "Midianites have no honor."

Reuel's sweat was pungent with fear.

"Maybe not, but we are men of honor," the man with the squint persisted.

The powerlessness Reuel felt was as unbearable as the pain in his leg.

Zura would say a prayer, but why would Yahveh ever listen to him? Reuel had never bowed to Yahveh. Yahveh had always seemed to prefer Yitzchak's side of the family rather than Keturah's offspring.

"Stand up!" the leader barked at Reuel.

Reuel turned over as carefully as he could. He crawled out from under the overhang and used the rock wall to stabilize himself, pulling himself upright. He let his broken leg dangle, for he didn't dare to touch it on the ground. He was an injured lamb before a pack of wolves.

"Uncover your head," the leader said.

Reuel would have loved to rebel even in this small way, but what was the point? If he were to die, they could look him in the face. He wouldn't cower or beg. He would have liked to see Reba and Hanok grow up and to have trained them in his craft. He would have liked to try out all the mirror designs Jael had drawn him, feel again her warm back pressed against his as they slept in their tent, and see her rare shy smile.

Reuel pulled off the head cover he'd worn to protect himself against the sun and insects. Things he need not be concerned about again. The cloth settled round his neck.

"I know you," said the short man. "You are Reuel, the coppersmith."

The man wasn't familiar.

"I saw the mirror you made at Naftali's daughter's wedding." He turned to the leader. "Naftali wouldn't be happy if this man were to die."

"Pah!" The leader spat and a globule of phlegm landed at Reuel's foot.

Reuel held his breath.

"It seems you have escaped feeling the bite from the edge of my sword."

Reuel's heartbeats were loud in his ears.

"Come," the leader said. "We will leave this man to hobble back to his home. Maybe someone else will finish him off."

The men mounted their camels, hung about with the gold they had recaptured from the Amalekites, and set off around the bend in the path.

Reuel exhaled. He reached out a shaky hand to touch the rock wall. Then he leaned over and dry-retched before easing himself onto the hot earth. His uninjured leg could no longer support his weight. He would drink a few mouthfuls of water and let the Israelites get well ahead of him. Then he must mount the camel and set off with all the speed his leg could handle toward the river. He'd be safer on the other side. Back onto paths and lands he knew as well as he knew the ridges of his own hand.

CHAPTER FIFTEEN

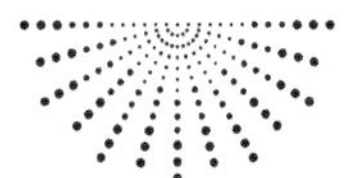

euel's camel slurped water from the Jordan River. He'd made it. He'd crossed into the eastern side of Canaan. The tension he'd felt since the encounter that almost ended everything began to recede. He had not seen anyone since meeting the five men. The trip had taken longer than he'd expected because he'd been careful to avoid all tracks. Avoided any places he might meet Israelites. He'd been favored once, but he'd rather not gamble with his life again.

A rock bounced down on the far side of the riverbed and Reuel glanced up. Another party of travelers began the descent to the river. Nausea surged in his stomach. He hauled on the camel's halter, but the animal pulled against him. It had no intention of moving on until it had drunk its fill. Stubborn beast. Reuel pulled his head covering across his face, hoping to appear as unworthy of notice as possible.

The group on the other side were getting closer. Reuel tried once again to move his camel on, but it only shook its head and kept slurping. Would the group on horseback now splashing across the river ignore him and keep going?

Tension gripped Reuel's shoulders, and he kept his head down. *Walk past. Ignore me.* The first of the horses stopped for a long drink then scrambled up the riverbank and passed by.

Keep going.

Whoever the group was, they were wealthy. Horses were uncommon. Common folk rode camels or donkeys, or they walked. The second and third riders passed, and the tension began to ease out of Reuel's shoulders.

"Good morning, blessings upon your head," called the last man of the group in a voice that was too familiar. Naftali of Jabesh Gilead. Had the short Israelite's words somehow conjured the man up? What could Reuel do? If he answered, there was a risk his voice would also be recognized, but if he didn't, the man might investigate further. Naftali wasn't used to being ignored.

"Good morning," Reuel said, partially lifting his head, so as not to appear rude.

"Where are you traveling to?" Naftali asked.

"Ramoth Gilead," Reuel answered, sweat breaking out along his hairline.

"Do I know you?" Naftali asked. "Your voice sounds familiar."

Now what? If Reuel said, "No," but Naftali found out he did indeed know Reuel, then Reuel would lose a valuable ally. If he said, "Yes," then Naftali would witness him in this pitiful state, and there might be more questions.

Reuel remembered how even facing death he had been determined to be proud of who he was. He took a deep breath and pulled off his head covering. "It is I, Reuel the coppersmith."

Naftali drew in a sharp breath. "My friend, you look terrible. Are you injured?"

Naftali had called him friend. Surely that was a good sign.

"I fell and broke my leg nearly a moon ago. I had to recover enough so I could ride home," Reuel said, mouth dry.

"Hmm," Naftali said. "You'd be safer traveling with us at least to

Jabesh Gilead. These are not days to be traveling alone, especially for someone of your ancestry."

"My ancestry?" The words fell out of Reuel's mouth because he couldn't clamp them in.

He was glad that the others traveling with Naftali were well ahead. Naftali had never given any indication that he took sides. Wealth was his main interest.

"We will not talk of that now," Naftali said. "There has been both great victory and loss."

Reuel said nothing, but his puzzlement must have shown on his face.

"Ah, so you don't know what has been happening." Naftali seemed relieved. "Gideon of Manasseh has wiped out all the Midianite and Amalekite raiders."

Impossible! How could a few hundred wipe out thousands?

"W-wiped out?" Reuel stuttered.

"It is true," Naftali said. "Was anyone you knew with the raiders?"

"I am sure there could have been," Reuel said cautiously. Was Ephah dead? Would Reuel have to be the one to carry the news home to his father and sister-in-law?

"Ride with me," Naftali said. "We traveled west wanting to confirm or deny the rumors swirling around our city."

Reuel let out a slow breath. He might be wary around Naftali, but he should be safe. He followed Naftali up the slope away from the river.

Naftali let Reuel catch up. "It will be better if you hear the real story from me rather than rumors. Then, if you have to tell anyone bad news, you'll know what really happened."

Did Naftali know about his brother, or did he assume Reuel should have been part of the massacre?

"I am glad you are mostly healthy," Naftali said. "I wouldn't want to lose my favorite coppersmith. My wife and daughter are sure to want more of your wares."

Reuel hadn't thought much about copper for days. He'd been too busy trying to avoid further damaging his leg, making sure his camel didn't run away, and avoiding detection so he could survive long enough to reach his family.

Naftali turned toward Reuel. "What I heard, I heard among a group of drinkers, but the story was so unlikely that it rings true. The story of Gideon is on everyone's lips on the other side of the Jordan and will soon be known on our side too."

"Who is this Gideon you speak of?" It was not a name Reuel recognized.

"Gideon is the son of Josh the Abiezrite, which will likely not mean anything to you. Abiezer was one of Manasseh's great-grandsons and is the name of one of our clans."

So this Gideon was likely related to Naftali.

"Like all our people on the western side of the Jordan, Gideon was trying to protect his family's harvest from the raiders. He was threshing wheat in a winepress to avoid discovery. An angel of Yahveh appeared to him and said, 'Mighty warrior, Yahveh is with you.' Gideon replied, 'Pardon me, my lord, but if Yahveh is with us, why has all this happened to us? Where are all the wonders that our ancestors told us about in Egypt and afterwards? Why has the Lord abandoned us and given us into Midian's hand?'"

Was this what the prophet in Jabesh Gilead had meant? Reuel recalled something about how the Israelites failed to worship Yahveh, loving instead the gods of Canaan.

"The angel said to Gideon, 'Go and save Israel out of the hand of the Midianites. Am I not sending you?' But Gideon said, 'How can I save Israel, for my clan is the weakest in Manasseh and I am the least of my family.' But the angel told him, 'I will be with you and you will strike down all the Midianites, leaving none alive.'"

None alive. Reuel swallowed a lump in his throat. While he was riding his camel, were Gideon and his men pursuing Jael, Reba,

Hanok, Zura, and any others who were of the blood of Midian? He must get home. *Curse this leg.*

"But Gideon must have been timid." Naftali shook his head. "Not someone I would have chosen to lead an army. He struggled to believe he was really being asked to fight. He said, 'If I have found favor in your eyes, please do not go away until I return with an offering to set before you.' Gideon went home, prepared a young goat and bread without yeast, and brought them back to the angel where he was standing under the biggest oak tree in Ophrah. The angel said to him, 'Take out the meat and bread and place them on this rock, then pour out the broth.' Then the angel touched the meat and bread with the tip of his staff and fire came out of the staff and consumed the offering and the angel disappeared. Gideon exclaimed, 'I have seen an angel face to face!' But Yahveh said to him, 'Peace. Do not be afraid. You are not going to die.'"

Living in these lands, everyone knew that the Israelites claimed their god was a miracle-working god, but Reuel had paid little attention. Early stories also told of angels, the messengers of Yahveh. The miracles had always seemed to happen long years ago. Those stories and this new one of Gideon sounded too fantastic to be true. Yet Naftali believed it, and he was no fool. A shiver went down Reuel's spine. This god who had decimated the Egyptians now seemed to have turned his gaze against the Midianites.

Naftali's horse stumbled, and Naftali patted its neck. "Peace. There is nothing to fear."

Reuel wished he had someone to whisper those words to him. There was much for him to fear. Reuel tugged his head covering around his face. He didn't believe Naftali would harm him, but one of his entourage might think they'd gain honor by killing him.

"Gideon built an altar to Yahveh. During the night, Yahveh told him to take the second bull, the one that was seven years old, from his father's herd, tear down his father's altar to Baal, and use the wood of the Asherah pole to offer the second bull as a burnt offering."

"I bet his father wasn't happy about that," Reuel said.

"He wasn't, and the people of the town demanded that Gideon must die for his actions, but his father said, 'Are you going to plead Baal's cause? If he truly is a god, he can defend himself.'"

Reuel found himself agreeing with Gideon's father. The gods, if they actually existed, should be more than able to fight to protect their own honor.

"Yahveh's spirit came on Gideon. He called on his own clan to follow him and sent messages to all in Manasseh, Asher, Zebulun, and Naphtali."

Reuel swallowed. He'd warned Ephah that the Israelites would be dangerous if they united.

"Many of our young men crossed the river to help, but most of them came home without fighting."

Reuel wrinkled his forehead. "Came home?"

"We'll get to that. First, there is another interesting part to the story. Gideon was still afraid, despite all the times Yahveh had reassured him. He begged Yahveh for some signs that he should be the one to save Israel."

Reuel shifted his leg trying to get comfortable.

"First, Gideon said he would place a wool fleece on the threshing floor. He asked Yahveh to allow the fleece to be wet with dew and the ground all around it to be bone dry."

Reuel leaned forward. "And was it?"

Naftali nodded. "He wrung a full bowl of water out of the fleece. But he still doubted, so he asked that the next night the ground be wet, and the fleece be dry. Yahveh also granted this request."

Reuel's throat tightened. Who was this god, who listened to the requests of a timid man and took the time to reassure him?

"More than thirty thousand men gathered in answer to Gideon's summons, but Yahveh said, 'You have too many men. If Midian is defeated your men would say, "Our own strength has saved us." So tell your men that anyone who trembles with fear may go home.'"

Naftali tutted. "And twenty-two thousand men admitted their fear and went home, including most of our young men. But Yahveh said, 'There are still too many men. Take the remaining ten thousand down to drink at the water, and I will thin out your army.' So Gideon obeyed. And Yahveh said. 'Separate the ones who lap the water as a dog laps from those who kneel down to drink.' Only three hundred scooped up the water in their hands and drank. All the others kneeled down and leaned over the surface of the water."

It was a clever test. Only those who scooped the water up to their mouths were alert to the danger that might be around them.

"Then Yahveh said to Gideon, 'With the remaining three hundred men I will save you and give the Midianites into your hands. Let all the others go home.'"

A ripple of fear spread through Reuel's belly. Three hundred had been his estimate of the number of men who'd passed by his cave. He had looked on their miserly numbers and despised them. He hadn't reckoned on Yahveh fighting for them.

"One man had been telling our party this story, but then another spoke up. Said his name was Purah and that he was Gideon's personal servant. He said that Yahveh had given Gideon one more sign that the victory would belong to Israel. Yahveh told Gideon and Purah to go down to the outskirts of the camp and listen to what they were saying."

Another ripple of fear assailed Reuel. He'd seen two men pass his cave and return shortly afterwards.

"Purah said that they arrived at the camp just as a man was telling another his dream. 'I had a dream of a round loaf of barley bread that came tumbling into our camp. It struck our tent with such force that the tent overturned and collapsed.'"

What a strange dream.

Purah continued, "The Midianite friend said, 'This can mean

nothing other than the sword of Gideon, son of Joash, will come, for their god has given the Midianites and this whole camp into his hands.'"

And it had been only a little while later that Reuel had seen the armed men pass his cave.

"Gideon gathered up his three hundred men and split them into three groups. Each was given a clay jar with a torch inside, a trumpet, and a sword. At the same moment they broke the jars and cried 'For Yahveh and for Gideon'—"

Reuel blocked out Naftali's voice. He knew what had happened next for he had seen it, although he'd misinterpreted it in his pride and ignorance. In the darkness, he had assumed that the Midianites had triumphed, but the sounds he'd heard had not been victory but a terrible defeat.

"Yahveh sent the Midianites and the Amalekites into panic. They killed each other and fled south. Gideon sent messengers to the other Israelites and asked them to go and block the crossings of the Jordan, and Gideon won the battle." Naftali's voice trailed off as though he recalled he was speaking to a Midianite.

"And the kings?" Reuel asked. He didn't dare to call them "our kings," in case it reminded Naftali that Reuel too belonged to the new enemy.

"They killed Zebah and Zalmunna and also the leaders Oreb and Zeeb," Naftali said.

That was it. There was no hope. The Midianite leaders wouldn't have died unless there was no one left to defend them. And Ephah? The trickle of hope Reuel had clung to was escaping through his fingers like sand, and only a few grains remained.

CHAPTER SIXTEEN

*J*ael had not had a moment to herself since the messenger had arrived. Abida was prostrate with grief, so Jael was kept busy fetching and carrying for him. Zipporah had withdrawn into caring for her own children and was pale and silent.

Noticing that Zura had been missing for a long time, Jael left Reba and Hanok with their cousins and went to find her sister. She asked several people before one directed her to the stairs leading up to the top of the wall. Here she found Zura. "What are you doing, Zura?" Someone must have brought her up here, for Zura wouldn't be foolish enough to climb the stairs on her own.

"I guessed this would be the coolest place in Ramoth Gilead," Zura said, fanning herself with a big leaf. "And it's also a good place to pray."

"Don't tell Abida or Zipporah you've been praying," Jael said.

"I'm not that foolish," Zura said. "They would ask me why Yahveh didn't protect Ephah."

Jael leaned back against the sun-warmed stone. "It's a reasonable question."

"And one to which I don't know the answer," Zura said.

"How do you worship a god whose ways seem random and unjust and cruel?" Jael asked. Ephah was dead but Reuel might be too. If that wasn't cruel, what was? Depriving two women of their husbands and four children of their fathers.

"I have learned he can be trusted, that even if things don't make sense to me, he knows all things and is working out his purposes through both the good and bad."

Jael snorted. "Some people would assume you were mad."

"Because Yahveh allowed me to be blind?"

"Something like that." Jael paused.

"Don't be afraid to say what you're thinking." Zura pushed her hair back off her face.

"You being blind meant no one wanted to marry you and you didn't have the opportunity to be a mother. You even have to rely on others to get up here to enjoy the breeze."

"That is true. I could choose to focus on everything I don't have and can't do, but what good would that do? I'd end up like Abida, prostrate and moaning on my bed."

A breeze blew and brought with it the smell of dried grass. Zura lifted her chin and sighed with pleasure. "I choose to focus on all that I have."

"And what's that?" Jael asked.

"You, for one. Not everyone has a sister like you. A sister who refused to leave me alone and has taken me along and made me part of the family."

Zura gave her too much credit. Jael had taken Zura with her because she was frightened of leaving home.

"And I have a brother-in-law who doesn't look at what I can't do but gives me worthwhile work."

"You've earned every bit of respect he gives you." Jael tried to keep the envy out of her tone. She wished Reuel gave her as much respect as he gave Zura.

"And you have generously allowed me to help you with the boys," Zura said.

It wasn't generosity. The boys tired Jael out, and Zura was much better with getting them to calm down and at sorting out their petty arguments.

"Besides which, I benefit from your good cooking and the beauty around me."

"How can you talk of beauty?" Jael said. "You can't even see it."

"Beauty is found in far more than color and shape," Zura said. "There is beauty in the sound of birds, and the whisper of the wind through the trees." She tilted her head as if to listen and feel the wind on her cheek. "There is beauty in the scent of flowers and the feel of a child's hand in mine."

And Zura took the time to enjoy all that was around her. Even though her life was as full as Jael's, Zura never allowed the busyness to prevent her sucking the juice out of each mouthful.

"Sometimes I think you're too good to be true," Jael said. "I so often want to grumble and complain. I often wish I wasn't married to Reuel and wasn't the mother to two energetic boys. Sometimes I just want to sit down and do nothing."

"I'm not as good as you think I am," Zura said. "Complaints and worries are often in my heart, too, but I take the time to turn them all over to Yahveh in prayer. That helps."

"So Yahveh is a sort of crutch?" Jael asked.

"He's much more than a crutch. Even if he is a crutch, then he is one that never breaks. He has never let me down yet." Zura touched Jael's arm. "Praying keeps me focused on him. It shows my weakness and dependence. It reminds me who he is and how he has worked in the past."

"I admire your faith, but I think it might be misplaced," Jael said.

Zura shook her head. "It's not misplaced, and I pray that you will one day have what I have."

It was hard not to be moved by Zura's absolute sincerity and confidence, but Jael wouldn't be fooled by such a god. She was better off without one.

"Do you pray for the others too?" Jael asked.

"I pray for every member of the family."

Jael would like to know what Zura prayed for each of them but wasn't going to ask, for that would keep the conversation going. Talking of Yahveh always made Jael feel uncomfortable. Yahveh seemed unknowable, and she wasn't sure of his intentions.

"I pray Abida and Zipporah will grieve properly," Zura continued. "And I pray they will have everything they need."

"I don't think Abida wants to live," Jael said.

"Perhaps, but he is needed to help Zipporah. Perhaps that is part of his grief—the one he relied upon is gone. I pray he will find Yahveh and find that he provides all the strength that is needed."

Abida had never shown the slightest interest in Yahveh. Not that the Israelites around here seemed to follow him either. Their mouths might say his name, but they also readily talked of Baal and Astarte. If Yahveh didn't answer their prayers, they simply moved on to someone else.

"Do you think Reuel is still alive?" Jael asked.

"I am praying he is and that he'll find his way home."

"If only we had an idea where to search," Jael said. Reuel might be increasingly unkind, but he had looked after her well while she waited for the birth of the boys, and he was a good provider. She didn't like to think of him unable to move and starving to death.

"We have more than enough worries without imagining the worst." Zura stood. "Help me down those stairs. They weren't too bad coming up, but going down will be worse."

Jael took Zura's arm. She couldn't imagine life without her sister. A sister whose beliefs puzzled her but which gave her sister peace and joy.

Things that eluded Jael.

CHAPTER SEVENTEEN

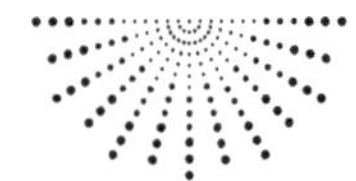

The camel grumbled all the way up the final hill.

Reuel patted its neck. "I know, girl. I'm ready to stop traveling as well." The camel turned its head to look at Reuel. "Yes, I know I'm talking too much, but there is no one else to talk to."

Reuel had traveled with Naftali to Jabesh Gilead. After the best meal he'd had in too long, he'd set off for Ramoth Gilead. The thought of reaching the town didn't fill him with joy. He hoped Jael and the boys would be happy to see him, but would his father? He was not the son Abida wanted to see come home.

Had news of the total destruction of the Midianite force reached his family? Would he need to break the news that his brother was lost, likely dead? He had to keep banishing the thought of Zipporah and his father's faces collapsing in grief. And his Jael, so cold and set against him, would she express any gladness on his return? At least he could trust that his boys would be joyful to see him.

Reuel's leg had throbbed badly for several days after the Israelite had kicked him. Naftali had insisted that several of his servants temporarily remove the splint so his leg could be washed. There'd been widespread bruising but no lasting damage. Even with riding, the ache had subsided to a dull discomfort. Soon he would try to put a little weight on it.

The stones of Ramoth Gilead's walls were now in sight. Reuel blinked back a surge of emotion he didn't expect. This was not his home, but his family was within.

"Not long now, girl," Reuel said, "and you'll get a well-deserved rest."

Reuel took a breath to steady himself. He wouldn't be getting any rest. If Ephah truly was gone, then the burden of the whole family would fall on him. A burden that might yet break him. He was not returning a hero with plenty of spoils. He was a man with a useless leg and no guarantees that it would ever again support weight and allow him to return to the travel required by his trade. Reuel almost envied those like Zura who thought gods existed to receive their prayers.

* * *

"Ima, Ima, Abba is home!" Reba shouted as he descended from the tree he'd been climbing.

Jael's heart raced. She scrambled to her feet, laying the washing aside. Reuel was alive!

"Leave the washing with me," Zura said, her voice full of joy. "You go."

Jael climbed out of the bed of the stream. Reba swung from the lower branch of the tree, dropped, and took off toward his father.

"Ima, help me down," Hanok wailed.

Jael went to the bottom of the tree and watched Hanok descend. "Be careful. Abba will wait."

It looked like one of Zura's prayers had been answered.

Hanok reached the lowest branch. Jael reached up and lifted him down. "Get on my back and I'll carry you." She crouched down so he could clamber up, then set off for where the camel was now approaching the yelling and jumping figure of Reba.

Hanok tapped Jael on the back as though she were a donkey. "Hurry, Ima, hurry."

Jael didn't need the urging. She was going as fast as she could manage. Reuel seemed to sit well on the camel. Maybe the messenger was incorrect about his injuries.

Reuel had reached Reba. He halted the camel and had it lower itself to the ground. Reba threw himself at his father.

"Careful, Reba. Abba has a broken leg."

Hanok slid off Jael's back and ran to hug his father. She stood back, watching Reuel embrace his sons like a man who had never expected to hold them again. She swallowed a lump of feeling she wished to numb, wondering what it would be like if her husband had embraced her with such emotion, but he'd never been affectionate with her.

"Welcome back," Jael said with a careful lack of emotion. "We've been so worried."

Reuel looked up at her over their boys' shoulders and she was startled at how thin he was. His eyes were circled with dark lines and his clothes dirty and dishevelled. He stared at her with a fixed intensity, such an intensity that she was forced to look away.

"Have you heard?" Reuel asked in a quiet, heavy voice.

"About the battle?" she asked, glancing up.

He nodded. He released the boys and waited until they were distracted petting the camel. "Any news of Ephah?"

"Not here," she mouthed at him, a tremble to her lip.

The grains of hope Reuel had retained vanished with this gesture of grief.

Such news was not to be spoken of in front of the boys.

"Come on, boys," Jael said. "Let's go and collect Aunt Zura and we'll go with Abba to the house."

Seeing Reuel try to adjust his weight on the camel, Jael jumped forward to offer her arm. He welcomed her help, gripping her with a trust that surprised her. She noticed his splint, the bruising on his injured leg, and the twinge of pain on his face he was trying to repress. She'd hated that he'd left, leaving her feeling uncared for, abandoned. Yet she had also enjoyed his absence, the break from his harsh tongue and constant disappointment. Now she felt a flash of guilt. What had it taken him to get home to all of them?

* * *

As they entered the small courtyard, Zipporah came out of the doorway, eyes wide and tears glistening down her cheeks. She'd cried off and on since she had heard the news about Ephah. Her children rushed past her to greet Reuel. Did they hope for another camel to be following behind? Did they not understand about their father? Zipporah gave Reuel a tight nod, then went back inside.

Reuel ordered his camel to crouch, then hugged his nieces and ruffled his nephews' hair. "Reba and Hanok are fetching me some water. Will you help them?" The children nodded and scuttled off with their cousins.

When Reuel gingerly lifted his splinted leg over his camel, Jael offered her arm again.

"How did you hear about the battle?" he asked her.

"A man survived and brought the news to us." Jael wished he'd hold her like he'd held their boys instead of just asking for news.

"I didn't think anyone survived," Reuel said. Using her for balance, he used his other arm to pull the two sticks off the camel. The camel lumbered to its feet, and Reuel used the sticks to leave her side and hop toward the hay supply.

Once the camel was eating, he lowered himself onto an old tree log. He touched the place beside him, rather than direct her to sit as he would have once done. "Tell me."

Jael crossed the courtyard and sat beside him. "The messenger survived because he was knocked out and no one noticed he wasn't dead. When he awoke, he found himself surrounded by dead Midianites."

"And one of them was Ephah?"

She nodded. "He brought home his ring."

"I kept hoping Ephah had somehow escaped," he said with such depth of sorrow she almost hugged him. "I should have been with him."

"How did you break your leg?" Jael asked.

"In the silliest way possible. I tripped over a rock."

She touched his arm. "It saved your life."

"I'm not sure it was a good thing," he said.

He sounded so full of despair. "Don't say that. We need you."

"Yes." The word sounded like a curse. She moved her hand from his arm.

Jael was about to offer to help Reuel wash when the sound of dragging steps sounded from inside the darkened entrance. It could only be Abida. He hadn't been out of his bed since the messenger's news.

Abida came out into the sunshine, squinting at the glare. His tunic was crushed and his beard unkempt. He looked like a man who no longer cared about his appearance. He gripped the doorpost. Reuel stood up to greet his father.

"You have returned," said the old man.

"Yes, Father, I have returned." Reuel hopped forward using his sticks.

"You are injured but not from fighting, I fear," Abida said.

"A moment of clumsiness," Reuel said.

"A moment that cost your brother his life."

The harsh words cut into Jael on Reuel's behalf.

"You can be sure I have deeply regretted it," Reuel said.

"Not as much as I have," Abida said.

Jael heard Reuel's quick intake of breath.

"If I had not been injured and hidden in the cave, you would have lost two sons."

"If I had to lose one son, then I wish it had not been Ephah," Abida said.

Reuel flinched as though he'd been struck. How cruel. What father would say such words to his son? Jael stepped forward and touched her husband's arm. This time, he shook her off, stinging her heart, reminding her why she tried so hard to numb it.

"I am sorry that my living has inconvenienced you," Reuel said.

Abida snorted and turned to shuffle back into the darkened room behind him.

Beside her, Reuel held himself stiffly as though to do otherwise might mean he would shatter like a broken pottery jar.

Oh Reuel, my husband, don't listen. Don't let those words sink into your heart. But even as she thought the words, Jael heard her husband draw a deep breath and knew the words had pierced deep. What damage would they do inside him? She knew only too well, for she knew the damage Reuel's words over the years had done inside her.

She stepped forward toward the entrance of the house, not daring to again offer Reuel her arm for support. He had always been independent and closed off. He would never open up to her. His flesh would close around the wound his father had dealt, and it would fester alongside all the other wounds.

CHAPTER EIGHTEEN

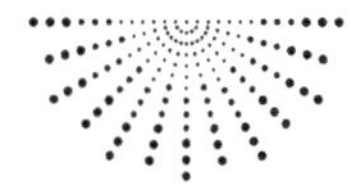

"Another drink!"

The man serving turned slowly. "Don't you think you've had enough?"

"Who are you to tell me when I've had enough?" Reuel thumped his fist on the wooden plank in front of him. "Another drink."

"If you fall over with that injured leg of yours, you'll regret it," the man said.

"I already regret it," Reuel said. "Regret is what I do best."

Self-pity rose in his throat and threatened to choke him. He regretted breaking his leg. He regretted not being in the battle. At least he could have died alongside his brother. Then his father would have mourned them both instead of looking at him with loathing. Since Reuel had arrived home, his father had not left his room again. Abida obviously had no desire to be anywhere near his remaining son.

Home! What a joke! Ramoth Gilead wasn't home. It never would be, not while his father mourned Ephah. Ephah, who had always been the favorite, who was now elevated to perfection. A perfection Reuel could never hope to equal. He'd hoped going on the raid would please his father. He'd hoped the sheer craftsmanship of the mirrors would be admired, but no. His father would never care about anything he did. It wouldn't matter how well he did with smithing or how wealthy he became. His father would always love Ephah best.

The drink came. Reuel dropped some copper on the plank to pay then slurped another mouthful. He didn't know why he bothered. The drink was as bitter as the emotions churning inside him.

Most of the patrons had already left this drinking place. One man remained, a man whose drinking kept pace with Reuel's.

The man turned his face suddenly in Reuel's direction. "Whaddya looking at?"

"Nothing. Nothing," Reuel said.

The man pushed back his bench and lurched to his feet, still clutching his drink. "Nothing, you say. I say you were looking at me." He burped loud and long. "I don't need anyone looking at me."

"And I don't want anyone fighting in here," said the drink server.

"I won't be fighting," Reuel said, standing to his feet. The room swirled around him, and he squeezed his eyes shut for a moment.

Reuel opened his eyes to find the man staring at his leg, still in its splint.

"Are you Ephah's brother?" the man asked.

"Why do you want to know?" Reuel asked, relieved the man wasn't about to take a swing at him.

"Ephah was my friend. I was there with him. With him when Gideon came," the man said.

It looked like this man had some regrets too.

"But you didn't save him?" Reuel sat down again.

The man shook his head, seated himself opposite Reuel. "Fell over in the confusion," he said in an undertone as he wiped the froth off his beard. "The Israelites didn't notice I wasn't dead."

The man took a few big mouthfuls of his drink.

"So we are the survivors," Reuel said. Jael had said the messenger was named Dedan, so this must be him. Surviving didn't seem to have done either of them any good.

"I can't seem to get over that they're all gone," the man said.

Reuel didn't say anything. There wasn't much point.

"Glad you made it home. Your wife was worrying," the man continued.

Reuel wanted to be glad. He knew his family needed him, but in his darkest moments he wished he'd been killed by the Israelites who'd found him asleep. Living now didn't feel like mercy.

After he'd woken up at around midday today, he'd attempted to do some work, but the metal seemed to have turned against him, as it had at every attempt over the past two moons. He'd ended up throwing everything back into the furnace. He'd been crafting copper since he was Reba's age, but now all his hands seemed good for were tossing back drinks. He'd made a mess of everything he'd tried. Even little Hanok had ended up in tears, running to Jael for comfort. The sight of Hanok's hurt and confusion had almost made him want to bawl himself.

"Your wife is a nice woman," the man said. "She could see I was hungry and thirsty, and gave me food and drink."

Reuel didn't know what it was that made him keep on being cruel to Jael. Hanok had barely finished crying and run off to play when Reuel had taunted Jael about her name. It wasn't her fault her parents had given her a heroine's name, a name most women couldn't live up to. The famous Jael had won a battle by putting a tent peg through the enemy commander's head. Jael would have been more likely to give him the goat's milk and let him sleep before sending him on his way. His Jael was not the kind to kill the enemy, and it was wrong to expect her to be different. Why couldn't he be thankful for who she was? After he'd hurt her with the cutting words of his tongue, she'd looked at him with the hurt eyes of a child and turned away, although not before he'd seen her lip tremble.

Reuel took another gulp of his now warm drink. It turned his stomach. More regret. He tried to drown his regrets, but he should have known better. All hard drink did was befuddle him and increase the likelihood that he'd snap at his wife and sons. A mountain of regret threatened to topple over and bury him like a landslide.

"Never thought it would be so hard to survive," the man said, staring into the depths of his drink. "I don't seem to know how to go forward."

Neither did Reuel. He couldn't go back to the way things were before, couldn't pretend nothing had happened, but he didn't seem to be able to live today either. Then there was the future which loomed in front of him. He'd wanted to make his name, provide for his family, and earn his father's respect, but now he couldn't even make the simplest object in copper. The future? He seemed unable to walk toward that either.

CHAPTER NINETEEN

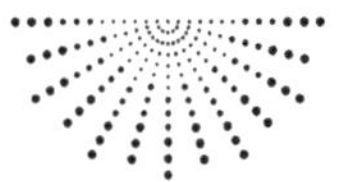

*J*ael had been lying in the dark waiting for hours. Waiting, knowing Reuel was somewhere out there in the town, trying to drown his griefs and his memories.

Why didn't he find someone to talk to? Instead, he stuffed his thoughts down and refused to spit out the poison working its way deep inside him. This seemed to be the way men were. Abida was the same.

She and Zura were different. If they had a problem, they talked about it. Somehow the poison diluted, and they could face the next day. Even Zipporah had opened her mouth and poured out some of what she felt inside after the loss of Ephah. Jael and Zura had listened and held her while she wept.

Now Zipporah was up and working in the home again. Cooking and cleaning and mending, turning her grief into good. She might not yet laugh or smile, but she was making progress. Zura would encourage her to tell stories about Ephah, to keep his memory alive for their children. Jael had first disagreed, thinking they should avoid speaking of Ephah at all, but she noticed how Zipporah would brighten when his name was spoken.

But Abida and Reuel? Both of them were stuck. Abida stayed alone in his inner room and stared at the wall, moaning, "Oh, my son, my son," as though he was the only person in all of history who had lost someone he loved. She thought of her mother when her father died, how much she had wept, how strong she had been to continue to build a life for Jael and Zura. It wasn't right to give up when people were depending on you to survive.

And Reuel was drinking to forget his father's words. It was such a waste. A waste of two men who were perfectly healthy and able to help, if they only were willing to do so. Instead, every burden fell on the women's shoulders, Zipporah, Zura, and Jael, plus the unnecessary burdens of caring for two men who wouldn't help themselves. She and Zipporah had been weaving extra cloth for sale and selling their excess goat milk. Zipporah had wanted to sell some of the copper, but Jael still hoped Reuel would be able to return to making mirrors. If the men didn't start working soon, the family would struggle to survive.

Jael turned over and strained her ears, trying to hear the noises outside. Somewhere water dripped and an owl called. *Reuel, come home. Don't be a fool.*

She must have fallen into a restless doze for she was awakened by the sound of Reuel vomiting in the courtyard. More work for her. Jael slipped out of bed, threw a cloak over her shoulders, and went outside. Reuel was moaning as he leaned against the stable wall.

"Jael, iss-thas-you?"

She didn't answer but went over and tugged on his arm. Reuel pushed himself off the wall, leaning heavily on her as he stumbled toward the house. Once inside, she pushed him onto the sleeping mat and covered him with a sheepskin rug. He was asleep in moments and would remain there until the sun was high in the sky.

Jael shivered and went to clean up the vomit. So far the boys hadn't worked out where their father spent his time because he left after they were asleep. Did he still care what the children thought of him? She wished he cared enough to stop his slide into the pit he was digging for himself.

The chill of the early morning air bit into Jael's exposed skin, and she rubbed her arms vigorously. The stars above seemed so cold and distant. Did they see her here, dipping out water to wash away the evidence of her husband's weakness? Zura said Yahveh cared, but he was yet to answer most of the prayers Zura faithfully offered him.

Next door, the newborn baby whimpered. Jael looked back at the house where Reba and Hanok would be sleeping, deeply and innocently. They didn't have the worries of where food or clothes would come from. They didn't yet know how tenuous life was. Reuel had told her about how timid Gideon had been when Yahveh asked him to unite his tribe to fight against the raiders. Maybe Yahveh didn't reject the timid.

"God of the heavens," Jael whispered. "I don't know if you see me or even care, but save our family. Don't let Reuel continue on the way he is going."

She looked up at the stars overhead. They still seemed unchanged. Still cold, still distant, still glittering in disdain.

She sighed and headed into the house. She'd curl up with the boys and try to get some more rest before another day began with little chance of hope.

* * *

"*A*bba, let me help you," Reba said to Reuel.

Reba wiped the perspiration off his forehead with his lower arm.

"I'm not sure I need your help today." He didn't think he had the patience to slow down his work speed to match a beginner. Already the sun was past its highest point, and he'd only just crawled out of bed, head splitting, and tongue furry. He had decided that today he had to try to start working again. He had to get some stock made to sell or he'd never leave here. And leave here he must. He couldn't stand to be around his father much longer. Not that he actually saw his father, but he could hear him moaning and crying in the dimness of his room.

"I want to help you, Abba," Reba said. "Like you used to help Grandpa."

His father had been a hard man to please, but Reuel had struggled and worked to earn his praise. It had never come in words, but after many years of perfecting his craft, Reuel had seen the glow of grudging respect in his father's eyes. He'd had to settle for that while Ephah had received endless praise and encouragement for far inferior work.

"I need to work fast today so I have goods to sell," Reuel said.

Reba sighed. Dragging his feet, he left Reuel working at his forge. Regret. Here was more of it. Reuel's father had constantly disappointed Reuel, and now Reuel was doing the same to his son. Would Reba and Hanok also look back at their father in disappointment?

Reuel turned back to his work but found no pleasure in it. He needed to get back to the open road. Away from the mounting regrets. Away from this house of grief.

CHAPTER TWENTY

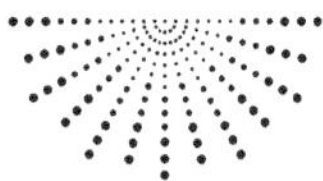

"Buzz."

Reuel swatted at his face and groaned. He'd once again come home in the dark hours before dawn and had the humiliation of having Jael wash him and put him to bed like a baby. He'd tried to push her aside and insist he could get to bed himself but soon proved he couldn't.

"Buzz, buzz."

Was the thing disturbing him a mosquito? Reuel's head pounded. He squeezed his eyelids shut to block out the brightness that threatened to pull him out of sleep.

"Buzz, buzz. I'm a hornet and I'm going to sting you." The shrill voice of an overexcited Hanok burrowed into Reuel's already aching head. He cursed and rolled into a sitting position. The room spun around him and nausea swirled in his gut.

"Don't sting me," Zipporah's youngest cried.

"Buzz, buzz, I'm coming to get you," Hanok persisted.

Why couldn't Jael keep the children away? How was a man supposed to sleep?

Outside there was a squeal and sound of running feet.

Curse the boy.

Reuel staggered to his feet, leaned on the wall and navigated his way to the doorway. He held the doorframe as he covered his eyes. The blinding sunlight seared into the back of his eyeballs, and his head pounded even more.

"Can't catch me, can't catch me," taunted another child.

"I will." Hanok dashed across the front of the doorway.

"Hanok! What do you think you're doing?" Reuel shouted.

Hanok stopped abruptly and seemed to notice Reuel in the doorway for the first time. "Playing, Abba."

"Why are you playing outside my room when I'm trying to sleep?"

"Im ... Ima." Hanok looked to the ground. "Ima couldn't take us out to play."

"So you thought you could play here?"

"Yes, Abba." He raised his head and looked around, but the other children had scattered. "I mean, no Abba."

"Did you not know I was trying to sleep?"

Hanok kept his eyes on the ground and nibbled his thumb. "Ima said you were sick, but I forgot."

Sick. So that was how Jael was describing him. He guessed he should feel thankful, but he didn't. It made him angry that she was talking about him at all. Why couldn't the boys mind their own business? They were probably telling all their little friends about him. Townsfolk loved nothing better than to gossip. Soon he wouldn't be able to hold his head up in this town.

Reuel's neck throbbed and the pain spread up his skull.

"Look at me when you answer," Reuel barked.

"Yes, Abba." Hanok's voice trembled.

"Where is your mother?"

"She went next door to visit someone who is sick."

Her job was to be here with her family keeping the children from disturbing him.

"I'm sick. She should be looking after me."

"Reba says you're not sick, just d-drunk," Hanok said, stumbling over the unfamiliar word.

"Did he?" Reuel said, his voice hard-edged.

"Drunk," Hanok said again.

Reuel's head pounded. Did he see a look of disgust on his son's face? How dare he? Anger rose in Reuel's chest. He'd teach the boy to respect him. A long branch leaned against the wall. Reuel grabbed it at the same time as he lunged to lay hold of Hanok.

"No, Abba!" Hanok yelled, fear written all over his face.

Reuel clenched his teeth and raised the stick to bring it down. It whistled through the air and thwacked into Hanok's back and buttocks.

Hanok screamed but Reuel ignored him. It felt good to lash out. To release the frustration that had been building in him for too long. To hear the whoosh of the stick and Hanok's yell as the stick slashed across his bottom. Reuel raised his arm and brought down the stick again. Hanok screamed and twisted, trying to escape, but Reuel had no intention of letting him go. The boy had cheeked him. He deserved a good thrashing.

"Stop!" Reba yelled as he ran across the courtyard toward them.

Reuel struck out at Reba as he dashed past, but the stick hit the ground just behind him. Reba fled.

Hanok whimpered and Reuel raised the stick again. The boy wasn't going to forget this lesson in a while.

"No!" Jael came out of nowhere from somewhere behind him. "Don't you hurt him."

Reuel didn't have time to hit Hanok again before Jael had grabbed his arm, hanging on to prevent him lifting the stick. She dug her nails into his skin. With a curse, he dropped the stick and shoved her away.

She stumbled backwards, fell over a rock, and hit the ground with a thud. For a moment as she lay there, he thought he'd killed her. He felt physically ill.

"Ima!" Hanok ran to her side, falling to his knees beside her and grasping her clothes.

"I'm alright, son." She rolled herself over and pushed herself up onto her hands and knees. A trickle of blood ran down her forearm from a cut on her elbow.

"I'll help you, Ima," Hanok said. He strained to pull her upright.

Reuel saw Jael take a big breath and struggle to stand up.

"Thank you, Hanok," she said as she gently pushed Hanok behind her.

Zura came into the courtyard. "Jael, are you alright?" She stretched out her hands. "Where are you?"

"I'm here," Jael said, moving to her sister's side but also making sure Hanok was still behind them, protecting him from the wild beast Reuel had become.

Zura patted Jael's face and arms, wincing when she felt the blood on Jael's arm. "I'm so sorry," Zura murmured. She bent down and whispered to Hanok, who clung to her and burst into tears. She let him cry until finally turning toward where Reuel was still standing.

"We are not your enemies," Zura said.

"I know it," Reuel said, voice low.

"Well, you have strange ways of showing it. It's impossible to drink your problems away. Your enemy is within. You need to face him."

"I'll keep away from the drink," Reuel muttered.

Jael took a deep breath and straightened. "You need to leave."

"I was planning to go as soon as you could get things ready," Reuel said.

Jael took a step closer to Zura, as though wanting support. "No, you need to leave. We are not going with you."

Reuel peered at Jael. What was she saying? He'd always thought her timid, weak even, but she stood there like the mother fox he'd once backed into a corner, protecting its cubs.

"But I can't do everything on my own." Reuel despised himself for the self-pitying whine in his voice, despised himself for admitting this aloud.

"You should have thought about that before," Jael said.

"Zura and the boys?"

She was trembling but still spoke clearly. "No, they will stay here with me. We can't leave your father and Zipporah alone at this time."

She couldn't talk to him like this. She couldn't tell him what to do. Yet she was.

The woman he'd always thought of as timid was proving to be as strong as a tower of bronze and as implacable. He'd be wise to retreat before he shamed himself further. Maybe when everything had cooled down, she'd reconsider.

Maybe.

But by the look on her face, he doubted it.

CHAPTER TWENTY-ONE

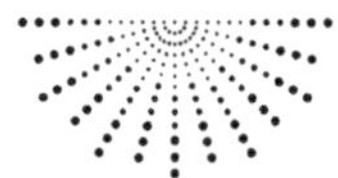

There it was again.

Reuel tilted his head to listen for the trickle of stones disturbed by whoever or whatever was behind him on the trail. Not long after he had left Ramoth Gilead, he began to suspect someone was coming after him. Whether it was simply another traveler moving in the same direction as Reuel or someone actually following him, he didn't know. Yet why would someone be following him? Besides raw metal, he had little that was worth stealing.

When Reuel had gotten up at dawn this morning, he'd hoped against all hope that Jael had changed her mind and decided to join him. Life on the road wouldn't be the same without his family and Zura along.

The boys sometimes irritated him with their endless energy and noise, but the journey was going to be much worse without it. Too silent, too boring, too lonely. He would also have to do everything himself. Setting up camp, carrying water, cooking, all in addition to the polishing and other tasks Zura and Jael normally did. And his leg was still weak, and he hadn't worked copper in two moons.

Reuel slapped the nearest camel on its backside, and it trotted forward. The goat protested a bit but allowed itself to be tugged on by the long lead attached to the camel. He'd been delayed as he left Ramoth Gilead because the goat had been reluctant to leave its stablemates and tried to butt one of the camels. The camel had kicked the goat, and that seemed to have settled things between them.

Reuel was still riding, but he had tried keeping pace with his livestock on foot over the last few days. His leg ached, but he thought it was more from weakness and disuse. Once the camp was set up, he'd make sure to practice walking every morning and evening until his leg was strong again. But this was a promise he'd made before, only to drink and sleep instead.

Reuel checked over his shoulder, hoping to catch sight of something moving, but there was nothing and no sound either. Maybe he was being fanciful. Reuel continued along the barely discernible path. Every now and then he stopped and listened but didn't hear any more sounds behind him.

The sun baked the back of his neck and gave him a pounding headache. When was the last time he'd been this sober? It did not feel good. Drink numbed his body and mind. But Jael and Zura were right—he had been a fool. Every morning after drinking he'd woken up to regrets compounded not diluted, then he had hurt his wife and young Hanok. Jael was right to send him out on the road. Once he reached the next town, he'd be too busy repairing the town's metalware to have time to drink to avoid the results of too much thinking. He'd have no one to provide his food or clean up his vomit but himself.

The path went over a small rise and dropped down to a spring and a shady tree. Time for something to eat and a rest. The animals immediately went over to the nearest patch of grass. He slid off the camel and then froze. He'd definitely heard the scrape of something on a rock and another slither of falling pebbles. Reuel looked back at the ridge and saw a flash of clothing as a man ducked behind a tree.

"Come out and show yourself," Reuel shouted. What was the man so frightened of?

The man came out from behind the rock leading a donkey and walked toward Reuel. He looked familiar. Reuel shaded his eyes and squinted toward the man.

"Oh, it's you, is it?" Reuel said.

Dedan, the messenger. His drinking companion of many nights.

Dedan came up the hill toward Reuel. "Thought you could do with some help."

"What kind of help?" Reuel asked, not at all sure he wanted to be around someone as depressed and out of control as himself.

"I'll do whatever you want. Like you, I couldn't stay in town any longer."

"Can you cook?" Reuel asked.

"I'll cook," Dedan said.

That wasn't exactly the question Reuel had asked. It probably meant Dedan had never cooked a day in his life. No matter. He couldn't be any worse at cooking than Reuel. Last night he'd had to douse the meal in a bucket of water to put out the flames.

"I can't promise it will be exciting," Reuel said. "Carrying water, milking the goat, and looking after the animals. I'll give you a go at polishing and see how you go with that."

"I'll do it," Dedan said.

"And no beer or wine. We drink water or goat's milk." Zura's words echoed in Reuel's mind. Getting drunk was no way to deal with problems. Dedan must agree or he'd be a danger rather than an asset.

"Agreed." Dedan picketed his donkey and rummaged through his load. He drew out some bread and onions.

"How did you know I was leaving?" Reuel asked.

Dedan avoided eye contact. "I was passing your place when I heard raised voices."

Reuel's face warmed. There was no privacy in a town. He doubted Dedan was the only person who'd heard the fight. "Why didn't you just come and ask to join me?"

Dedan shrugged. "I wasn't sure you'd say yes."

"And you thought I'd be less likely to say no out here."

Dedan nodded.

"Let's see how it goes," Reuel said. "If we can't make it work, I'll ask you to leave."

If it worked, it would be a huge help to have someone around to do all the tasks Jael and Zura usually did—cooking, cleaning, and setting up the tent. That would allow him to concentrate on his craft.

* * *

"If you hold up that corner, I'll get the first tent pegs into the ground," Reuel said to Dedan.

Dedan did what he was asked, and Reuel used the big hammer to pull one side of the work tent tight. Then Reuel used his walking stick to walk to the next corner. Dedan moved wherever he was directed, and erecting the first tent didn't take much longer than usual.

Jael had worked out the perfect place to put the cooking fire in relation to the tents. Reuel sent Dedan to light the fire while he laid out his tools and prepared the furnace to smelt the copper.

Reuel left Dedan making flatbread at the campsite while he rode the donkey toward the town. It had been too long since he'd been here, and the townspeople would have been waiting for several moons past when they expected him. He wouldn't ring the gong that signaled his arrival until he'd had a less heavy day to see how he'd manage.

The town gate was open, in contrast to his last visit. Two guards were standing and idly chatting but looked up when he approached.

"It's been a long time, Reuel," one of them said. "What have you done to your leg?"

"I fought with a camel and lost," Reuel said. "But I can now put weight on it, and it should soon gain strength."

"Hopefully it won't impede your work," the guard said. "My mother has two pots needing mending."

"Bring them along first thing in the morning and you can be at the head of the line," Reuel said as he entered the gate.

It didn't take long to buy some pomegranates and fresh vegetables. Back at the campsite, Dedan looked sheepish. "I burned the first two, but I'm getting the hang of it." There were two blackened lumps in the fireplace.

"You'd better," Reuel said. "If you want to stay, you have to be useful." He looked around for the walking sticks he'd brought along.

"I'm going to practice walking," Reuel said. He hopped over to where the walking sticks were laid and picked them up. Dedan flipped another flatbread while Reuel put his foot to the ground and gently put more weight on it. It felt like the knee would crumple if he took the splint off, so he left it on. He walked slowly forward, making sure each step was well supported by the sticks in his hands. His leg felt awkward and shaky, but there was no pain. He took that as a good sign.

"Need any help?" Dedan called out.

"Not this time. I'll keep the splint on but I will get you to help me on the day I take it off." Hopefully this town would provide enough work to keep him here until his leg was functioning well again.

Reuel walked up and down. By the last lap, his leg was shaking with fatigue and aching fiercely. He went over to the fire and spent the mealtime explaining his work routine so Dedan would be prepared for the morning.

* * *

*R*euel mopped his brow with his forearm. His leg ached, his shoulders ached, and he wished he'd never been raiding. He was so out of shape. His customers, headed by the guard's mother, had started to arrive soon after daybreak. She must have told her friends that the coppersmith had arrived, for the day had been heavier than he'd planned.

"More wood for the furnace," Reuel called to Dedan, who was chatting to the people in line.

Apart from stopping too often to talk to the customers, Dedan was learning fast. Today they were only dealing with copper, for bronze required the extra step of putting in a proportion of tin, and Reuel's concentration wasn't as good as it had been. Would he ever get back to crafting mirrors?

Reuel went over to those waiting in line. They huddled in the meager shade cast by the tent and fanned themselves with leaves.

"Four more. You, you, you, and you," he said, pointing. "I'm recovering from a broken leg, and I haven't the stamina to do more."

"I've been waiting half the day," an older man said.

"It's up to you. If I keep working, I won't do a good job," Reuel said. "Look at your order in line. You'll be in the first three tomorrow."

"I guess that will have to do." The man got to his feet.

Reuel wasn't worried. It wasn't as if there was any other coppersmith around, and copper objects were rare and precious. Most households only had a few objects made out of metal. The man would be back.

Once he was finished for the day, Reuel would give Dedan a few more pointers, and hopefully he'd improve his abilities every day. He wasn't Jael or Zura, but he was a whole lot better than no one.

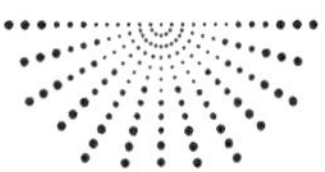

CHAPTER TWENTY-TWO

*J*ael woke to the sound of Hanok whimpering in his sleep again. Ever since the beating, Hanok had been having nightmares and wetting the bed.

She stood up from the sleeping mat and reached for her cloak. If she took Hanok outside now, they might avoid the wetness and the smell that embarrassed him. This morning he'd kept saying, "But I'm not a little boy, Ima," as she tried to clean up and get the smell out of the room.

Hanok woke up as she scooped him up. "Ima where are we going?"

"Outside, so you can pee."

It didn't take long. Once he'd finished, Hanok held up his arms to be carried. "I had the bad dream again."

"The one about Abba?"

Hanok put his arms around her neck and nestled in. "Uh-huh. He's always so angry."

It was bad enough having endured one undeserved beating, but Hanok also had to relive it in his dreams.

"Abba knows he shouldn't have hit you," Jael said. She hoped she wasn't lying, but Reuel had barely been able to look at her when she said farewell. Perhaps he at least felt ashamed. Hanok had refused to come out of the house to say goodbye, his soft little boy skin bruised with the welts she'd been too slow to prevent. If only she hadn't been next door and could have intervened earlier.

Reba was standing at the window when they came back into the room. He whirled around. "I was afraid you'd gone and left me."

"I wouldn't do that," Jael said. "We just went out for a few moments."

She lowered Hanok to the mat and then settled them both down before putting an arm around each of them. She sighed. Reuel had no idea what his actions had done to the boys. Their energy and zest were gone. No laughter, no running around, no petty arguments She longed for a need to tell either boy to be quiet. Neither wanted to leave her side. Reba was ashamed he hadn't been able to stop the beating and dismissed his running to call her as a poor substitute. There was no way a slight boy could have stopped his well-muscled father. How could she help them? She had no words. She didn't know if Reuel would return. Even if he did, she couldn't stop him from getting angry. She'd done everything to keep him calm and happy, given everything, yet it had been no use.

"Ima, I don't want to go to sleep again," Hanok said. "I don't want Abba to be angry with me again."

"You shouldn't have called him a drunk," Reba said.

"Hanok doesn't even know what the word means," Jael said. "Where did you hear the word, Hanok?"

He burrowed more deeply under her arm without saying a word.

"That's what the bigger children further down the laneway called Abba," Reba said.

Which meant that despite her trying to keep Reuel's situation quiet, someone had seen him stumbling home early in the morning. It was never going to be possible to keep anything secret in such a small place. The neighbors had probably heard and passed on all the details—the drinking, the fight, and the fact that she'd sent Reuel away. Shame heated her face. What kind of woman sent her husband away?

"It wasn't your fault, Hanok." She wanted to reassure him, but how?

Hanok lifted his head and propped it up on his elbows. "Why was Abba so angry when I said that word? Is it a bad word?"

His face was a pale blur in the moonlight filtering through the window. He needed reassurance, but would explaining help? Zura had a much better way with words than she did, but Zura was sleeping with Zipporah and the other children.

"There's nothing wrong with the word, Hanok, but it describes something that isn't so nice." How could she explain drunkenness and the reasons for it to one so young?

"Sometimes …" Jael paused to gather her thoughts. "Sometimes when someone is very sad, like your Abba is about his brother, sometimes people want to forget."

"I can't forget Uncle Ephah," Hanok said.

"Abba doesn't want to forget Uncle Ephah either, but he doesn't want to be sad …" Jael's voice trailed off. She was making a mess of this.

"But we're all sad," Hanok said. "And Uncle Ephah's children are sad."

"Have they talked to you?" Jael asked.

"Sometimes they do," Reba said. "But sometimes they get all quiet and we know they're thinking about their father."

"And sometimes they cry," Hanok said.

"Those are normal and good ways to be sad," Jael said. "But sometimes people won't talk or cry. Then they don't deal with their sadness. They try to forget their sadness."

"Like Grandpa. He just stays in his room and moans," Reba said. "I don't think it helps him."

"No, it doesn't help," Jael said.

Reba sighed. "Because you can't forget, can you?"

Jael shook her head. "No, you can't. But some people try, and they might succeed for a short while."

"Was that what Abba was trying to do?" Reba asked.

"I think so," Jael answered. He was probably trying to forget his guilt—guilt that he had broken his leg and missed the battle, and guilt that he'd survived. It was complicated enough for her. She wasn't going to try and explain all that to the boys.

"In the evenings, after you were asleep, Abba was going out and buying a kind of drink that makes people forget, at least for a short time."

"Could I try that?" Hanok asked.

Oh dear. How could she explain that drinking made people feel terrible afterwards? She frowned, forcing herself to think back to an experience that might help. Yes, there was one horrible experience Hanok might remember.

"Do you remember that time when it was really hot and that older boy was spinning you around?" Jael asked.

"And I vomited all over you?" Hanok asked.

"Yes, you did. Do you remember how you felt?"

Hanok nodded. "All hot and shivery. And dizzy." He touched his head. "And my head ached."

"Well, that is what it feels like to be drunk," Jael said. "It is not a nice feeling at all."

"Then why do people drink?" Reba asked.

"It's a bit like the spinning. It feels fine at the beginning, but the more you drink, the worse you feel."

"Then I'm never going to drink," Hanok said.

Jael hugged the boys close to her side. "That's a wise decision. It's much better to talk and cry when we feel sad."

"The others laugh at me when I cry," Hanok said. "They call me a baby, but I'm not!"

Jael gave Hanok a squeeze. "You're not a baby. Anyone who talks like you're talking to me is a mature young man. If you need to cry about something, you come and cry with me. I won't call you a baby."

Hanok curled up next to her, and she ruffled his hair. Before long, she heard the little snuffles that signaled that he'd fallen asleep. Reba too seemed to have drifted off. Jael moved to get comfortable. Where was Reuel on this night? Was he lonely? Was he getting enough to eat? The man definitely couldn't cook, but maybe he'd found food to buy.

Zura would be praying about all these things. Jael sighed. She'd now heard the full story of Gideon's victory from an Israelite neighbor. She'd confirmed that Gideon had been extremely reluctant to believe the angel's words and had needed many reassurances. Jael had always thought the stories about Mosheh were exaggerated to justify the Israelites conquest of the Canaanites, but she'd confirmed Gideon's story from multiple people.

Yahveh obviously cared about timid Israelites. He probably had more than enough to do looking after the Israelites. She was a Midianite, and a woman. Women weren't important in anyone's eyes, let alone the eyes of a great god who'd made everything.

CHAPTER TWENTY-THREE

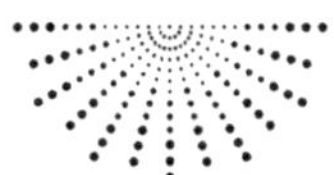

*R*euel had gone to the well outside the town walls. They'd already been here many days, and he no longer needed the splint on his leg. It remained sore and stiff but was no longer useless. He couldn't yet work a full day, but it wouldn't be long before he could.

Reuel dropped a clay pitcher attached to a long rope into the depths of the well and hauled it up once it was filled with fresh water. His arms were sore from even this little weight, softened by his months of shirking his work. His pride stung along with his weakened muscles.

As he drew the water he needed to fill his waterskins, he heard a giggle.

"Don't tickle me," came a little girl's voice.

Reuel turned his head. The giggles sounded just like Hanok. Reuel used to find the giggles annoying, but now he'd love to hear such sounds.

Reuel loved his sons, of course he did, but he hadn't known how hard it would be to be separated from them day after day. Reba was at an age that he should be working alongside his father every day, but that wasn't happening. Instead, Jael said that while Reuel had been away on the raid, Father had started to train Reba in the basic skills. But would it continue? Could Abba lift his head out of his grief to see to Reba's education? Zura had already begun to teach Reba buffing and polishing. Even Hanok sometimes clamored for a go at it.

An older girl, presumably the little one's sister, spoke next. "You can tickle me if you catch me." She took off running round the well.

"Not too far," called a young woman as she put down her water jar. Another woman, much older, who accompanied her, also put down her water jar, and sat down on the stone wall. Reuel dropped the clay pitcher back into the well to draw them some water. The younger woman gave a shy nod of thanks, then followed after her daughters, who had raced toward a stream.

"Which is your favorite?" Reuel asked the older woman.

The woman looked up at him, eyebrows knotted in the middle. "Favorite? I don't have favorites."

"Everyone has favorites," Reuel said. He'd known he wasn't his father's favorite from early childhood. Many of the painful times in Reuel's childhood had been from receiving the punishment that should have fallen on his older brother. Ephah just had to proclaim his innocence and he was believed.

"I made up my mind as a child that I'd never have favorites," the older woman said. "My father played favorites in our family. It spoiled my sister. And myself too, because my mother, seeing I was loved less, loved me too much."

"Surely a parent can't love too much?" Reuel asked, pouring the pitcher into one of her water jars.

"It depends on how you explain love," the woman said. "A parent can certainly love unwisely."

Reuel dropped the pitcher back into the well. "In what ways?"

"Favoritism turns a family into a war, competing for love and attention."

This described Reuel's family well. He'd seen the injustice of his father's love of Ephah, and Reuel had spent his years competing for that love. Trying to get his father's attention to turn on him and away from Ephah. It had never worked. Reuel had not wanted a share of his father's love. He'd wanted it all. Every single bit.

"I chose not to play favorites with my children. Now I have grandchildren, I work hard at showing them love equally. At least, as equally as I can."

One little girl waved at her grandmother, and the old woman waved back. "It helps them love each other and others if they know that they both have my love." She turned toward Reuel. "My parents did not love wisely. My father's love for my little sister meant I tried desperately to win his attention. I didn't value the love my mother offered because it was given too freely." She chuckled. "Foolishly, I valued what I did not have and looked down on what I'd been given."

She sighed and stared at the ground. "Our family was like that of Yitzchak and Rivkah's."

Reuel raised an eyebrow as he emptied another pitcher into a water jar.

"You don't know that story? Yitzchak was the son of Avraham."

"I know who Avraham was," Reuel said. "But I know little of the story of Yitzchak's marriage or his family."

"I wonder what part of Avraham's story you know?" the woman said. "There are so many angles to it. He was the husband of three women and eight sons, but he loved Yitzchak the best."

Sourness filled Reuel's mouth. For the love of Yitzchak, Avraham had sent his other sons away. Away to scrape out a livelihood in the desert when they should have all been heirs of promised blessings. Blessings which included being a great nation and eventually owning all the land toward the sunset and the great water he had heard was there.

"Yitzchak was sixty when he and Rivkah finally had their twin boys. Yitzchak favored the elder, Esau, and his wife heaped her love on the younger, Yaacov." She sighed. "Yitzchak should have learned from the injustices among his own brothers, but perhaps the favored one finds it more difficult to learn, for they have more to lose. Certainly, my sister has never seen anything wrong in the way she was treated. Favoritism had big consequences in Yitzchak and Rivkah's family."

"How so?" Reuel asked as he watched the two children throwing twigs into the stream and following them as they bobbed along on the current.

"Yaacov used trickery to grab anything he could. First his brother's right as eldest son, then even more."

Reuel raised an eyebrow.

"Rivkah overheard Yitzchak saying he planned to bless his older son and telling Esau, who was a great hunter, to prepare a meal of tender venison." The woman shifted her seat on the wall. "Rivkah then hatched a plan to get the blessing for her favored son."

This Yaacov was a grasping man. Like Reuel, he'd wanted as much favor and blessing as he could get. Yet looking around, apart from the large number of Avraham's descendants, the promised blessings seemed to have disappeared like water into the desert sands.

"Rivkah told Yaacov he must kill a goat and she would prepare it."

Reuel snorted. "Surely Yitzchak would know the difference between venison and goat?"

"By this stage, Yitzchak was very old and blind. His tastebuds were also not as keen. Perhaps Rivkah knew how to disguise the flavor of the meat with certain sauces."

"Perhaps, but surely even a blind man would know the difference between his sons. Their voices must have been different."

"Rivkah had thought of everything. She even bound goat hair on

Yaacov, so he felt like his hairier brother. It also meant Yaacov smelled more like an outdoorsy man."

"And did it work?" Reuel asked. His arms were throbbing now from repeatedly hauling water, but it felt good to feel pain that wasn't related to drink or injury or sorrow, but from honest work.

"They succeeded in their trick, but it also destroyed any hope of a relationship between the brothers, and they were estranged for most of their lives. But sadly–" The woman clicked her tongue. "Sadly, Yaacov didn't learn his lesson, for he continued showing favoritism into the next generation. First, by showing favoritism to one of his wives. That ended any hope of peace in the household, for the women became so competitive for his attention that they even used their servants as concubines to win favor with Yaacov."

Reuel whistled. "I'd have hated to live in that situation."

"One of the results of four women in the household was that there were many sons—twelve, in fact—but even there Yaacov played favorites. He loved the younger sons, Yosef and Benyamin, the sons of his favorite wife, more than the others. It led to all sorts of jealousy. Eventually the older brothers sold their younger brother, Yosef, into slavery."

"Isn't Yosef the one who rose to power in Egypt?" Reuel asked.

She nodded. "Later, Yosef would say that though his brothers had meant to harm him, Yahveh had planned that Yosef would be in Egypt to save many lives, including all his family."

Reuel blinked. "That is an interesting way to look at things."

"Yosef has taught me many lessons. I have come to see that we must trust that Yahveh is always in control of the circumstances in our lives."

"Even the bad?" Reuel asked.

"Perhaps especially the bad," she said. "Yosef experienced much injustice. He was sold into slavery by his jealous brothers, then falsely accused and ended up in prison."

The children were now splashing in the stream and squealing

with excitement. Reuel recalled a memory of him rebuking Hanok for making a similar sound when playing with his cousins. He gave his head a sudden shake to chase the memory away.

"But everywhere Yosef went, he kept his eyes on Yahveh and lived in a way that pleased him." The grandmother fixed her bright eyes on her happy grandchildren.

"But it wasn't fair," Reuel said.

"Much in life isn't fair. If we focus on the hardship, we only end up resentful and bitter."

It all sounded so easy when she said it. Just keep trusting Yahveh. But Reuel didn't even know what that meant. He could see that resentment existed in his heart and that it was linked with his father and Ephah, but he didn't know how to begin sorting out the tangles. How did trusting Yahveh make a difference? How could he trust someone he couldn't see?

The two girls ran toward their grandmother.

"Can we go home now?" the eldest said.

"We can." The grandmother got to her feet, nodding at the water jars Reuel had filled.

Reuel's strength was spent, but he wished there'd been more jars to fill so he could have asked more questions.

CHAPTER TWENTY-FOUR

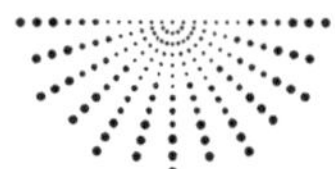

"Jael, I want to ask your forgiveness," Zura said.

"What for?" Jael couldn't think of anything Zura had done that required forgiveness.

"In my desire to help you in your marriage, I didn't understand how much Reuel had hurt you and how much he needed to put right. When you sent him away, I was proud of you for standing up to him. Reuel needs to deal with his brokenness before things get worse."

Jael blinked away tears. Since Zura had said nothing about Reuel's leaving, she'd assumed her sister disagreed with her.

"I appreciate your apology," Jael said.

"You must let me know if I ever say something that isn't helping."

Jael leaned in and hugged her sister. This woman was precious, even more so in this time with Reuel gone.

"Jael, I was just about to pray. Would you like to join me in praying for the family and Reuel?"

Jael pursed her lips. Jael had gone to find Zura because she needed someone to talk to about the boys and the things they'd said. The boys had slept late and seemed more settled and less clingy today. They'd gone to play with their cousins, so Jael finally had a moment to herself.

"I'm still not convinced that prayer is any use," Jael said.

Maybe Zura's prayers had brought Reuel home, but after that everything had gone sour.

Zura said nothing.

"After all, look at you!" Jael said. "You are so loyal to Yahveh, yet he does nothing." Her voice rose. "If he is as great as you say he is, why doesn't he heal you?"

Zura turned toward Jael, a look of infinite sadness across her scarred cheeks and eyes.

"I don't know all the answers, but I've learned to trust."

Jael suspected that Zura's sadness was not for her own blindness or lack of healing but for Jael's hardness of heart. The anger rose in Jael's throat.

"Yahveh is not worthy of your trust."

Zura's hand came up to cover her mouth. "Oh, Jael, I know you've been hurt, but please don't ever say such a thing. Yahveh has always been worthy of my trust. True, he didn't heal me, but when I poured out my hurt and bitterness, he gave me peace. He's taught me to see the good and to be thankful. The more I've done that, the more joy I've found."

Hot tears stung Jael's eyes. She hadn't meant to hurt her beloved sister. She might not have taken up a stick, but she'd beaten Zura just the same. Words could do just as much damage as sticks. Just look at the damage Reuel had done to her spirit, and the damage Abida had done to Reuel. Abida's words had been like a knife let loose inside Reuel's body, still slashing and cutting their way deep within. Jael would never want to do this to another person, especially not her ever kind sister. She knelt to embrace her sister.

"Forgive me, Zura. I may not believe in Yahveh's strength, but I believe in yours. When you pray, I hear the good you want for us, good I dare not desire because my life is so hard and I've been so hurt. Without you, dear sister, I wouldn't have hope."

Zura held Jael as if they were again just two small girls. "But Yahveh is my strength and my hope, Jael. Yahveh wants so much good for all of us."

* * *

*J*ael woke deep in the night to see Zura at her praying post in the moonlight. The boys were sleeping, faces peaceful, Hanok finding rest from his nightmares. Zura's face was streaked with tears, cutting Jael's heart.

"Zura," she whispered. "Again, I am so, so sorry. I've been angry at Reuel for his lack of kindness toward me and the children, yet then I was unkind to you, the person who least deserves it."

"You were speaking out of your brokenness," Zura said.

"But it was no excuse to use my hurt as a weapon to beat you."

"You did hurt me, but I reminded myself that we are all broken in some way." Zura gestured toward her face. "Some of our brokenness is visible, but most of it is hidden somewhere deep inside of us. Much of it we don't even know about."

"Then how can we deal with things we're ignorant about?"

"Brokenness usually reveals itself at some point, like yours did. That's when we can start to deal with it and allow it to heal."

Broken was how Jael felt. She had a broken marriage and two hurting children. The wounds Reuel had dealt her ached, yet he had wounds as well. Most had been inflicted by his father, but some were from his mother. His mother had wounded him in more subtle ways.

Jael got to her feet and sat next to her sister. The window shutter was open to let in the cool night air. Together they looked at the moon, shining like a bright round mirror. Reuel had hoped their mirrors would bring their family a bright future. Did he still have these dreams? Did he still want good for them, or was he broken beyond repair?

"Do you remember that cow that limped?" Zura broke the silence. "Reuel thought the problem was the cow's hip, but in the end, he found a stone in its hoof and all that pus underneath. The pus was released when he pulled the stone out and dug around with his knife, and eventually it healed. I'm praying everyone will heal. You and Reuel, the boys, and Abida, and Zipporah and the children too."

Jael sighed. "I don't see how."

"It won't be easy," Zura said. "In fact, it needs a power much greater than ourselves."

Yes, Zura was going to talk about Yahveh. Yesterday, Jael would have gotten up at this point of the conversation and walked away. But she remembered her own words, that she didn't trust Yahveh but she did trust Zura. It had been unkind to always be so scathing when Zura spoke of her trust in Yahveh. Even if Yahveh was a story which gave comfort, not a real power, these stories had given Zura unnatural strength. It was becoming clearer and clearer that Jael could do nothing to fix her brokenness in her own strength.

"Your words yesterday gave me a bit of a challenge," Zura said.

"Please don't think of them. I should not have said them."

"Maybe not, but there was good in them because it forced me to think back to all the stories of Yahveh I know. I went right back to the beginning of our world, and there are remarkably few stories of Yahveh healing individuals. There are plenty of miracle stories, so his power is not in doubt, but they are mostly stories of rescue, like Noach in his ark and the plagues God sent to rescue the people of Israel from Egypt."

Jael remembered the stories of Noach and the plagues.

"The only healing miracles I could think of were when Mosheh was leading the people through the wilderness." Zura turned toward Jael. "Even these were healings after judgments. Yahveh healed Mosheh's sister, Miryam, after she was struck with leprosy for defying Yahveh's choice of Mosheh as Yahveh's leader."

"But that shows he has the power to heal if he wants to," Jael said.

"Yes. The clearest story I was thinking of was about one of the many times that the Israelites complained. They said, 'There is no bread! There is no water! And we detest this miserable food.'"

Jael laughed softly. Even whispering so as not to wake the boys, Zura had got the whine of their complaints perfectly into her voice.

"I tell you, it was no laughing matter for Mosheh. He had heard all these kinds of complaints before. The Israelites were always talking about returning to Egypt to eat cucumbers and pomegranates, and forgetting they were slaves back in Egypt. Yahveh sent poisonous snakes to bite the people. Many died."

Jael's eyes widened. Snakes were a harsh punishment for whining. She imagined Israelite mothers telling their whining children that snakes were coming if they didn't hush up.

"The Israelites were chronic complainers. Yahveh wanted them to learn to ask him when they had problems, not complain about it."

"I thought you said this story was about healing," Jael said.

"Have patience, little sister!" Zura smiled in the moonlight. "The people asked Mosheh to plead to Yahveh to save them, and Yahveh told Mosheh to make a snake out of bronze."

"Bronze? Maybe Hobab or one of our ancestors made it," Jael said. Hobab would have been traveling with the Israelites all this time.

"I never thought of that, but you might be right," Zura said. "Mosheh was told to put the snake up on a pole. If anyone was bitten by a snake, they could look toward the bronze snake and be cured."

"I wonder where that statue is now? Anyone who owned it would make a fortune."

"Do you really think the statue itself had healing power?" Zura said. "We work with bronze every day, and it has never healed anyone that I'm aware of."

"I guess you're going to tell me that it was the choice to trust Yahveh's words that saved them," Jael said.

Zura grinned in the moonlight. "I guess I am. That is one of the few stories that I can remember about healing. Like the story of Miryam, this story was the reversal of a judgment."

"So Yahveh doesn't heal people like you?" Jael asked.

"I am sure he could, but it was another story that I recalled and saw in a different light that gave me comfort."

"And?"

"And it is a fairly unusual one. What do you know about Yaacov?" Zura asked.

"Absolutely nothing," Jael said.

"Yaacov was one of Avraham's grandsons. He had plenty of his own brokenness, not helped by parents playing favorites between him and his brother. Yaacov was constantly deceiving others and greedily grabbing everything he could. It took him many years to learn to trust Yahveh. Along the way, Yahveh sent an angel to wrestle with him. When Yaacov refused to give up, the angel touched his hip and dislocated it. For the rest of his life, Yaacov walked with a limp."

Jael looked at her sister. "That doesn't sound like a healing story."

Zura nodded. "Your words yesterday unsettled me. I recalled the stories I mentioned, but it was Yaacov's that most spoke to me. Yaacov was always trusting his own deceitful plans to get his own way. Yes, he'd been given promises like the promises to Avraham, but he wanted to run his own life."

"Isn't that like most of us?" Jael asked. She had been relieved to marry Reuel because he didn't serve any god. Thus, she could avoid the kinds of demands the gods made for sacrifice and allegiance.

"Yahveh didn't heal Yaacov. Instead, he injured him for life."

Jael rubbed her eyebrow. "I am still not seeing why you find this encouraging."

"Maybe I'm not doing a good job of explaining," Zura said. "I feel like although Yaacov's body was hurt, his heart was healed. For the rest of his life, Yaacov would remember that he had met Yahveh. That Yahveh knew him and had blessed him." Zura sighed. "When I was first blinded, I was in so much pain, physically and in my heart. I was angry at the woman who spilled the boiling water. I was angry at the gods who had not prevented the injury and later failed to heal me. My inner brokenness was a bigger problem than the physical. Yaacov's story reminds me that sometimes Yahveh turns the harm we suffer into a way to heal us." Zura side-hugged Jael. "Yahveh can take bad happenings and use them for good. That's certainly been my experience and is what I'm praying for us all."

Zura's views on Yaacov's story were unexpected. The Canaanites around them either placated the gods to keep evil and harm away or pleaded for blessing. No one saw blessings in suffering. No one except Zura. Anyone else listening to their conversation might conclude Zura was delusional, but Jael envied Zura for her peace, joy, and contentment. Three priceless gifts Zura would say only came from Yahveh.

If only Jael could have the gifts...but they required belief in the giver. Jael couldn't trust what she didn't believe.

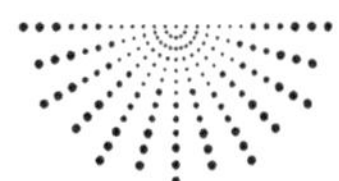

CHAPTER TWENTY-FIVE

Reuel leaned back against a log and gave a deep sigh of contentment. "That was a good meal."

"I'm working at it," Dedan said.

Reuel wiped the grease from the lamb off his chin. "You're certainly doing something right, because that was definitely not like your first efforts."

"I've found someone to teach me," Dedan said.

"Is that where you've been going after you've finished getting all the wood for the furnace and lighting the fire?" Reuel asked.

Dedan nodded.

"I was worried you were going against our agreement," Reuel said.

"Drinking, you mean?"

Reuel grunted. He'd made sure Dedan wasn't disappearing to drink for there'd been no physical signs and no smell of alcohol on him.

"Then I worried about…" Reuel flushed. "You know—"

Dedan sighed. "I wouldn't dishonor my wife."

Reuel sat up straight. "I didn't know you had a wife." He had wondered why not, for Dedan was strong and healthy and well past the age for taking a wife.

"Most men my age have a wife." Dedan's voice was low and sad. "I had a beautiful wife and a son, and my wife was expecting another child."

"I'm sorry. I've been so absorbed in my own problems that I never considered you might have suffered more than myself."

"Grief is like that," Dedan said. "It swallowed me for so long I barely noticed the sun was shining outside and I still had a life to live."

It sounded like Dedan's grief had prostrated him like it had Reuel's father. Reuel had not withdrawn into his room, but he'd withdrawn from being present for his family.

"I joined the raiders as a way to escape." Dedan clicked his tongue. "Stupid idea. Now I've got more grief to deal with. Tried alcohol this time, to help me forget."

All that the drinking had done was delay Reuel from dealing with his grief and regrets.

"We men are good at physical fighting but not nearly as good at fighting our griefs," Dedan said. "I am learning something I will never forget. I have to face up to what I've lost."

Reuel had not heard Dedan talk so much since they'd met. "How have you come to this new understanding?"

"My cooking teacher has proved to have more wisdom to impart than just the kneading of dough," Dedan said with a laugh.

Reuel leaned closer to the fire and clasped his knees. "Who is this teacher?"

"The other day I saw you talking with an older lady near the well. She recognized me when I went to buy some vegetables at the market and stopped to talk." Dedan added an extra log to the fire. "She asked if I was doing the cooking for us both. I shrugged and told her I was doing my best."

"Did she offer to help you?"

Dedan nodded. "I admitted I was finding it challenging but needed to help you out with something. I'd already proved to be not up to standard with coppersmithing."

"Don't be too hard on yourself. I was learning to work with copper soon after I could walk." Reuel pointed at the pile of wood near the furnace. "It helps a lot not to have to do all the wood collecting and chopping." Jael and the boys normally collected wood. Jael also collected their daily water, did all the cooking, made their clothes, set up and packed up the camp, and was at his side drawing the designs for his mirrors to further his dreams. He'd had nothing but harsh words for all her efforts.

"Grandma Dinah said I could come and help her each day with the meal, then come home and cook the same one immediately afterwards."

Reuel chuckled. This Dinah sounded quite shrewd.

"She tells me stories as we prepare the food. They've been helping me."

Reuel raised an eyebrow. "Stories from her history?"

"Yes. Stories of people like me. People who have suffered much loss but who continued to walk forward following Yahveh."

"I don't understand how people can continue to trust this god if he lets them down."

Dedan chuckled. "Believe me, I had the same questions, especially when she told me the story of Job."

"Job? I haven't heard that name."

"He was apparently a wealthy man probably in the time of Avraham. You know about Avraham, don't you?"

Reuel nodded. "He's our ancestor too. I knew a little about him, but the woman you're calling Grandma Dinah told me more that I didn't know."

"Dinah and her husband, Asher, take turns telling me stories. Let me see if I can remember the story of Job. It's the story of a man who suffered far more than I have."

"That doesn't sound very encouraging."

"Surprisingly I found it helpful. I'll try and explain why."

A half-burned log in the fire settled, and sparks flew up toward the stars above their heads. Dedan poked the fire with a stick then added another log.

"Job was the greatest man in the east, for Yahveh blessed him in every way. He owned vast herds of camels, sheep, oxen, and donkeys, and he had seven sons and three daughters."

Blessed indeed. Perhaps his father had left him a fine inheritance.

"Job was a follower of Adonai and would regularly offer sacrifices just in case he or any of his family had sinned against Adonai." Dedan looked across at Reuel. "This is where the story gets a little weird, for we are told that the angels in heaven gathered around Adonai and Satan joined them."

"Satan? I am not sure what I believe about him," Reuel said.

"I asked Asher. He said the stories don't speak of him much, but they believe he was one of the created angels who used his freedom to rebel against his creator. Now he works against Adonai, aiming to spread discord and evil wherever he can."

There was certainly plenty of evil in these lands. One of the reasons Reuel preferred traveling to staying in Ramoth Gilead was that they could avoid most of the festivals to Baal and his consorts. He didn't want Reba and Hanok to see the fear of the children who were being sent to be sacrificed or to see the revelry or drunkenness and debauchery that happened at those festivals. The Israelites had been wise to hide in their towns and mountain caves when the raiders crossed the Jordan at harvest time because women wouldn't have been safe if they'd been found. Shame filled his belly. Would he have had the courage to prevent any women who had been found from being raped or worse? He liked to think he would have, but he'd have been more likely to have turned a blind eye.

"Anyway, Satan came, and Adonai asked where he'd come from.

Satan replied, 'From wandering to and fro across the earth.' Adonai asked him, 'Did you see my servant, Job? There is no one else like him, for he is blameless and upright and fears me and shuns all evil.'"

Reuel's eyes widened. Blameless. Upright. What must it have been like to have such a man for a father, for a spouse? Reuel was not such a man.

"'Yes, I saw him, and of course he follows you for you have given him everything,' Satan scoffed. 'You've put a protective hedge around him so nothing can touch him. He worships you because you've blessed him but take away everything he has and he will curse you.'"

Satan had a point. What person wouldn't follow a god if they received riches and blessings?

"So Adonai said to Satan, 'I give you permission to do what you want, but you must not lay a finger on the man himself.'"

"What did Satan do?" Reuel asked.

"A servant arrived and said, 'Sabeans came and stole all your oxen and donkeys. They killed all the other servants, and I am the only one who escaped.'"

"How did Job respond?" Reuel asked.

"He didn't have any time to respond, for another servant came running in and said, 'The fire of God fell from the heavens and burned up all your sheep and those caring for them and I am the only one who escaped to tell you.'"

"Satan is clever to allow one survivor each time."

"Clever and cruel, for while the second messenger was still speaking, the third arrived and said, 'The Chaldeans formed three raiding parties and swept down and stole all your camels and killed your servants and I was the only one to escape and tell you.'"

"So that's all the oxen, donkeys, sheep, and camels gone." Reuel ticked off on his fingers. "What's left?"

"The most precious of all. Another messenger came running in and said, 'Your sons and daughters were feasting in your elder son's house when suddenly a mighty wind swept in from the desert and struck the corners of the house.'"

Reuel held his breath, dread gripping his belly.

"'The house collapsed, and all of your sons and daughters are dead. I am the only one who escaped to tell you.'"

"So, Satan won," Reuel said and picked up a stick to stab at the fire.

"He might have won if he was fighting against you or me, but the story doesn't end there."

Reuel lifted his head to look across at Dedan.

"Job got up, tore his robe into shreds, and shaved his head. Then he fell to the ground in worship and said, 'Naked I came from my mother's womb, and naked I will depart. Adonai gave and he has taken away. May his name be praised.'"

"You must be joking," Reuel said. "What man would continue to worship this god?"

"A man very different from you and me," Dedan said. "And Job remained steadfast through all the rest of the story."

"You mean there's more?" Reuel poked the glowing coals in front of him. The action seemed to help him express the emotions swirling inside him.

"Satan went back to Adonai's court, and Adonai said to him, 'Did you see Job, still blameless and upright? Even after all you have done to him, he still remains faithful.'"

Reuel looked at Dedan. "Did Satan have an answer?"

"'Skin for skin,' Satan scoffed. 'A man will give anything as long as he lives, but stretch out your hand and strike his body and he will curse you.' And so, Adonai said, 'You may do anything you like, but you must not kill him.'"

Reuel had never heard a story like this.

"Satan struck Job with boils. The pain was so bad that he went outside and sat on the ash heap and scraped his sores with a piece of pottery. Even his wife came and said to him, 'Curse God and die!' but Job replied, 'You are speaking like a fool. Shall we only accept good from God and not trouble?'"

"So, Job and his god won?" Reuel said.

"We're still not at the end of the story," Dedan said.

"Don't stop now." Reuel shifted his position to stretch out his aching leg. "What happened?"

"Three of Job's friends came to comfort him. When they saw the horror of his body, they wept, tore their robes, and sprinkled ashes on their heads."

"Probably as little use as drinking, hey Dedan?" Reuel slapped Dedan's shoulder, trying to lighten the tension.

Dedan stared into the fire. "At least they were showing that they could see the enormity of Job's losses. They followed it up by just sitting with him in silence for seven days. It might not have looked like they were doing anything, but I think I'd have appreciated someone just sitting with me that long. My house was so quiet and empty without my wife and son." Dedan sighed.

"What happened to them?" Reuel asked.

"They were struck down by a fever that swept through the town," Dedan said, voice low. "They were gone so quickly. I didn't even have time to say goodbye."

Reuel hadn't had an opportunity to say goodbye to Ephah either. Not that his loss could be compared to Dedan's. He didn't even know what he thought about Ephah. Had he even loved his brother? They'd been rivals more than brothers. Rivals for their father's attention. Ephah had won every time, and it looked like he was winning even in death, for their Father didn't seem inclined to rejoice that he still had one son left. And Jael? Maybe she'd welcome him back. Maybe? He couldn't be confident about that because he hadn't expected her to send him away in the first place. He hadn't thought she would have had that much backbone. Maybe she had more of their ancestress, Jael, in her than he'd thought.

"Dinah and Asher said the rest of Job's story is a long poem they haven't memorized. The friends try to convince Job that he must have done something wrong for Adonai to allow such suffering to come upon him."

Reuel frowned. "But the suffering has nothing to do with Job. It's all to do with the challenge Satan gave Adonai. A sort of competition to see if people worship Adonai for what they can get or simply because he is worthy of worship."

"That's the most profound thing I've heard you say," Dedan said.

Reuel rubbed his head. "What? What did I say?"

"Those words about Adonai and Satan being in a competition. The people in Canaan worship Baal and the other gods because of what they can get or to avoid being cursed. Job's god seems different. He wants to be worshiped because of who he is, not just for the gifts he gives."

"But isn't that what we all want?" Reuel said. "I don't want my sons to love me because of what I give them or do for them." He wasn't sure they loved him at all. They might even be afraid of him now. He stabbed at the fire again. He wanted another chance to be a better father, a better husband. Would he ever get the chance, or had his behavior ensured he would never be welcomed home?

"Job keeps insisting he hasn't done anything wrong, but neither he nor any of his friends know about the background to what is happening. They can only see the disasters that have fallen on Job and smell the stench of his sores. The friends keep insisting Job must have sinned, and Job keeps insisting he hasn't. He does plead with Adonai to speak with him and give him answers though."

Reuel snorted. "Well, that's not going to happen. The gods don't speak with men."

Dedan grinned. "This time you're wrong, because Adonai spoke to Job out of a storm. Again, Dinah and Asher have not memorized all the words Adonai spoke."

"It sounds like there are Israelites who do memorize the words of these stories."

Dedan nodded, "Asher said that clever young people are sent to memorize the words of Mosheh from older people who have recited the words over and over again, and can teach others."

"Are none of these things written down?" Reuel asked. Not that he could read, but there were people who could.

"There are very few written copies of Mosheh's words, but there are scribes who copy them. Then there are those who memorize the words and teach others. Asher doesn't think the story of Job has yet been written down."

Reuel blinked. Then the people who memorized the words were very important indeed. If all of them were to die, the story of Job would be lost. He turned toward Dedan. "What did Asher and Dinah remember of the words of Adonai?"

"The words made me laugh because Job wanted Adonai to speak and answer his questions but instead Adonai asked him hundreds of questions."

"What kinds of questions?"

"He said something like, 'Who is this who speaks words without knowledge? Brace yourself like a man, and I will question you and you shall answer me. Where were you when I laid the foundations of the earth?' and lots of questions like, 'Have you journeyed to the depths of the sea? Do you know when the mountain goats give birth? Are you in control of the seasons?' At the end he says to Job, 'Come on, answer me!' and Job repents and says, 'Surely I spoke of things I didn't understand, things too wonderful for me to know.'"

"Is that it? Doesn't Adonai tell Job about Satan's challenge?"

Dedan shook his head. "Asher said that what Job needed to learn was that he was a mere man. That there were many things far beyond his ability to know or control, and he must learn to trust that Adonai is in charge."

"Not an easy lesson to learn. When the boys push hard and want explanations, I do try and teach them that they need to trust I know more than they do and I have their best interests at heart." Reuel cleared his throat. He hadn't had Hanok's best interests at heart when he'd beaten him for naming him as the drunk he was. "The problem is that I don't know everything, so sometimes I get it very wrong."

"Maybe that is what makes Adonai different. If he truly is the creator and sustainer of all things, as Asher and Dinah believe, and he is also only ever good, then Job is able to trust him."

It was a big series of 'ifs'. Yes, Reuel liked the story, but liking the story was a long way from wanting to worship the god of the story. He'd always steered clear of coming under the bondage of any god. He'd not heard of any god with a nature worthy of trust, just gods with the power to bless and curse at whim. He had seen how much they asked and how fickle they were. He wanted to be free to make his own decisions and choices.

But that hasn't gone too well, has it?

The thought was troubling. He remembered Gideon, and how Yahveh was so patient with all Gideon's doubts and worries until Gideon had seen enough to trust. He remembered Yaacov attempting to manipulate blessings for himself when Yahveh had planned to give him blessings all along. Yaacov had just needed to trust. Reuel brushed these thoughts from his mind like an annoying fly. It was late, and he needed to be rested if he was going to work on some new mirrors tomorrow.

CHAPTER TWENTY-SIX

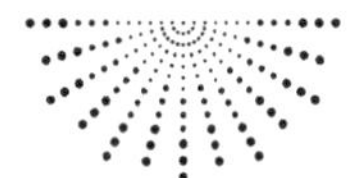

*J*ael and Zipporah had come to the nearest well to draw their day's water. Instead of a line of chattering women waiting their turn, it was quiet. Jael glanced around, looking for a reason for the silence.

"Where is everyone?" Zipporah asked.

"Let's draw our water and get home," Jael said. Something didn't feel right, but she didn't want to worry Zipporah. She lowered the bag into the water. Once it was full, she pulled it hand over hand to the surface. Then they worked together to empty the bag into the containers slung on the sides of the donkey.

Zipporah took her turn and lowered the bag into the well.

Jael looked around. A shutter at one of the upstairs windows was open. Someone was watching. Why?

Zipporah pulled up the next load of water. The moment they'd emptied it, Jael took over. The hairs on the back of her neck rose. She wanted to get home as soon as possible.

They'd filled the last container to the top when something whizzed through the air, hitting the ground at their feet with a plop. Jael wrinkled her nose at the pungent smell of fresh manure.

"Duck!" Jael said as other clods flew through the air. One hit the donkey on its haunches, and it kicked, letting out a hee-haw of protest.

Heart racing, Jael grabbed the donkey's halter and turned it around to head for home.

"Stay close," Jael said. "And don't run."

They moved forward, one on either side of the donkey, as more lumps of manure fell around them. One splattered Jael's foot, another hit her back with a stinging blow. She placed her hand on Zipporah's. Zipporah was trembling.

"Mid, Mid, Midianites," a boy chanted, still out of sight.

Jael lifted her head. She still couldn't see anyone. Cowards!

Zipporah, eyes wide, was clutching the donkey's mane.

"Just keep walking," Jael whispered. "Slow and steady."

"Mid, Mid, Midianites. Gone a-raiding, won't come back," chanted another boy.

Zipporah gasped.

"Take no notice. Keep walking," Jael said through clenched teeth. "They're just children." Children whose parents had not come to the well and allowed their children to behave like this.

The donkey bucked and hee-hawed again. Jael stroked its shoulder. "You're alright. Slow and steady." She was talking to herself as much as the donkey.

More manure landed on Jael. Zipporah too had been hit. Tears were streaming down Zipporah's face, but Jael wouldn't give their tormentors such satisfaction. She held her head high and jerked the donkey's halter to turn it abruptly down a narrow side street. The sounds of the attack died down.

"Is it finished?" Zipporah whispered, wiping a stream of muck from her neck with the back of her hand.

"Hope so," Jael said in an undertone.

They walked in silence. Jael had often wondered what the Israelites in Ramoth Gilead thought of them. Now she knew. The parents might not be openly antagonistic, but they hadn't prevented their half-grown children from attacking.

They turned down the next street, closer to home.

"Good morning," someone called.

Jael startled, mouth dry. She managed to greet the woman in return. Not everyone was against them, but they'd be staying inside for a while. Inside until things calmed down. Reba had reminded her this morning that Reuel had already been gone one moon. Would they ever get back on the road again, or would she be stuck in this town with a household of grief and people who resented and rejected them?

* * *

"Well done, children." Jael stretched her back.

Since the attack, they'd stayed within the walls of their courtyard. Their neighbor had been willing to collect water for them in exchange for their excess goat milk.

The children found being confined hard. Seeing there was a good breeze today, Jael had suggested they do the annual washing of the carpets.

Jael looked at the sopping wet children, covered in suds. "We'll finish the last carpet. Zipporah, would you be willing to take the children onto the roof for a while?" It would be easier to work without the young ones around. Fewer water fights.

Once the children left, Jael and Zura scrubbed side by side on their hands and knees.

"Zura, I've been meaning to ask you. Do you think Yahveh cares about our little problems? Like the fact that our neighbors don't like us." Jael blew her hair from her eyes.

"I think you're confusing care with giving us what we want," Zura said.

Jael scrubbed another section of carpet, trying to understand what Zura was getting at. She gave up. "What do you mean?"

"We often have a list of wants, but we sometimes ask for things that won't be the best for us. Or sometimes Yahveh says no because he has a bigger purpose."

"I still find it puzzling that Yahveh hasn't healed you and you don't seem to mind." Jael moved backwards to scrub the next section of carpet.

"It's too strong to say I don't mind," Zura said. "Sometimes it is more of a struggle than other times."

"You've never told me why you became a follower of Yahveh when so few others follow him."

Zura chuckled. "You've never asked."

Zura was right. All her talk of Yahveh this and Yahveh that had only annoyed Jael.

Zura scrubbed the next section of carpet then sat back on her haunches. "When I was first injured, I was in a lot of pain from the burns and my heart was scorched too. Scorched with the anger I felt toward the woman who was so careless as to splash me with boiling water. I prayed to any and every god, demanding healing and also demanding that they punish the woman for what she did to me."

Jael had been too young to remember any of this. Zura had already been a young woman, well into her coppersmith training, when the accident happened.

"I would pray to one god for several days. When there was no response, I'd reject that god and try another. For the first time in my life, I encountered something Ima and Abba couldn't solve for me." Zura sniffed. "I felt so alone in my struggles. So powerless. All my effort was concentrated on getting my eyesight back so I could be useful and have a chance at marriage." She sighed. "I had to reach a low point where I wanted to die before I began to see."

"See?" Jael asked, checking she hadn't missed scrubbing any parts of the carpet.

"I needed to see that the desire for revenge isn't good for anyone, and there is a difference between willful harm and accidents. My anger prevented me from seeing that the woman who caused my blindness was also suffering. She blamed herself."

"So she should," Jael said. "If she hadn't been talking and had looked where she was going, she'd have seen the mat was uneven."

"Yes, that's true, but she also needed my forgiveness. More than that, she needed Yahveh."

Jael helped Zura to her feet and rinsed off the carpet and together they hoisted its dripping heaviness over a pole so it would dry more quickly. Then they sat in the shade.

"Why did you eventually choose Yahveh?" Jael asked.

"I suspect he chose me," Zura said with a smile. "He waited until I'd exhausted myself, running in every direction but toward him. Then he sent his messenger."

"His messenger?" Jael asked, confused.

"I didn't know she would turn out to be a messenger from Yahveh. In fact, I was a little annoyed when she came and offered to massage wool fat into my scars. Kozbah was one of Ima's many friends. She started coming every afternoon with her little jar of ointment. As I lay there and she massaged my face and throat, she would tell me stories and sing songs about the stories."

"Stories about Yahveh?" Jael asked.

Zura nodded. "Some I knew and some I didn't. She started at the beginning, with the creation of the world, and Adam and Havah. How they rebelled against Yahveh, and tried to be independent and make their own decisions."

Jael nodded. Zura had told her many stories before Jael had hardened her heart against the god of the stories.

"There were stories of Avraham and Mosheh and Yehoshua. The

story that really changed my thinking was the story of Yosef. Yosef was one of the twelve sons of Yaacov."

Since they'd talked about Yaacov the other day, the history no longer seemed unfamiliar. Jael knew of Avraham, of course, but Midianite stories usually focused on Keturah, his third wife, not Yitzchak, the son of Sara.

"Yaacov had four wives, and the women fought among themselves for his favor. Yaacov foolishly loved his son, Yosef, best and showed it by giving him a beautiful multicolored coat. Eventually Yosef's elder brothers sold him to Midianite traders to get rid of him, and our ancestors sold him into slavery in Egypt."

"It sounds like a depressing story," Jael said.

"Be patient," Zura said. "Yosef suffered many injustices. First, his own brothers sold him, then he was falsely accused of a crime and thrown into jail. Yet, he never saw these things as evidence that Yahveh didn't care. Rather, he trusted in Yahveh, year after year, in the tough times. Eventually he was miraculously taken out of the prison and raised to one of the highest positions in the land. While he was in that position, his brothers arrived in Egypt looking for help."

"I hope he had them thrown into prison," Jael said.

"That may have been what they deserved and how many people would have responded, but Yosef forgave them. He said something like this to them, 'You intended to harm me, but God intended everything for good so that many lives would be saved.'" Zura shook her head. "Yosef's attitude surprised me. He had suffered for years because of other people, yet he hadn't become bitter as I was becoming. I longed for the freedom from bitterness that Yosef had. Kozbah urged me to trust that Yahveh had a plan for my blindness and to trust him to give me the strength to forgive the woman who had injured me."

The newly washed carpet dripped.

"How could you possibly forgive her?" Jael asked.

"It wasn't easy. I struggled for a few days, but I knew my way wasn't working. Eventually I prayed and asked Yahveh to change me."

"And did he?"

Zura nodded. "From the day I trusted him to change me, he has. Not all at once, but bit by bit. It took years for me to understand that I can see more clearly because I'm blind."

"It sounds like a contradiction," Jael said.

"It does, doesn't it? Yahveh used my blindness to take away my independence. He made me aware how much I needed him. Yahveh has taught me to listen to what he wants me to do and to listen to others. I am often tempted to run ahead of him, but I've learned to wait and trust his timing and his ways."

Jael had always tried to dismiss her sister's character as just who she was, but Zura had just claimed she was the way she was because she followed Yahveh.

"Yosef and Mosheh, and all those men were famous, but does Yahveh care about ordinary people? For women like me?" Jael said.

Zura laughed. "Yes, sometimes it does seem like most of the stories are about men, but none of them were famous before they met Yahveh. It was Yahveh who chose them and used them to bless many others. But does he care about women like you and me? That's a good question, you know the Canaanite gods do not. Even though our parents kept us away from the temples, surely you noticed it was women who were kidnapped to work there, and it's usually girls who become offerings to the gods. Yahveh's a God who sees women."

"I know you say that but does Yahveh really care? For if he doesn't, then I don't want to serve him," Jael said.

Zura paused for a long moment. Probably praying.

"Do you remember hearing about Hagar?" Zura asked.

The name sounded familiar. Jael squinted in concentration and thought back to the bits and pieces of stories Zura had told her over the years. "Wasn't she the second wife of Avraham?"

"She certainly was. She was a slave. Probably given by the Egyptian pharaoh to Avraham as a gift. When Avraham's wife failed to have a child, Sara came to Avraham and suggested he take Hagar as a second wife so they could try and gain a son through her."

"Like our neighbor did. He gained three sons from his second wife," Jael said. Three sons who had been among Jael's playmates.

"I can think of several other families," Zura said. "Avraham and Sara forgot to rely on Yahveh, so they used Hagar to gain the son they wanted."

"What do you mean?" Jael asked.

"Hagar ended up being with child, but when Sara discovered this, she was overcome by jealousy, forgetting that giving Hagar to Avraham had been her own idea. She mistreated Hagar and made Hagar's life so miserable that Hagar fled into the desert."

Jael leaned forward. "Then what happened?"

"Yahveh sent an angel to Hagar, and told her to return to Sara and submit to her."

"That doesn't sound fair," Jael said. "Maybe he didn't know Sara had been mistreating her."

"Oh, he knew, for when the angel first saw Hagar he said, 'Hagar, slave of Sara, where have you come from and where are you going?' Hagar then said she was running away from her mistress."

"Oh," Jael said. "So the angel was telling her to go back to her miserable existence. If I'd been her, I wouldn't have gone."

"Lots of people would agree with you, but I told you Yahveh doesn't always do what we expect. The angel told Hagar Yahveh would increase her descendants so much that they would be too numerous to count. She was already with child and was to name this son Yishmael. The angel then added, 'For Yahveh has seen your misery.'"

"So he did see her?" Jael said.

"Yes, and Hagar knew it, for she actually gave Yahveh a special name, Beer Lahai Roi, which means 'Yahveh sees me.' She must have believed it, for she went back to Sara and lived in Avraham's household. It wasn't easy. Many years later, she had to leave again for good because Sara had her own son and didn't want Avraham's attention divided. Sara demanded that Avraham send Hagar and Yishmael away. Avraham was upset about it, but Yahveh reassured Avraham that he was still in control and told Avraham to listen to Sara in this matter."

Jael wasn't impressed by Sara.

"Hagar and Yishmael soon ran out of food and water. Hagar laid Yishmael under a bush to die. She went away and cried, and the Lord rescued her a second time, for he provided a well of water and promised Hagar that Yishmael would also become a great nation."

"It's a sad story," Jael said.

"Sad in some ways, but it is also a special story, for this Egyptian slave saw messengers from God twice. I've never seen an angel. No one I know has ever seen an angel. Yet this woman, this nobody, this slave, talked with angels twice." Zura turned toward Jael and took her hand. "You ask if Yahveh sees and cares about ordinary people. This story tells us that indeed he does. Yahveh cares for those that no one else cares about. Yahveh calls them by name. Hagar found the God who sees. I want you to find Yahveh too. Won't you turn to him? He will provide everything you ever need."

"Will he change my husband and return him to me?" Jael asked.

"I cannot promise you that. But I can promise you that God will work for good in your life."

"I don't know if I can trust him if the way is hard and difficult," Jael said.

"I have found Yahveh to be enough for my every need," Zura said, face shining. "It hasn't been easy, but he has never let me down. I trust that one day I will be with him forever and that I will truly enter his promised land."

It was obvious that following Yahveh had nothing in common with the way the Canaanites worshiped their gods. For it wasn't some sort of transaction, where a person made an offering and got things in return. It was much more about learning to trust in a god whose character was trustworthy.

One problem remained for Jael was not yet convinced Yahveh was trustworthy.

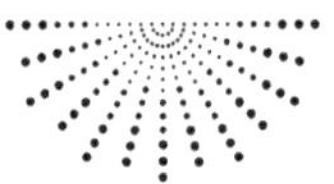

"Reuel, can I watch you work?"

Reuel mopped the sweat dripping off his forehead and cheeks, and glanced toward the older man who had just entered his work area. "It's not very interesting."

"It is to me. My grandfather made plows, and I spent most of my childhood watching him work. It always amazes me when I see something appear out of wood or metal."

It still amazed Reuel, and he was the one who could make it happen. He'd finished all the fixing of pots and metal objects, so now he was taking the time to make more mirrors. Jael's designs were stunning and just looking at them again the previous afternoon had rekindled his desire to make the objects the drawings represented.

"I hear you are being better fed nowadays," the older man said.

Reuel looked up. "You must be Asher."

Asher nodded as he sat on a rock.

"Dedan is always talking about you and Dinah." Reuel headed back to the furnace to remove some molten metal.

Asher looked on quietly as Reuel ladled out the metal and

rapidly worked it into the series of flowers that would surround the oval of the actual mirror. Making flowers was much easier than fruit because flowers didn't have to be recognizable as a specific species. Naftali might get his wish after all as the mirror surrounded by fruit might always be the only one of its kind.

When Reuel had finished, he put more metal into the furnace, then wiped his face and neck with a cloth. "Thank you for not talking during the tricky bits."

"My grandfather drilled into me that I must be quiet whenever the molten metal came out of the furnace."

"Dedan says you have done so much for him." Reuel glanced at the furnace to check things were going as they should.

"People often attribute help and change to the wrong source," Asher said. "Dinah and I have only listened and let him talk."

"Perhaps that is all that is needed," Reuel said.

"It would be nice to think so, but people tend to think things can be sorted out with a few changes on the surface, but most issues are much deeper. Yahveh is the only one capable of bringing deep healing, right down to the roots of issues."

Reuel could sense a deep well of wisdom in Asher, but was this man someone he could trust? Someone he could allow to probe into the deeper issues that Reuel suspected were hidden within himself and leaking their poison?

"I hope you don't mind, but my wife told me that she'd spoken to you and told you some stories from our history." Asher said. "And you shared a little about your own past."

"I don't mind," Reuel said. "What did she tell you?"

"That, like her, you'd come from a family where your parents each showed favoritism."

Asher looked like he was about to say more, but Reuel had to rush to the furnace.

Asher sat still while Reuel worked the molten metal with his tongs and clippers, forming petals and buds and leaves. He was getting back into the rhythms of his work, but this first mirror wouldn't be his best work. He'd keep it to show to potential buyers or sell it for a lower price.

Once he'd finished the next part in the process, Reuel took a long drink from a dipper filled with water and offered it to Asher as well.

"Your wife told me about Yitzchak and Yaacov, and how their favoritism harmed their families. My family was the same. I've spent my life trying to win my father's approval, but he has always been focused on my elder brother. Now that my brother has died, Father has collapsed and won't leave his room. Just lies there staring at the wall."

"I'm sorry to hear that. I am going to start praying he gets out of his room."

"Pardon my rudeness, but do you think your god actually hears and answers prayer?"

"I do," Asher said, "for I myself have experienced too many answers to doubt."

"What kinds of answers?" Reuel took a seat on a convenient rock.

"Dinah is my second wife," Asher said. "She was an answer to prayer. I was devastated when my first wife died after a long illness. She just got thinner and thinner until she faded away."

"So your god didn't answer those prayers?" It felt rude to point this out.

"I prayed for a long time for my wife, but eventually she taught me that going to face her maker was not the tragedy for her it felt like to me. We had so many precious times together during her illness. Times we likely wouldn't have had if she hadn't become ill. Before then, I worked too long and too hard and neglected to spend enough time with her."

"Did you have children?"

"We were not blessed with children together," Asher said. "In the beginning, I was angry about that. But when my wife died, I was grateful I had no family around who needed my help, for I was lost without my wife. But I don't know. Maybe it would have helped me to have someone else to care for."

Asher reached for the ladle and took a drink. "It was during those years of loneliness that I really learned to pray. I prayed just for strength to get through each day. I prayed Yahveh would provide for me, encourage me, and give me a sense of purpose once again." He smiled. "And eventually he brought Dinah, a widow with three children, into my life. And he gave me a second happy marriage with a woman who has clung to Yahveh when many of those around us have abandoned him."

"I was going to ask you about that," Reuel said. "Most of the Israelites I know follow the Baals and Asherah. The prophet I heard in Jabesh Gilead said the drought was because the Israelites had abandoned Yahveh."

Asher sighed. "Yes, too many try to combine the worship of Yahveh with the local gods. They might pray to Yahveh, but in their hearts they only do it because they remember he is powerful and hope he might help them. They are not truly committed. Instead, they pray to all the gods to make sure they don't offend one. My people must bring Yahveh much pain because they don't understand he is the only one worthy of worship. When they worship other gods, they are really worshiping the powers of darkness."

Reuel blinked.

"Would any good god demand that children be sacrificed or demand sacrifices that impoverished people? The gods of Canaan couldn't possibly be good, for worshiping them leads to much evil."

"But do you truly think your god is good? Why would he allow your wife to die and you to be childless?"

"I don't know," Asher said. "But I've found peace in following him. I've discovered he is working for my good and that he loves and cares, even when all around me is dark and I can't see that it will ever be morning. But look, just as morning comes each day, Yahveh has given me new blessings. It's like that story of Job. After all his trials and pain, Yahveh gave him more sons and daughters and put a new song in his heart."

"But he must still have grieved for his seven sons and three daughters who were killed."

"Yes, as I still miss my first wife. When Yahveh spoke to Job, he gave him a new perspective. He never told him why he had to suffer, but somehow Job came to a position in which he trusted Yahveh even if he didn't fully understand. That's where I have come to. Who knows? Maybe my choosing to trust Yahveh even when times are dark achieves something in the heavens as it did with Job."

Reuel's eyes caught on the first star appearing in the dusk sky as he thought about this.

"Perhaps there are many things we can't learn unless we go through dark times and are forced to trust in Yahveh," Asher said.

"What did you learn through your hard times?" Reuel asked.

"Do you need to add more wood to your furnace?" Asher pointed at the dying fire.

"The work will always be there," Reuel said. Perhaps he too had learned something recently.

"I mentioned that I worked too hard before my wife's illness," Asher began. "I always excused my neglect of her by saying my main job was to provide for her and any children we had. I didn't see there was so much more to life than work. Her illness forced me to shorten my workdays, and we learned to talk, really talk, and encourage each other. We prayed together and laughed together and, yes, cried together. Everything brought us closer and closer until she became my best friend, my greatest encourager."

Is this what Jael had hoped their marriage would be like? Reuel had thought she was to be his helper but maybe Jael had expected something like this kind of companionship from him, but he'd never known how to be a companion to her. Or was it that he'd never considered companionship important enough to bother about?

"Together we learned to love Yahveh's world." Asher pointed toward the sun which was just beginning to go down. "We reveled in each sunset, in each bird song, in each cool mist in the morning. Even food tasted better than I could ever remember when I learned to savor it instead of eating as fast as I could to get back to whatever I thought was important."

"Were you still able to celebrate these gifts after she…" Reuel paused, not sure if his question was insensitive.

"After I passed through the initial grief, it was a great encouragement to go to the places we'd loved and look again at the beauty she had shown me. It made me feel closer to her. Later, when I met Dinah, the gifts my wife had given me were turned into blessings in my new marriage. I have learned to squeeze every drop out of the blessings and beauties Yahveh gives."

It all sounded so different from Reuel's life that he could scarcely imagine it. Yet Asher's words tugged at Reuel's heart.

"The Sabbath rest day used to be a day I endured, impatient to get on with the work waiting for me. Now the Sabbath is a day to enjoy. The very best day of the week, when Dinah and I can spend time with each other, and remind each other of our great and very, very good God."

Reuel was sure he'd think of more questions later, but for now he needed space to think on Asher's words. The man was so sincere and so joyous. He was what Reuel had always longed for in a father. It was hard to believe he'd passed through many hardships. But what if life was like smithing? What if people had to pass through the fire in order to become pure and beautiful?

CHAPTER TWENTY-EIGHT

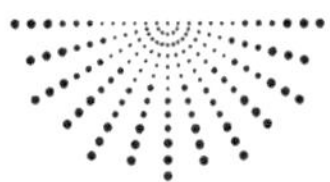

ael knew where to find her sister at this time in the morning. She'd be under the tree in the courtyard, praying.

"Zura, what are we going to do about Reuel's father?" Jael sat down next to her sister. "Besides praying, of course."

"I didn't know you were praying." The corner of Zura's mouth twitched.

"You do more than enough for the both of us," Jael said.

"You don't get any benefits if you don't actually pray," Zura said.

"I haven't observed any benefits from all your prayers."

"Haven't you? Then you aren't very observant. I can feel the difference between when I pray and when I don't." Zura took Jael's hand. "My spirit needs prayer. Without prayer, I am unsettled. I worry one way then turn and worry the other. I think I have to solve my problems."

"And don't you?"

"Many of our problems can't be solved by us. They need a God who can see all things and to whom nothing is impossible. I can't bring Ephah back, but Yahveh can help Zipporah and Abida to want to live again."

"He doesn't seem to be doing anything that I can see." Jael removed her hand from her sister's. "If I worked as slowly as he does, nothing would happen in this family."

"Then Yahveh's sense of speed is different from ours. Avraham had to wait twenty-five harvests for the son he was promised, but eventually they had a son when it was well past possible."

"If that story is true, Yahveh wasn't very kind to Avraham and his wife."

"What if there were lessons Avraham and Sara had to learn before they were ready to be parents?" Zura asked.

"How do you know that? You assume that Yahveh is both powerful and good, so you always give him the benefit of the doubt. I am not making that assumption."

"I know, and I often pray about it," Zura said.

"Don't waste your prayers on me," Jael said. She didn't know what she thought about Zura praying for her lack of faith. It felt invasive.

"I never waste my prayers," Zura said with a laugh.

"Has Yahveh given you any ideas about what to do about Abida?" Jael asked, keen to direct the focus away from herself.

Zura nodded. "I think so. I know we need to get Abida out of that room, but I hadn't thought about how it might be possible."

"And you have now?" Jael looked at her sister. "How are you going to do it?"

"I'm going to appeal to his basic sense of goodness and desire to help the weak. I am sure it is deep down inside him somewhere," Zura said. "But I need you and Zipporah to take the boys and the goats out to the stream."

Jael stood. "I'm more than happy to do that. I'm tired of being trapped inside, and so are the boys. I'll get something ready for us all to eat first."

The sunshine outside would do them all good. It couldn't be healthy to be stuck inside all the time, gradually driving each other crazy. She'd make sure the boys ran off all their energy.

Zura helped them get ready. When they were ready to leave, Jael said to Zipporah, "Goats or children?"

"Us, us," the children yelled.

"Goats." Zipporah put her hands over her ears. "Let me get the goats."

Jael laughed. "Good choice." She clapped her hands for attention and handed a bag to each of the older children. "Now pair up, hold hands, and let's go."

Outside the gates, Jael drew in a deep breath. The wind brought the smell of dried grass, and poppies tossed their red and yellow heads along the edge of the stream. Ahead of them a fish jumped, light flashing silver off its side. Out here, the grief and worry they lived with seemed a little less heavy. Grief for Ephah. Worry and concern for Reuel. Was his leg healed enough so he could stand and work? Was he selling his wares? Would her sending him away make him think and change?

"Ima, can we build a dam?" Reba asked.

"You can certainly build a dam." Jael turned to Zipporah. "I'll help you tether the goats first." Taking some of the leads in her hands, Jael led the way to the lushest grass. Once there, she tied the leads around some sturdy branches and left the goats to forage. With a series of bleats, they trotted out to the end of their leads and settled to eating as much and as fast as they could. Obviously, they hadn't appreciated being stuck inside either.

Jael walked toward the stream where the children were working together as she'd taught the boys, finding bigger rocks to lay down first. Jael tucked her tunic into her belt and waded into the water, placing her feet carefully among the rocks. "What do you want me to do Reba?"

"Find us some more bigger rocks."

Jael waved toward Zipporah. "Come and help."

Zipporah shook her head. "I'm fine here."

"Ima, we want you to help," said her youngest daughter.

"Yes, Ima, come and help," cried the middle child.

Zipporah gave in and came to join them. Her youngest took her hand and led her into the deepening pool. "Find sand to fill the gaps, Ima."

The walls of the dam were nearly complete and the water was rising up their legs when Reba yelled, "Look who's coming."

Jael stood up straight, stretching out her back and shading her eyes with her hand. Zura had done it. There was Abida, wearing a clean tunic and with his hair and beard tidied, arm in arm with Zura.

Clever Zura. Abida had had an affection for her ever since she'd been a young woman and started working in his workshop. Abida appreciated women who were useful, and Jael guessed what Zura had done. She'd probably expressed sadness that she'd been left behind and asked if he'd be kind enough to take her to join the rest of the family. He wouldn't have had the heart to turn her down.

Jael clambered up the bank and adjusted her tunic before going forward with a smile. "Welcome, Abba. The only thing missing from our expedition was you."

His lip trembled and he patted her hand without a word. Perhaps he didn't dare speak or had simply fallen out of the habit. What did it matter? He was here. A bird caroled nearby and darted across his line of sight.

"The food is over here in the shade," Jael said leading Zura in that direction. "Over here you'll be close enough to hear the kids and Abida can help them if they need it."

"Perfect." Zura flashed a smile toward Jael. She'd probably want to claim that Yahveh had heard her prayers. Jael was going to reserve judgment. She'd need to see far more prayer answered as she'd like it before she'd consider that Yahveh was not only powerful but cared for someone like her.

"Come, children," Jael called a short while later. "Let's leave the dam to fill up on its own while we eat."

"Can we paddle in the pool after we eat?" Reba asked.

"You can." Jael sat down and unwrapped the flat breads from their cloth.

Zipporah came over to them with a healthy flush on her face and helped Jael unpack cucumbers and goat cheese. She handed the first portion to Abida. Without thinking, he ate some, then looked surprised that it tasted good and kept on eating. He'd lost a lot of weight since Ephah's death.

"Me next, me next," Hanok said. "I'm this much hungry." He spread his arms wide to demonstrate.

"What do I always say? Adults first." Jael handed the next portion to Zura then quickly distributed the food to the children. They proceeded to munch and chatter as though nothing untoward had ever happened in their lives.

Abida watched them in silence, but Jael couldn't help noticing that his eyes were brighter and he was paying attention. If they could convince him to come out into the sunshine every day, the birds and flowers and children's laughter would do the rest.

CHAPTER TWENTY-NINE

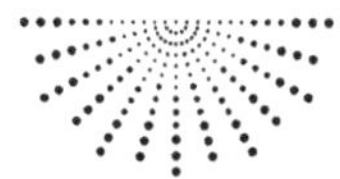

"Reuel, are you about to finish for the day?" Asher asked.

Reuel looked around his work area. "I just have to tidy up. What are you wanting me to do?"

"I'd like you and Dedan to come for a walk with me to one of my favorite lookouts," Asher said.

Asher had been to visit them nearly every day while they were outside his town. Tomorrow, they would move on, and Reuel's heart was heavy. He and Dedan had found a family where they hadn't expected one.

Reuel busied himself dampening the furnace fire and putting away all his tools. After he and Asher left the open-sided tent, Reuel unrolled the final wall and laced it closed.

Dedan was waiting for them under a tree, and they set off in the warm orange light of early evening. The three of them walked through the olive groves, lined with trees with ancient, twisted trunks and silvery-green leaves. The ground slowly rose toward the highest ridge in the area. Dedan and Asher chatted, and Reuel trailed behind them. Dedan would find it even harder to leave than Reuel. He'd spent nearly all his spare time with Asher and Dinah, listening to every story they knew. He had shared some of them with Reuel when he returned to cook the evening meal.

As the ridge steepened, they slowed their pace. Finally, they scrambled up the last of the rocks and stood on the top. Before them lay hill after hill and field after field. Greens and browns, and the speckled gray of rocks tumbled across the landscape.

"What do you see?" Asher asked.

"Apart from fields, hills, trees, and sheep?" Reuel asked, sensing Asher was digging deeper.

"A place for insects and birds and worms to hide," Dedan said.

"It is all those things, but what I mean is that I see the land promised to Avraham's descendants."

"To Yitzchak's, you mean," Reuel said, throat tight.

"I think that is what we need to talk about," Asher said. "We've known each other for a while and have talked a lot, but I sense a troubled man behind your friendliness. When I come up here and see the land spread out below me, it fills me with thankfulness. Thankfulness that I live in Yahveh's promised land. The land he promised to Avraham and his descendants. As I look at this land, even in drought, I see it as evidence of Yahveh's blessings." Asher peered at Reuel. "I don't think you see that, and it is raising a barrier in your heart between us. More importantly, it is raising a barrier between yourself and Yahveh."

An angry lump filled Reuel's throat. He liked Asher and Dinah in spite of the fact that they were Israelites. He didn't like most of the Israelites he sold his wares to. He resented that they were Yitzchak's descendants and that he was one of the despised descendants of Keturah. A wave of anger surged up his throat. As he stood here, looking at the land, all he saw was a place where Midianites were always the outsiders. Outsiders who were despised and sometimes cursed.

Asher laid his hand on Reuel's shoulder. "As a young man, I had many misunderstandings about Yahveh. I refused to listen to those who said there were answers. I am asking for you to listen to me today in the hope that what I have to say might mend some of those wounds inside you."

"Please speak," Dedan said.

Reuel couldn't voice agreement, but he'd listen because of the respect he had for Asher.

"Reuel, you carry one of the two names of Mosheh's father-in-law. Do you remember that Mosheh asked Hobab, his wife's brother, to join the Israelites?"

Reuel nodded.

"Mosheh said to Hobab, 'We are setting out for the place that Yahveh promised to give us. Now come with us and we will treat you well, for Yahveh has promised good things to Israel.'"

Of course Reuel knew the story, for it was the reason he and his ancestors lived in these lands rather than remaining out in the desert lands far to the south. Remembering this story always made him angry, for Mosheh's promise had not been kept.

"Say what is in your heart," Asher said. "It is only when you are willing to speak your thoughts that we can examine them to see what is true and what is false."

"Are you telling me I'm wrong?" Reuel asked. "Before I've even spoken?"

Asher chuckled. "All of us believe some lies. I once believed Yahveh was unfaithful for when I looked around my land, I could not see the blessings he had promised."

"I have been confused about the same thing," Dedan said. He pointed toward the nearest waterway. It contained a mere trickle of water, and many of the fields around them were parched from lack of water. "I see little blessing in this land that is supposed to flow with milk and honey."

"Interesting, isn't it? We all seem to have selective hearing. As a youth, I remembered that Yahveh had promised to bless us, but I forgot the blessings were dependent on our obedience."

Reuel looked around and settled himself on a rock. This sounded as if it would take some time. Dedan and Asher also found rocks and seated themselves.

"I looked around me and saw only signs that Yahveh wasn't happy with us, so I doubted he cared. I even doubted sometimes that he truly existed."

"Can you explain what you meant about the blessings being dependent on obedience?" Dedan asked.

"Mosheh led my ancestors to Sinai, the mountain of God, where Yahveh revealed himself in fire on the top of the mountain. He asked Mosheh to go up to the top and talk with him. While he was there, Yahveh gave Mosheh the ten commandments and expanded on them in the law. Part of the law included the covenant between Yahveh and Israel."

Covenants weren't uncommon, but why would the creator of the universe bind himself in an agreement with Mosheh and his descendants?

"Too often, Mosheh's generation failed to obey Yahveh's commands." Asher shook his head as if talking about his own disappointing child. "They lived out their lives in the desert. It would be their children, raised in the desert and fed the stories of Yahveh delivering them from slavery in Egypt, whom Yahveh would lead into the promised land. But before his death, Mosheh gave this new generation an instruction." Asher pointed to the horizon. "Look toward the sunset and a little north. Your young eyes may be able to discern two peaks."

Reuel shaded his eyes with a hand, and squinted to where Asher pointed. He couldn't see the mountains. It might be possible on a clearer day.

"Half the Israelites were to climb Mount Gerazim. Half were to climb Mount Ebal. The blessings for keeping the covenant to follow and obey Yahveh were to be recited from Mount Gerazim. The curses Yahveh would send on them if they failed to obey the good commands of the covenant were to be declared from Mount Ebal. Mosheh did not want this new generation to fail as his generation had failed. He wanted them to follow Yahveh with full hearts in the land of milk and honey they had been promised. Mosheh told the new generation how Yahveh was giving them a path to destruction and death, or a path to life and prosperity, and begged them to choose life." Asher gestured with his hand toward the dusty fields. "Behold the fruit of my people's choices, the curses that reveal our lack of faithfulness."

The old man's voice broke and his eyes filled with tears. Dedan stared at the barren horizon, as if only considering the full breadth of the drought for the first time. Reuel turned Asher's words over in his mind. The old man saw the thirsty earth as evidence of Israel's lack of faithfulness to the covenant they had made with their god. Not just evidence, but punishment. The shame he must feel, the shame all Israelites who believed in the old ways and old stories of their people must feel—it must be crushing.

Asher sighed. "I have seldom seen prosperity in the land, but I believe that when Yehoshua entered the land it was fertile and beautiful beyond belief. Truly a promised land."

Reuel remembered hearing stories of the beauty of the land in times past. He too had only ever seen it impacted by drought.

"Yehoshua, Mosheh's successor, followed Yahveh, but even he did not fully finish the work he'd been asked to do. Yahveh clearly instructed that the people within the borders of Canaan must be fully wiped out."

"Why?" Reuel felt sick and anger churned within him.

"As a youth, I had the same question. An old man whom I greatly respected reminded me of something that happened in Avraham's time. Yahveh spoke with Avraham and said it was going to be many hundreds of years before his descendants would receive their inheritance in the promised land."

"Your Yahveh doesn't rush to fulfill his promises," said Dedan.

"That's because he always has a plan," Asher said. "He told Avraham his descendants would be slaves in Egypt for four hundred years before they were rescued and brought into the promised land, and he told Avraham why they had to wait."

This had never made sense to Reuel; why the god who had promised their ancestors this land had waited so long to give it to them.

"Because the sins of the Amorites had not yet reached their full measure," Asher said. "When I first heard this reason, I didn't know what it meant. It seemed obscure."

"I don't understand either," Reuel dared to admit.

"For a start, I thought it was just talking about the Amorite people, those around Kiriath Arba, but the elderly man explained that Amorite was a term that could mean Canaanite and thus was much broader than one kind of people."

"And the line about sin not yet having reached its full measure?" Dedan raised one eyebrow.

"It means the Canaanites were not yet evil enough for Yahveh to judge. He was not going to simply wipe out the people within Canaan and give the land to Avraham. No, Yahveh would wait to fulfill his promise until the people of Canaan were so evil that they deserved to be judged. Yehoshua was to be the means of Yahveh's judgment."

Reuel's mouth went dry at this thought. A god who would wait with a cup of judgment, like a cup of melted copper, ready to pour on the heads of the wicked was terrifying to consider. And he knew some of the stories of what this god had done in Egypt.

"But there are still Canaanites around," Reuel said, pushing away his fear.

"There are, and that is because Yehoshua did not fully carry out Yahveh's commands. Not only did he get overconfident and allow himself to be tricked by some Hivites living somewhere over there." Asher gestured toward the southwest. "But the whole conquest slowed down, and eventually everyone settled down among the remaining Canaanites." Asher sighed audibly. "It's been a disaster for our people, for they all too easily followed Canaanite customs and gods. Some ..." Asher's voice slowed to a sigh. "Some people even offered their own children as sacrifices to Baal."

Child sacrifice was one of the main reasons Reuel had steered clear of religion. He wanted nothing to do with such barbaric and cruel practices.

"There are so few Israelites who follow Yahveh wholeheartedly."

"But some do, like you and Dinah," Dedan said.

Asher smiled. "Yahveh has demonstrated his power and compassion over so many past generations. Still, I had shut my heart to these stories. I went into my first marriage an unbeliever, but my wife prayed for me for years, and slowly I came to see that Yahveh really was the one she claimed him to be."

Jael wouldn't be praying for Reuel. He had been determined his family would have no gods, and she had never challenged him. But Zura? She'd never made a secret of the fact that she prayed for all those she knew. It used to irritate him, but hearing Asher, he wasn't sure it did anymore. If Zura followed this Yahveh, maybe it made total sense.

"I was a fool for so long," Asher said. "I wouldn't listen to my wife. But I could not ignore the fact that she had genuine peace and calmness about her. She took her worries and put them into Yahveh's capable hands."

Zura had the same peace about her. Despite the difficulties of being blind, she never complained, at least not in Reuel's hearing.

"But Yahveh had a way around my pride. He allowed the words from that old man I met to clear the rubble that prevented me from listening. Once he dealt with the lies I had believed to be true, then I was once again willing to listen to the stories of Yahveh from the beginning. The more I listened, the more I came to trust the God of the stories."

Dedan was nodding, looking like a man in deep agreement. But Reuel could not yet understand clearly. If Yahveh truly had the power these stories suggested, there was someone else Reuel had to blame for the Midianites always being the outsiders in these lands.

"I know you look at this land under your feet and don't see your inheritance," said Asher, as if aware of what he was thinking. "I have been praying for you both ever since my wife first talked to you. She thinks you are like many Israelites who focus on blood relationship. My people get it wrong because they think being a descendant of Yitzchak means they are automatically guaranteed blessing. I suspect you think that because you're descended from Keturah and Midian and not Sara and Yitzchak, that you miss out on blessing. Am I right?"

Reuel nodded.

"Before Mosheh died, he spoke to my ancestors as they waited to enter Canaan. He said something I have found most helpful. He said Yahveh did not choose the Israelites because they were more numerous or powerful than other peoples. He chose them because he wanted their blessings to attract other nations to enquire which god they followed. They were chosen to bless the world and attract all peoples to know the Creator."

Reuel's eyes widened. "Then it looks like the Israelites have failed."

Asher sighed. "Yes, most of the time we have gone our own way and refused to follow Yahveh. We have failed to fulfill our purpose. It makes me sad to think about it because our failure has meant many other peoples have not seen the blessings that would have led them toward Yahveh."

"We have not seen the blessings Mosheh promised our ancestor, Hobab, for we have not been given good things," Reuel said.

Asher shifted his seat on the rock and looked thoughtful. Perhaps he was praying. Dinah and Asher seemed to do that a lot.

"How do I explain?" Asher said. "Yahveh's people are not his people by blood. We could be in the direct line of Yitzchak and Yaacov, but if we do not follow and obey Yahveh, then it is the same as if we were a Canaanite. Or…" He paused. "We could be of those who have no relationship to Avraham, yet follow and obey and love Yahveh and so belong to Yahveh's people."

Reuel rubbed his head. "One of the things we Midianites have in common with you is that all our sons are circumcised on the eighth day. It was something Avraham was commanded to do for all of Keturah's sons, and we have continued the custom. We thought it made us acceptable to Yitzchak's descendants, but it never has."

"There are many people who are circumcised but whose hearts are far from Yahveh's," Asher said. "Under those circumstances, circumcision simply becomes an empty custom. The key thing is where our heart is. Is it turned toward Yahveh or away?"

That was an easy enough question for Reuel to answer. His heart had always been turned away from Yahveh. Turned away in anger and a burning resentment.

CHAPTER THIRTY

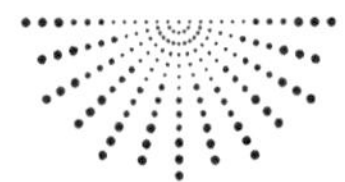

"Can I join you?" Jael asked Zura, who was sitting under the tree in the courtyard as she did early every morning. "The boys are still asleep, and I wanted to ask you more about Yahveh answering prayer."

"What would you like to know?"

Jael pursed her lips. "I want examples of people's prayers being answered."

"You'll have to give me time to think," Zura said.

While Zura thought, Jael enjoyed the peace of the early morning with the sky the palest of pinks and birds twittering.

"You've made me think. When I go through the stories in my head, I can't think of many instances of people praying at all. Maybe that is because they use other words. I can think of one phrase that is often used."

"Which is?"

"When a person or group of people 'cried out to Yahveh.' It's quite common in the stories about Mosheh. The Israelites were oppressed by the Egyptians, so they cried out to Yahveh. He heard them and sent Mosheh to speak to Pharaoh, and God used Mosheh to send ten plagues on Egypt."

"I have heard you telling those stories to the boys before they sleep," Jael said.

"You don't mind, do you?" Zura asked.

"No, I don't mind. They're not the only ones enjoying them." Jael found the stories fascinating. It seemed incredible that no one had told her the stories before. If the Israelites were supposed to be followers of Yahveh, why had none of them told her these things?

"Well, there are lots of mentions of prayer during the ten plagues. What do you remember?"

Jael thought back to the blood and the frogs, and the hail and the locusts. "Wasn't it Pharaoh who asked Mosheh to pray?"

"It's interesting, isn't it? Pharaoh never prays himself. He always asks Mosheh to mediate with God. Why do you think that is?"

Jael stared at the ground. "I don't know. Maybe it was simply because Pharaoh was used to connecting to the spiritual world through mediators like his magicians and enchanters."

"I don't know the answer either, but your suggestion is a good possibility."

"Or maybe he didn't want to actually interact with Mosheh's god, for then he would have to admit Yahveh was more powerful than the Egyptian gods and he would be under an obligation to listen to him. Maybe asking Mosheh was his way of keeping Yahveh at a distance."

"There's so much we don't know, but you raise some good possibilities. We never see Pharaoh praying to Yahveh himself, but each time he requests that Mosheh does, Yahveh answers. Sometimes he even answers at the exact time that Pharaoh makes the request."

The sky above was now brightening, and someone was chopping wood next door.

"After the tenth plague, when Pharaoh tells Mosheh and Aharon to get out, and take their people with them, Pharaoh changes his mind again," Zura continued. "He summons his army, and they pursue the Israelites and catch up to them on the edge of the Red Sea. The Israelites see the Egyptian army coming and they cry out to Yahveh." Zura paused. "No, that isn't really a prayer. It's more of a cry of desperation. Yahveh rescues them anyway, by opening a pathway through the sea and drowning Pharaoh's army."

"You'll have to tell that story tonight. I don't know the details."

Zura smiled. "I'll make sure I include as many details as I remember. After crossing the Red Sea, the Israelites spend the next forty years wandering around in the desert. Mosheh often cries out to Yahveh, asking that he stop plagues and disasters from wiping them all out."

Jael narrowed her eyes. "Why were there plagues falling upon the Israelites? I thought they were Yahveh's special chosen people."

"They are, but they often forgot the privilege, and they grumbled and complained so many times rather than speaking to Yahveh and letting him know their struggles."

"Like the boys do when they don't like the food they're given or it's been raining and they haven't gone out to play," Jael said. "I hate it."

"But don't you think we complain too?" Zura asked. "Most of my complaints are never voiced, but it is easy for me to complain when I don't know where I am or trip over things."

Things members of the family carelessly left around.

"Yahveh obviously values thankfulness," Jael said.

Zura nodded. "Like we do when the boys are thankful. The more thankful we are, the less resentment, grumbling, and bitterness can flourish."

"I like that idea. I want to water the good plants and neglect the bad ones or dig them out."

"Exactly," Zura said. She cocked her head to listen. "The boys will be out here soon."

"Is that a hint that if we're going to pray, we should do it soon?" Jael asked.

"Something like that." Zura laughed.

Jael wriggled her shoulders. The thought of praying out loud made her nervous. "How do you pray?"

"I have never heard any instructions about it. How do you think you should address Yahveh?"

"I think I should stand and maybe hold my hands up," Jael said. She hadn't seen Zura doing that, but perhaps Zura had never wanted to draw attention to what she was doing, or maybe she prayed differently when none of them could see her.

"You do what you think is right. It is Yahveh you have to please, not me, but I'll stand with you." Zura stood. "Why don't you pray first? Then you won't be trying to copy me. It's refreshing to hear someone new to it pray."

It might be refreshing for Zura, but Jael felt like a little baby lisping out her first words. How did one even address the creator of everything? A god she was just tentatively getting to know.

"Creator and great God of wonders." Jael took a big breath, and Zura reached over and put a hand on her shoulder. "Thank you. Thank you for giving me Zura for a sister. Thank you for Reba and Hanok, and thank you for helping Father and Zipporah begin to take an interest in life again."

Abida was going for a daily walk with Zura and apparently listening to stories of Yahveh too.

"Thank you that Father is talking of restarting the lessons in the workshop for the boys. They'll love that."

It was interesting how once she started being thankful, Jael could think of many more things to be thankful for.

"Thank you for a place to live. Thank you for caring and giving me a chance to get to know you." She didn't know how to end her prayer, so hopefully that was good enough.

She paused until Zura said, "See, it wasn't that bad, was it?"

"Not really."

"It gets easier the more you pray. Would you like me to pray too?"

"Yes, please. I want to hear how you do it."

Zura raised her hands. "Great God of all who trust you, thank you for seeing us here in Ramoth Gilead. Thank you that Jael is finally letting me talk about you."

Jael had never thought how her indifference and resistance to Yahveh might have hurt Zura.

"Thank you that you gave Jael courage to confront Reuel. I ask you for mercy for him. Help him not to just work as usual, but help him to take the time to ask why he started drinking. Help him to forgive his father, and restore that relationship. Let him encounter you and allow you to change him."

If Yahveh changed her husband, Jael would know this god truly cared. But was it possible? Reuel had always been so against any of the gods. *Yahveh, do the impossible. Please!*

CHAPTER THIRTY-ONE

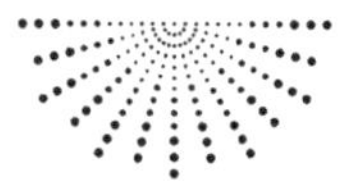

"Sorry we are late," Reuel said as he and Dedan rushed up to the doorway of Asher and Dinah's home. "We had goat trouble."

Dinah laughed. "Escaped again, did it?"

"Uh-huh," Reuel said.

Asher smiled broadly. "Welcome. We're so glad you can be our guests before you leave."

Reuel's throat tightened. He didn't want to be reminded that they were going to leave this couple who'd welcomed them when others would be more likely to spit on them as Midianites. Reuel and Dedan went through the doorway into the room beyond. The smell of roast lamb wafted through the air, and Reuel's mouth watered. Dedan's cooking had improved, but he still had a lot to learn.

A servant came to wash and dry their feet, then Asher led them into the best room and made sure they were each seated with a cushion behind their back. Reuel carefully placed the sack with its gift out of the way.

Dinah and a servant entered the room carrying fresh bread and a mound of fragrant lamb to join the cucumbers, lentils, curds, and herbs that were already laid on the floor cloth.

Asher stood and waited for the servant to leave before taking the bread from Dinah and making sure she was comfortable. Reuel swallowed the lump in his throat. Dinah eating with them signaled they were being treated as close family.

Asher held the bread up. "Thank you, mighty Creator and Holy One, for all your gifts to us. Of bread and meat, and family and friends. Guide our conversation and bless our friends as they go on their way tomorrow."

Lowering the bread in his hands, Asher tore each round and handed it to Dedan first, as the eldest guest, and then Reuel. Finally, he offered some of the bread to Dinah. Dinah's smile toward her husband made Reuel nearly lose control of his emotions. Would Jael ever look at him like that? Like he was the biggest blessing in her life, and she never wanted to be apart from him? Reuel had seen Jael's expectant joy on their wedding day, but it had soon faded. If he returned home now, Jael might turn away from him. It wouldn't be unjustified, for he had scared her badly.

"Would you like some lamb?" Asher asked, passing Reuel the dish.

Reuel took some pieces and placed them in his bread with cucumber and herbs. He took a big bite. It tasted as good as it smelled.

"Do eat some more," Dinah said. "There's plenty. I do love to see young folk eating."

Reuel took some more. "The rest of your family weren't able to join us?"

Dinah smiled. "We sent a meal to them, but the children can be a little noisy and Dedan wanted to hear my story. Not all of it is suitable for little ears."

Dinah rang a little bell. The servant came in, bringing nuts and dried dates and figs. Again, Dinah waited until they were alone before speaking.

"My childhood wasn't an easy one. I've told you how my parents played favorites, but things got worse. I had a loss similar to Dedan's, when all my family died of fever."

Reuel's throat tightened. So much tragedy in so few words. Dedan had said Dinah was the first person he'd felt comfortable to talk with about his family. Maybe it was because she had experienced similar losses to his own.

"I went to live with my father's sister. She was not happy to have responsibility for a crying girl who was younger than all her own children. When I arrived, she locked me in a room until she was certain I wasn't carrying the fever that killed my family."

"Dinah had never been left alone before," Asher said. "And being locked up by herself gave her terrible nightmares."

"I still get nightmares occasionally," Dinah said. "My aunt made me feel like an unwelcome burden and an outsider."

Outsider. Interesting that Dinah used that word, for Reuel had felt like an outsider within his own family after his mother died. It hadn't helped that he also felt like an outsider among the Israelites.

"Once my aunt was certain I was not carrying the fever, she made me work like a slave. I often cried myself to sleep."

Asher reached sideways and gave his wife's hand a squeeze. Again, their obvious connection brought a lump to Reuel's throat.

"All I wanted to do was escape from the family. When I heard that my aunt and uncle had arranged a marriage for me, I was delighted." Dinah sighed. "But I rejoiced too early, for the man they'd accepted a proposal from was looking for a second wife after his first had died. He had three children, and he wanted them looked after and kept out of his way. It was not easy, but eventually I came to love the children."

"It was not their fault their father was a brute," Asher said, voice a growl.

"He wasn't a brute at the beginning," Dinah said. "But he made some bad financial decisions and drank to forget his sense of failure."

Just as Reuel and Dedan had done, only they had drunk to forget their guilt at surviving.

"Once he started drinking, things quickly started going from bad to worse."

"You can say that again," Asher said. "It's a good thing he died before I met you."

Dinah smiled. "I'm not sure beating him up would have helped, dear."

"It would have helped me," Asher muttered.

"I'd grown up in a family that said they followed Yahveh, but it was just an outer show, not a deep commitment from the heart. My husband tried to force me to worship Baal and Asherah. The more he pushed me to make the sacrifices, the less I wanted to. Maybe it was the only way I could rebel."

"How did you finally come to know and follow Yahveh?" Dedan asked.

"My husband had been drinking even more than usual and had beaten me several times. I was feeling as low as I'd ever felt and was considering whether to end my life when I went out to the well. There was a stranger there. He took hold of my shoulders and looked me in the eyes and said, 'You are loved and precious to your Creator.'"

"Who was the man?" Reuel asked.

"I don't know," Dinah said. "But afterwards I wondered if it was an angel, for he set off toward the town, but the other women coming toward me didn't see him and I never saw him again."

Angels! Did Dinah really think Yahveh sent angels to talk to people?

"Of course, I don't know if I saw an angel, but Hagar saw angels twice. Both times were when she was as alone and feeling as hopeless as I was. Perhaps Yahveh has a special kindness toward women in despair."

"Tell Dedan and Reuel what happened next," Asher said.

"I can't describe it really. It was like I'd been stumbling around in the dark and suddenly the sun had risen, or like being enveloped in a warm hug. I was filled with certainty that Yahveh had stooped down to touch me. That he had seen me and had plans for my life."

Reuel reached for a fig. It was hard to dismiss what Dinah was saying because sincerity was in every word.

"What happened next?" Dedan asked.

"Some things got worse. My husband plunged further into drunkenness, but I felt totally different. The situation didn't change, but I had changed."

"Tell them about Miryam," Asher said.

"Miryam was another gift from Yahveh. She was one of the sellers in the market. I had asked Yahveh for a friend who would help me know and follow him. Every time I went to buy her fruit or olive oil, she would tell me a story. We never had long, but we made the most of every opportunity. I asked her to tell me the same story every day until I could tell it myself."

"And Dinah passed on every story to the children," Asher said. "And later to me and many others."

Like Reuel and Dedan.

"When I'd learned one story, then Miryam would tell me another. The more I learned, the more I wanted to know and the more I prayed." Dinah sighed. "My husband could beat my body, but he couldn't take away my confidence that Yahveh saw me and loved me. And he couldn't stop me from praying." She looked across at Asher. "You're getting upset again. I'm sorry."

"Of course I'm upset. How could a man treat you as your husband did?"

Reuel's face warmed. He hadn't treated Jael or little Hanok well either. He might try to justify himself and say it was only once, but who knows what would have happened if he'd stayed in Ramoth Gilead and kept drinking? Jael had done the right thing by sending him away, but what if she was becoming used to his being absent? What if he was never allowed home?

"Did your husband ever notice the change in you?" Dedan asked.

"I prayed he would, but I don't know. One morning, after a heavy bout of drinking, he had a fit and died." She sighed. "I wished I'd been able to talk about Yahveh with him."

Reuel opened his eyes wide. If he'd have been in Dinah's place, he would have wished the man dead. Maybe Jael now wished him dead so she could start again with someone else.

"And eventually you married Asher," Dedan said.

"Yes, but not for some years. I had to learn to trust that Yahveh would provide for me and the children."

"And how did he do that?" Reuel asked.

"In many different ways. Sometimes I could work in the harvest and be given part of it. Sometimes it was from my own garden being especially fruitful. Other times a neighbor would give me something. Many times, the children and I would pray and ask Yahveh to help as we had nothing to eat. He always provided." Dinah looked around at them all. "I have been following Yahveh for many years, and he has never let me down. He doesn't usually provide in the way I expect, but he always provides."

"And does he accept those who are not Israelites?" Dedan asked.

Reuel looked across at the man who had appeared from nowhere to help Reuel at his lowest. Dinah would tell him Dedan was evidence that Yahveh provided for everyone.

"He has always accepted anyone who submits themselves to him," Asher said. "Any who choose to obey and follow him. Midianites like Hobab and, I think, the original Reuel. Mosheh's father-in-law seemed to understand who Yahveh was."

"And there have been other non-Israelites too," Dinah said. "Rahab of Jericho, and the Gibeonites."

Reuel looked across at Dedan who nodded as if those names were familiar to him. Perhaps Dedan would tell him about these people as they traveled on to the next town.

Dedan leaned forward. "Could I become one of Yahveh's followers?"

Reuel's eyebrows rose. He'd known Dedan was coming to talk with Dinah and Asher every day, but he had not expected this.

"Of course," Asher said. "If you are willing to love Yahveh with all your heart and with all your soul and with all your strength."

"I am," Dedan said.

Reuel swallowed. He had only just found a friend, and now it felt like Dedan was running away. Or was he running ahead?

"What do I need to do?" Dedan asked.

Dinah looked at her husband.

"Normally you would declare your allegiance by being circumcised, as a visible sign of your decision," Asher said. "But you've been circumcised. At the time it was only a meaningless following of custom for custom's sake but now you'll look back and it will have meaning."

Reuel leaned back against his cushion. Listening to Dedan and seeing his desire to follow Yahveh, made Reuel feel quite alone as if Dedan had left for a distant land and he'd been left behind. It was confusing. If the original Reuel and Hobab had truly aligned themselves with Yahveh, then maybe he was the one who'd wandered from the right track. But was following Yahveh the right way?

CHAPTER THIRTY-TWO

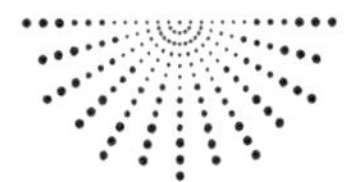

"Come on, boys." Jael shook out the bedcovers and folded them out of the way. "Your grandfather is going to continue teaching you to make bells."

Reba looked up at her. "You mean bigger bells for the goats and oxen?"

Jael nodded.

"Ima, I don't want to." Hanok moved to stand as close to her side as possible.

Hanok was still having nightmares, and he wouldn't let her out of his sight.

Jael looked down at him. "Do you want to sit with me and watch?"

He nodded without saying anything and popped his thumb in his mouth. He hadn't sucked his thumb for several seasons.

Hearing Abida heading for the workshop, Jael picked up Hanok and followed Reba, who was bouncing with excitement.

At the workshop, Abida greeted them. "Ready to heat up the furnace, Reba?"

Reba nodded enthusiastically and followed his grandfather. Jael sat on the bench and pulled Hanok onto her lap. He usually loved anything to do with fire.

Abida uncovered the mouth of the furnace where the fire was banked from the day before. Reba had already picked up the kindling and held it ready.

"Help me with the tongs," Abida said.

The tongs were too heavy for Reba to manage on his own, but with Reba in front and Abida leaning from behind him, they picked up each small piece of wood and laid it against the hot coals.

"Now let's use the bellows," Abida said.

Abida had invented a foot pedal to send air into the clay furnace, and Reba loved to work it. He didn't seem to notice that Abida's foot provided the extra oomph.

"Look, Grandpa, I'm doing it."

Already the flames were licking at the dry wood.

"Keep going, Reba," Abida said. "We'll add more wood once the flames are bigger."

Hanok's hair tickled Jael's neck.

If things were going well, Reuel would also be waking up his furnace about this time. Jael swallowed. She missed the rhythms of life on the road. *Oh, God who saw Hagar, can you see me? If you will listen to the prayers of one such as I, please change Reuel. Make him a new man and restore him to us.*

The flames were now eating into any wood that was fed to them.

"That's enough wood for now," Abida said. "Are we going to make the bells out of copper or bronze?"

Reba put his head to one side. "Bronze."

"Correct," Abida said. "But why?"

"Because it melts at a lower temperature."

Abida nodded. "And?"

"And because this is going to be around the goat's neck."

"And?" Abida asked again.

"And bronze is harder. It will last even in the wind and rain."

"You've been listening." Abida ruffled Reba's hair.

Pride welled up in Jael's heart, then sadness. It should be Reuel training his son. Reuel had said his father had seldom praised him, but Abida offered praise now. Had Abida changed, or was this going to be a case of favoritism again? Jael hugged Hanok to herself. Not favoritism. Not if she had anything to do with it.

"Can you remember what amount of tin to add?" Abida asked.

"Nine scoops of copper and one of tin," Hanok muttered under Jael's chin.

"Clever boy," Jael whispered to him as Reba gave the same answer.

Abida checked the fire and handed the scoop to Reba. "You do it."

Reba scooped up copper pellets. Abida checked each time that the scoop was full. The right quantities of pellets were added to the crucible.

Once the crucible was ready, Abida asked, "Where do you put the mold?"

"Here." Reba patted the bench. "It's the closest place to the mouth of the furnace."

Abida helped Reba put the mold in place. Together, the two took the long handle of the crucible and slid it into the furnace.

As Jael watched Abida guiding Reba, the sadness welled up again. *Bring Reuel home. Change him and give us a new start.*

Later, once the molten metal was poured, Abida said, "Tomorrow, when the bells have cooled, we'll be able to look at them. Now we will make the little clapper that actually makes the sound."

Hanok leaned up and whispered in Jael's ear. "Ima, I'm hungry. Can we go now?"

* * *

*T*hat evening, Jael and the entire family were sitting on the roof to avoid the stifling rooms below and to be in the best position to catch any slight breezes. Below, the animals were restless in their stalls.

Hanok put his head on Jael's lap. If he slept up here, perhaps he wouldn't have nightmares.

Zura waited until they were all comfortable. "Hanok asked me to tell you the story of Noach."

"But we've heard that one," Reba whined.

"Every time we hear a story, we learn new things." Zura leaned against the rooftop wall and crossed her legs. "I've told this story many times, but I'm still learning new things."

The group who'd been hearing the stories had grown every evening. Even Abida had joined them last night, after hearing many stories on his own.

Zura took a deep breath. "Long, long ago, Yahveh created the heavens and earth, but the first people rebelled against Yahveh and went their own way. As the generations passed, the peoples of the earth grew in wickedness. When Yahveh saw how great the wickedness of people had become, he was deeply troubled and regretted that he'd made people. He said, 'I will wipe all people off the face of the earth, for I wish I had not created them.' But Noach found favor in the eyes of Yahveh."

There was total silence on the rooftop as everyone listened.

Zura told how Yahveh instructed Noach to build an ark. "'Build it out of cypress and coat it with pitch both inside and out. Three hundred cubits long, fifty cubits wide, and thirty cubits high, with upper, middle, and lower decks. I am going to bring floodwaters and all creatures on the earth will die. But with you I will establish my covenant, and you will enter the ark with two of all kinds of living creatures.'"

Zura's voice painted pictures in Jael's mind. She saw the ark being built and felt as though she were there, experiencing the rain and the flood, the utter devastation.

"The waters rose and covered even the highest mountains to a depth of fifteen cubits. Every living thing that moved on land perished—birds, livestock, wild animals, all the creatures that swarmed over the earth, and all mankind … only Noach was left, and those with him in the ark." Zura paused. "But Yahveh remembered Noach."

Jael let the story flow over her as Zura described how the flood receded and Yahveh promised Noach he'd never flood the entire earth again. The boys were completely gripped by the story. For a moment, life in Ramoth Gilead was forgotten.

"Aunt Zura, what's our ark?" Reba asked.

"What do you mean?" Zura asked.

"Well, in Noach's day, the only way to escape Yahveh's judgment was to be on the boat. So how do we escape Yahveh's judgment?" Reba asked.

"An excellent question. I told you we can learn new things each time. Does anyone have an answer?" Zura asked.

"Do you think Yahveh is going to judge us?" Zipporah asked.

"There was that prophet we heard at Jabesh Gilead," Jael said. "He said that Yahveh was judging the Israelites because they had abandoned him. The people threw manure at him and cast him out of the city."

"Prophets who speak of judgment aren't always popular," Zura said.

"Israelite prophets always call the people back to follow and honor Yahveh. Perhaps that is how we escape judgment," Abida said.

Zura nodded. "Yes, the way to avoid judgment is to repent."

"Ima, what does re-pent mean?" Hanok asked, looking up at Jael.

Children always thought their parents knew everything. "I think it means being sorry," Jael said.

"It includes being sorry," Zura said. "But we can feel sorry without actually repenting."

Abida leaned forward. "How would you explain it?"

"Being sorry for what we've done against Yahveh but also deciding to completely change direction. Instead of walking away from Yahveh"—Zura pointed to her left—"we choose to turn toward him." She pointed to her right.

It was what Jael longed for Reuel and for all of them. Reuel had been sorry the morning he left, but perhaps it was more being sorry for the consequences of having to go away on his own. By now, he would have noticed that his work had more than doubled without her and Zura's contributions, and he'd never been able to cook. But had he been sorry enough to actually repent and walk in a different direction? And did he have the willpower to do so? Zura would say people could never change completely, for they needed the power of Yahveh. The power that had opened the Red Sea and created the universe. The Reuel she knew would never admit he needed that kind of help.

CHAPTER THIRTY-THREE

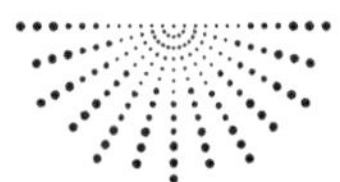

*R*euel trudged along behind the overly cheerful Dedan. A Dedan who'd woken before dawn and was now whistling. It was getting on Reuel's nerves. Reuel was once again the outsider, which Dedan reinforced every time he whistled a jaunty tune.

The evening before, Asher had walked them to the city gate and hugged them goodbye. Reuel didn't know what Asher had whispered to Dedan, but to Reuel, Asher had said, "You don't need to be on the outside. Yahveh is waiting to welcome you home."

The words had given Reuel a sleepless night, which might be why he was so cranky this morning. His mood wasn't helped by the goat who'd yanked the rope out of Reuel's hand as he was untethering it. They'd had to waste time as they worked together to trap it between some big rocks next to the stream.

It was a two-day journey to the next town. Before sunset they found some rocks on a little hillock, removed the burdens from the animals, then tethered them near grass and water.

It didn't take long to collect wood, set the fire, and cook a pot of lentils.

Dedan lifted the pot off the fire. "Dinah loved the pot you gave her yesterday."

"They gave us much more," Reuel mumbled. If only they'd had longer. Longer for him to understand what Dedan now had.

Once the fire died down to its coals, they laid out their sleeping mats and sat on either side of the fire.

The fire popped and sent a shower of sparks into the darkness. Tomorrow they should arrive at the next town, and there'd be the usual stream of customers for days. There wouldn't be much time for anything but hard work.

"When Dinah mentioned some of the non-Israelites who'd decided to follow Yahveh, you seemed to know who she was talking about," Reuel said.

"Rahab and the Gibeonites, you mean," Dedan said. "Dinah had told me their stories, but I won't be able to tell them as well as she did."

"You can't cook as well either," Reuel said. "But I manage to put up with your efforts."

Dedan threw a dried fig across the fire. "I cook a whole lot better than you do."

That was true enough.

Dedan took a deep breath. "Let's start with Mosheh. He had led the Israelites out of Egypt and through forty years of wandering in the wilderness. When he died and Yehoshua had succeeded him, they were about to cross the Jordan River."

Reuel's throat tightened. He himself had crossed the Jordan river twice, but he would always associate the river with Ephah's death.

"Before they crossed the river, Yehoshua sent two men to Jericho as spies. They met Rahab and discovered she knew all about the miracles Yahveh had done in Egypt. She knew Yahveh had promised the Israelites the whole land of Canaan and that all the Canaanites would be wiped out."

"How did she know?" Reuel asked.

"I guess the news of what happened in Egypt was carried by travelers and traders far and wide," Dedan said. "After all, it would have been the biggest news in the world. The destruction of Egypt and its gods by an unknown god, a god whose people were slaves."

Reuel placed another of the branches they'd collected onto the fire. They'd camped in the cluster of rocks for some extra protection. Travelers they'd met on the road said Gideon's victory had made the roads much safer, although it might not be safer for Midianites. He'd overheard people say the only good Midianite was a dead Midianite.

"Rahab said she knew Yahveh would destroy her city of Jericho, so she pleaded for her life. The men told her that as long as she didn't betray them and left a scarlet cord tied in her window, they would protect her."

"And was Rahab saved?" Reuel asked.

"She was, along with all her family. She even married an Israelite and had children and became one of them."

"Do you think we must become Israelites in order to be saved?" Reuel asked.

Dedan stared at the fire. "Didn't you say that your wife's sister is also a follower of Yahveh?"

"I did," Reuel said.

"And yet she travels with you? She has not married an Israelite?"

"She is unmarried."

Dedan looked across at Reuel, brow furrowed. "Isn't that unusual? Why hasn't her father found her a husband?"

"He died long ago."

"Is there no brother to take on the responsibility?"

"No, and I haven't found her a husband either. She's not easy to find a husband for."

"And why is that?" Dedan asked.

They seemed to have gotten off the topic.

"Zura is blind," Reuel said. "She is one of the finest women I know, and an excellent metal polisher, but she is blind and her face is scarred from an accident."

There was a long silence.

A log in the fire settled with a thud, sending up more sparks.

"My wife refused to marry me without bringing Zura with her," Reuel said.

"Your wife has courage," Dedan said. "She risked losing you to protect her sister."

An image of Jael defending Hanok and sending him away rose in his mind. Reuel had repeatedly taunted Jael for her timidity, but she'd had more courage than he had. He was afraid to look deeply inside himself and see the brokenness. The ugliness. He should have talked with Asher about it. Asher would have listened. Maybe he could have helped.

"What about the people you called Gibeonites?" Reuel asked.

Dedan added another branch to the fire and settled back on one elbow. "Gibeon was one of four Hivite towns west from where the Israelites first crossed the Jordan. Like Rahab, they had heard of the ten plagues of Egypt, but they also heard terrifying stories of the defeats of Sihon and Og, powerful Amorite kings to the east of the Jordan, and later about the defeats of Jericho and Ai. Like Rahab, they also knew that Yehoshua had been told to annihilate all of those within the borders of Canaan."

Reuel picked his teeth with a grass stem. "Why didn't they all get together to fight the Israelites?"

"Believe me, that was tried a few times, but it soon became obvious that Yahveh was fighting for the Israelites and victory had nothing to do with military strength."

"What did they end up doing?" Reuel asked.

Dedan sat up and crossed his legs. "They resorted to a trick."

Reuel tossed the blade of grass into the fire. "What kind of trick?"

"They pretended to have come from far outside the area to make a peace treaty with Yehoshua because they'd heard of the fame of the Israelites and their god," Dedan said.

"I doubt Yehoshua would have been tricked so easily."

"Yehoshua did ask them for proof and the Hivites showed them their worn-out shoes and moldy bread as evidence."

"I still doubt Yehoshua would have been fooled," Reuel said.

"Asher emphasized that Yehoshua had not asked Yahveh but had relied on his own judgment. He made the peace treaty without praying and only found out three days later that he'd been tricked."

Reuel whistled. "Did he honor the treaty?"

"He did, despite some of the elders saying they shouldn't honor any treaty that was the result of a deception."

"What happened to the Hivites?" Reuel asked.

"Asher said Yehoshua gave them their lives, but said they had to work as woodcutters and water carriers for their place of worship which is based at Shiloh."

Reuel thought for a few moments. "Couldn't Yahveh have alerted Yehoshua that he was about to make a mistake?"

"Yahveh looks at our heart. Maybe there were Hivites who were truly seeking him, so he had mercy."

Reuel stood and stretched his legs. Asher had said Yahveh had invited all peoples to call on him for rescue and commit themselves to obeying his law. Rahab and the Hivites had had an opportunity to do that. Dedan had also chosen that road.

It did not promise to be an easy road. The Israelites wouldn't all be as accepting as Asher and Dinah or the god they followed. Too few truly aligned their hearts with Yahveh. Reuel would watch Dedan and see where his choices led. There was no need for a hasty decision.

CHAPTER THIRTY-FOUR

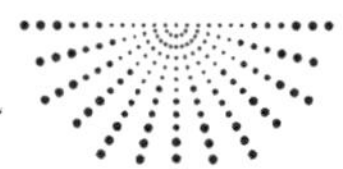

A scream ripped through Jael's room. Jael woke staring into the darkness. She wrinkled her nose in distaste. The pungent smell of urine filled the room, and Hanok was now beside her whimpering.

"No, Abba, no."

"Ima," Reba whispered. "It stinks in here."

"Get up and take your blanket onto the roof with the others," Jael said. "I'll look after Hanok."

As Reba followed her instructions, Jael stood, picked up a spare tunic, and scooped Hanok into her arms. He was drenched both with sweat and urine, and he clung to her as if he'd never let her go. She moved the hair from his forehead and leaned down to kiss him. "Do not fear, Ima is here."

"Ima?" His voice wavered. "I'm wet again."

She patted his back. "Don't worry. We'll go and wash."

"Ima, I'm scared. Abba is always angry at me."

Jael hugged Hanok closer. She couldn't promise Hanok that Reuel would never hurt him again for she didn't know if Reuel had changed, but she could hold her son tight tonight.

Hanok's weight was heavy in her arms as they walked out into the courtyard. Tonight, the stars were obscured by clouds. It was so dark; she was thankful she knew every stone and patch of earth outside.

They reached the bucket. "Take off your tunic, Hanok."

Hanok whimpered. "I'm cold, Ima."

Jael placed the clean tunic on a rock. Still holding Hanok's hand, she helped him slip off the wet tunic, wash, and get redressed.

"Jael, do you need some help?"

Jael looked across the courtyard to where her sister was a pale blur in the doorway.

"I need some dry clothes. Be careful, it's—" She'd been about to say "dark" but day or night made no difference to Zura.

Zura disappeared back inside and was soon back and handing Jael dry clothes. Jael tried to disentangle her hand from Hanok's, but he clung harder. "Auntie Zura will hug you now. Ima needs to wash too."

Hanok grabbed his aunt's hand, and Zura sat down and held him. Jael shed her wet clothes, changed into the new tunic, and washed the old ones before laying them out to dry.

"Leave cleaning the room until tomorrow," Zura said. "Come up to the roof for the rest of the night."

Jael doubted she'd sleep, but Hanok was already almost asleep again.

"Let's pray together for Hanok," Zura said. "And let's gather everyone together each night before bed to pray, particularly for Hanok."

"Do you think Yahveh cares about my little Hanok's nightmares?" Jael asked.

"If he cared about how Hagar was treated in Avraham's household, even as a slave and a foreigner, he cares about Hanok."

A breeze ruffled their hair and Jael moved closer to her sister's side. "Can you pray first?"

Zura put her arm around Jael. "Great Creator who sees and knows all things, we ask for your kindness on our precious Hanok."

Jael swallowed a lump in her throat. Hanok was precious. Seeing his struggles and his fears broke her heart.

"Please protect Hanok's dreams and allow him to sleep through the night. Help him to know he is safe and that you have him in your care. Show him how much you love and care for him. You formed him within Jael, and you know how to help him."

Jael waited until Zura finished. "I always thought of myself and Reuel as having formed our children, but maybe that is wrong."

"Yahveh is behind every human action and breath. He created your body so it can carry a child. He knows everything, and he looks after each one of us from before we are born."

Which helped explain why he cared.

"Are you going to pray?" Zura asked.

"I'll try," Jael said. She was now practiced at expressing her gratitude to Yahveh but still struggled to feel that her little needs were of interest to the creator of everything. She took a deep breath. "Thank you for creating my beautiful boy. Thank you that you see us sitting here under your night sky. Please give Hanok dreamless sleep for the rest of the night and for all the nights to come. Thank you for listening."

She turned toward Hanok. "Come on. I'll carry you up to the others."

"Shh," Zura said. "He's asleep already."

Jael gently disentangled Hanok from Zura's arms, and they all went quietly to the rooftop.

* * *

The next evening, Zura told them the first section of Avraham's story. Reba leaned against Jael on one side, and Hanok sat on her lap as she leaned against the rooftop parapet.

"Now who has got something they're thankful for?" Zura asked.

"Me, me," one of Zipporah's girls said.

"And me," Reba said. "I made some more bells. Grandpa says they're good enough to sell."

"Well done," Jael said to Reba.

"Then let's start with thanksgiving,' Zura said. "You don't have to say much, but let's see if we can all say something."

Jael's heart rate increased. Up until now, Jael had only ever prayed out loud with Zura. She took a deep breath.

"How do we start?" Reba asked.

"Why don't I start?" Zura said. "I won't finish the prayer but leave it open so you can just say your own thanksgiving. Then I'll finish off at the end. Does that make it easier?"

Reba nodded.

"And perhaps it will help if we all stand together in a circle," Zura said.

They all stood close together, an encouraging unity which made the absence of Reuel so much more noticeable. Would he ever be part of their circle again?

"Creator of all that is around us in the rivers, in the sky, and on the surface of the earth, we thank you for all your good gifts. For food and drink, and for Abida's home that shelters us all. Thank you that you called Avraham to follow you and that we too can follow." Zura gestured around the group. "Your turn."

"Thank you we could play at the stream today." Zipporah's youngest had an adorable lisp.

"And that I could make more bells," Reba said.

"Thank you I could make bread today and we could eat it," Zipporah's daughter said.

The children didn't seem to find this difficult. Why should Jael?

"Thank you for our family, and that we are all working well together," Jael said. Maybe she shouldn't have mentioned family because it reminded everyone of who was missing.

Hanok tugged on Jael's arm. She leaned down. "I can't do it," he whispered.

"Can I say something for you?" Jael asked.

He nodded and stretched up on his tiptoes to whisper in her ear. "Thank you for Auntie Zura."

"Hanok has one," Jael said. "He's thankful to Yahveh for his Auntie Zura."

Hanok wasn't the only one who was thankful for Zura. Zura was keeping the remains of this family together. Looking around, they were even moving forward from the tragedies that had fallen on them.

"Thank you for my children," Zipporah whispered. Her sons and daughters moved in close and clutched her legs.

It had been extremely hard for the children as their mother's grief had made her distant. Once again, Zura had made sure that she spent extra time with all the children.

Abida cleared his throat. "Thank you for Zipporah and Jael and Zura. Thank you that I am here on this rooftop under your stars instead of staring at my wall and wondering how I can face tomorrow. And thank you for Reba and how he loves to work with me."

Zura paused then finished their thanksgiving session. "Yahveh, thank you that you see us, and that you care, and that you welcome all to follow you."

Jael would have to ask Zura why she was so confident Yahveh welcomed all.

Zura shifted over next to Jael and Hanok and laid her hand on Hanok's head. "Hanok, can we especially pray for you to sleep well?"

Hanok nodded.

"Yahveh, you made us, your people, so we can sleep, and you are ruler over all our dreams. Please help Hanok to sleep well and without dreams. Help him to feel your peace."

When Zura had finished, Jael leaned down to Hanok. "What do you say to your aunt?"

"Thank you, Aunt Zura," Hanok said.

Jael covered him with a blanket. Abida and Zipporah also lay down. Abida's snores soon made their nightly music.

Jael shifted closer to Zura. "You sound so confident that Yahveh cares about our little concerns."

"I can see why you struggle with it. After all, if Yahveh made the sun, moon, and stars, his power is beyond anything we can imagine. He keeps everything functioning and—"

"And I can only just manage my household," Jael said.

"Our abilities are limited." Zura chuckled. "We don't always notice when the boys are feeling upset or grumpy, let alone knowing how to deal with it. But Yahveh notices everything. He noticed Hagar, which we know because the angel said to her, 'for Yahveh has seen your misery.' And he noticed Yosef in his prison cell."

Zura had told the boys this story some time ago.

"Can you think of other things Yahveh noticed?" Zura asked.

Jael thought back to the stories Zura had told the boys and the whole group.

"That Adam and Havah had eaten the fruit. That Cain had murdered his brother Abel."

"You're doing well," Zura said. "Yahveh doesn't just notice when people are miserable or need help. He notices all our sin, even the things we do that we think no one has seen."

If that was the case, Yahveh knew of the tensions in her marriage.

"Why don't we pray for Reuel?" Zura said.

"But Reuel doesn't follow Yahveh," Jael said.

"Yahveh wants everyone to come to know him. He will be actively pursuing your husband."

Like a prospector searching for new lodes of precious metal.

"Reuel was never interested in any gods. To be honest, it was a sort of relief to me. I never wanted anything to do with Yahveh either because—" Jael gestured around her. "I see nothing enviable or attractive about the way the Israelites worship."

"That's because most Israelites have compromised. They want Yahveh's blessings, but they don't give him their whole heart and mind." Zura shuddered. "They mix a holy God with the abhorrent evil of the Canaanites' religion. Yahveh must hate it."

"The only person whose faith I've envied is yours. Even then, it has only been in recent days."

Zura chuckled. "You certainly weren't open to listening to me in the early years, but I don't blame you. It's hard when someone wants to talk about Yahveh, but most people around you have corrupted his worship."

"There's so much dross that the pure metal can't shine through," Jael said. "But I think I'm seeing the shine now and it's beautiful. You've reflected Yahveh to me, and I find I'm hungry to know more."

Zura's smile lit up her face and she grasped Jael's arm. "I'm so, so glad. Sometimes I worried I was part of the barrier to you coming to know Yahveh." She gestured at her eyes. "I know you struggle to understand how a God I say is good could permit my blindness."

"I might always struggle with that because I love you so much and it hurts me to see what you miss out on."

"I have found it more helpful to focus on what I have, rather than what I don't have." Zura raised Jael's hands to her lips. "I have you and the children, and I have the moment-by-moment presence of Yahveh."

"How do you know Yahveh is with you?" Jael asked.

Zura paused. "It's hard to explain. Maybe I feel his presence more because I am blind. I don't have as many distractions, and I need him so much."

It was an intriguing thought. Jael yawned.

"We'd better get to sleep. First, let's pray for Reuel," Zura said. "Wherever he is, he needs Yahveh."

"Can you pray for him?" Jael asked. She wasn't sure that she wanted to pray blessings on Reuel. Not yet. Not when she still saw the impact of Reuel's anger on Hanok.

Zura sat up straight and raised her hands to the heavens. "Great and mighty Creator. We praise you not only for your greatness but for your care. You know everything and you care for all. You know where the hawks roost, and you provide for them. You know where the goats give birth and where the camel finds food, and you know where Reuel is now."

Jael loved the poetry of Zura's prayers. It always made Jael see the world in different ways.

"We ask that you help Reuel to deal with his grief and loss. Help him to take his brokenness to you and allow you to heal him. May he find friends who will walk alongside him."

Jael had always had Zura's companionship, but who were Reuel's friends? His father had favored Ephah, a decision that had prevented Reuel from being close to his brother. Reuel didn't have friends, and he hadn't treated her as a friend. She was merely the one who worked alongside him so he could concentrate on his craft, the one who bore his children and ensured they all ate and were clothed. She'd never thought of him as lonely, but he must be for he had no one to share his thoughts with. *Yahveh, bring him home, but only if he is changed. I can't deal with the man he used to be.*

CHAPTER THIRTY-FIVE

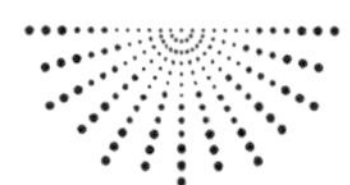

Reuel had been mending pots and copper objects since daybreak. The sun was dipping toward the hills as he polished the cooking pot he'd just repaired. Dedan had now become an expert at calculating how many repairs Reuel could do in a day. He'd sent the rest of the customers home around midday with instructions to return tomorrow.

With a final flourish of his cloth, Reuel held the gleaming pot out for inspection. It looked like new again. He handed it back to its owner. "That will last two hundred barley harvests. Just don't kick it down the stairs."

The customer laughed and paid for the repair. Reuel slipped the payment into a cloth bag hanging at his waist. Every night he hid the bag in a different place. He closed the mouth of the furnace and put away his tools, then turned to head out for a late afternoon walk. A silhouette blocked the doorway. Reuel squinted at the man. Naftali. And Naftali was not looking his usual affable self.

"Walk with me," Naftali said. "I have something I want to discuss with you."

Apprehension curled like a fist in Reuel's belly. He'd worried

Naftali might call in some favors sometime. Naftali had not only promoted Reuel's wares, but he'd protected his life when he could so easily have allowed his men to harm a hated Midianite. A Midianite Naftali must have known had been raiding on the western side of the Jordan River.

Naftali waited while Reuel laced up his work tent. Naftali's men were seated around the fireplace, and Dedan was serving them refreshments. Reuel glanced toward Dedan and hoped he communicated his need for prayer. He needed all the prayers he could get. Reuel had only ever seen Naftali's soft side, but no man had the kind of wealth Naftali had accumulated without a hard core of bronze beneath. The fist in Reuel's belly clenched.

"Your wife and family are well, I hope," Reuel forced himself to say.

"They are well," Naftali said. "I notice your family is not with you."

"They stayed with my father and sister-in-law, who have suffered loss," Reuel said. He didn't want to answer any more questions about his family.

"The loss of a son is always difficult," Naftali said.

Reuel controlled a grimace. His father wouldn't have cared if he had died instead of Ephah.

"Do you know what has been happening over the other side of the river?" Naftali asked.

Reuel shook his head. He and Dedan had done their job and no more. He didn't interact with the Israelites more than he had to. They didn't want to stir up any possible dangers among people who might consider it a good deed to kill two more Midianites.

"After Gideon's victories, many people wanted to make him our king."

Defeating and killing tens of thousands of raiders would make anyone a hero.

"But Gideon has steadfastly refused to take leadership. The

problem is that he has many wives and many children, and his sons are likely to be more ambitious than he is."

Reuel could see why Naftali was concerned. All it needed was more than one ambitious son and there would be a long, destructive war between factions. War would not only destroy Israelite lives but would make them vulnerable to outsiders returning to conquer them while their attention was focused elsewhere.

"You travel from place to place and can listen in to the local gossip. I want to know what is going on. I love my people and don't want to see them come to ruin," Naftali said.

Naftali had not said "again" although coming to ruin had been a continuous cycle in recent years. Even in Reuel's and his father's lifetimes, the Israelites had been oppressed by Moabites, Philistines, and the Amalekite-Midianite coalition.

"And if I can't send you this news?" Reuel asked.

Naftali placed a hand upon Reuel's shoulder. "Now, now, there is no need for such thoughts between us."

It all sounded innocuous, but Reuel had heard a few stories about Naftali that didn't relieve the tightness in his belly. Stories of others caught in a trap and being ruthlessly annihilated with the loss of their reputation and livelihood. He had much more to lose as a non-Israelite. Tension tightened in his neck and shoulders. Was Naftali wanting an immediate answer, or could he buy some time?

"When do you want my answer?" Reuel said.

"I have traveled to find you. I will wait," Naftali said.

That was what Reuel had been afraid of. There was no time to come up with a plan. He didn't want to be further beholden to this man, and yet was "no" even an option? He could not endanger his own life, for too many others depended on him: Jael and the boys, Zura, his father, and now his sister-in-law and her children too.

* * *

"Reuel, what are you doing here?" Dedan dropped into the seat next to Reuel.

Reuel peered at Dedan through bleary eyes.

"It took a long time to find you. I didn't expect to find you back in such a place."

Shame curdled in Reuel's stomach. He hadn't expected to be here either. He'd promised himself he wouldn't make this choice again, yet here he was. Trying to escape thinking about Naftali. Stupid. All he'd done was make sure he had less time to think clearly.

Dedan peered at Reuel. "What brought you back here?"

"Fear," Reuel muttered.

"Want to talk about it?" Dedan asked.

"Not here," Reuel whispered, pushing the remains of his drink away.

Dedan stood and waited for Reuel to do the same. They left together, with Dedan's hand under Reuel's elbow. Dedan stayed close even when Reuel vomited outside the city gate.

Back at their camp, Reuel rinsed his mouth and sluiced water over his head in an attempt to clear the befuddlement from too much strong drink on an empty stomach. Shivering, he went over to the fire which Dedan had stoked and warmed himself before sitting on a rock.

"Would your fear have anything to do with the man who visited late this afternoon?" Dedan asked.

Reuel sighed. "Do you know him?"

Dedan shook his head. "Should I?"

"That was Naftali of Jabesh Gilead," Reuel said.

"Ah," Dedan said. "I know that name. What did he want with you?"

"He's become a patron by choosing one of my mirrors for his

only child's wedding and promoting my work. He also protected my life after Gideon's destruction of our people."

Dedan scratched his nose. "Does he want a favor?"

"You seem to know how these things work." Reuel belched.

"He has a bit of a reputation."

"He's worried about the situation with Gideon and wants me to report any news I hear," Reuel said.

Dedan raised an eyebrow. "Is that a problem?"

"I've heard stories about the man that make me nervous." Reuel's gut rolled and he took a deep breath. "I don't want to be caught in a situation where I can't escape."

"And you can't say no?"

"I don't know. I can't afford to lose my livelihood or my reputation. Or worse. I have two families relying on me now, plus an elderly father." His stomach ached just thinking of his father's rejection.

"Asher told me I must learn to pray about everything," Dedan said. "This sounds like a sensible thing to do because I don't know how to advise you."

"Do you think Yahveh will answer prayers when—" Reuel shifted on the rock. "You know. I'm not one of his followers."

"Perhaps this will help you decide to follow him." Dedan grinned. "Seeing him answer your prayers, I mean."

Maybe. Reuel had rejected all the gods for so long it had become a habit, but he couldn't help envying Asher and Dinah and even Dedan. They seemed to have a peace he lacked.

"Shall I pray for you?" Dedan asked.

Reuel nodded and stared into the fire as Dedan began.

"Yahveh, God of all wisdom, we need your wisdom now for Reuel is afraid of agreeing to Naftali's request. He doesn't know Naftali's intentions and doesn't want to be obligated to him."

Reuel sighed. He didn't understand prayer, but he could see the attraction of turning his cares over to someone far above his own wisdom. His wisdom was so limited. If Asher was to be believed, Yahveh's wisdom was limitless.

"Yahveh, if Reuel is to say no to Naftali, give him the courage and protect him from any consequences. Please work in this situation for good. We remember Reuel's family. Keep them safe and provide everything they need. Help us to only be afraid of you. For fear of you will reduce all other fears to their proper size."

Somehow Reuel didn't think Dedan meant the kind of fear he felt when thinking of Naftali. Fear of Yahveh would be the awe he felt toward someone so much greater than himself. A fear tempered by the fact that Yahveh was good and his intentions were always for his people's best.

If only he could believe Yahveh was like his true followers proclaimed him to be.

* * *

*R*euel groaned when he woke in the morning. His mouth felt like it was full of rabbit fur, and his head pounded. Dedan was already up and getting the fire ready for the day's work.

Reuel rolled over and pushed himself to his knees. He'd go and bathe in the stream to clear his head. Naftali would be here before the first customers arrived, demanding his answer. Outside Reuel squinted in the light. Already the sky was streaked with gold, and the coolness was burning off the dawn.

He completed his wash in the brackish water and turned back to the campfire. Sure enough, Naftali was there, seated and talking to Dedan as if he didn't have a care in the world. Reuel's chest tightened, but he walked forward. Could Naftali sense his fear?

Naftali stood and met Reuel, and they walked away from the camp. Reuel willed his stomach to settle and took some slower breaths to calm himself. *Yahveh, if you're there and if you care for someone like me who has ignored you all my life, help!*

"Have you thought on my offer?" Naftali asked.

"I have," Reuel said, determined not to let his voice shake. "I am happy to pass on some news, but I will not pass on anything that will harm my own people." He didn't mention his concerns for his family. Better not to remind Naftali where he was vulnerable.

There was a long pause. Reuel's heart pounded in his chest. *Let my family be safe.*

Naftali suddenly turned and slapped him on the shoulder. "That is what I hoped you'd say. I could never trust a man who spoke against his own people. I came all this way because I believed you were man enough to set clear boundaries. I don't want men around me who tell me what I want to hear. I want men of integrity, and I hoped you might be one of them."

Reuel let out a deep breath of relief and Naftali looked sharply at him. "Were you afraid to say no to me?"

Did Reuel dare to admit it? He nodded.

Naftali guffawed. "You've heard rumors about what happened to folk who went against me, haven't you? Widely exaggerated." His eyes twinkled. "My wife and daughter call me a lamb in bear's fur."

It wasn't a description Reuel would have used. Relief surged through him. He'd been so afraid of what Naftali could do to him and his family. Dedan had said he should only be afraid of Yahveh and that would reduce all other fears to their correct size, like pebbles compared to a mountain. Maybe Dedan was right.

"Come and eat with us," Reuel said.

"I'd be delighted to do so," Naftali responded as they turned back to the camp.

Warmth filled Reuel's belly. Maybe Naftali would become a friend like Dedan and Asher.

CHAPTER THIRTY-SIX

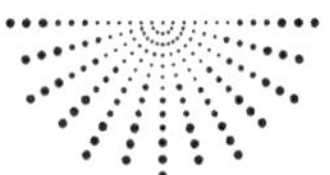

*J*ael left the boys sleeping peacefully on the roof and hurried down to pray in the courtyard with Zura. The early mornings had become her favorite time of day, a time to pour out her thanks for the changes she could see in the family and to turn her concerns over to Yahveh.

Zura was sitting with her head cocked to one side. She held up a finger to her lips and cupped a hand around her ear. Jael sat down and strained her ears to listen for whatever had caught Zura's attention. There it was. The excited chirps of young birds being fed by their parents, somewhere secure underneath the roof.

Zura smiled broadly. "I always love listening to their urgent demands. It reminds me of how much we desperately need Yahveh, even if we don't know it."

Jael smiled. "I look back and don't know how I survived all these years without Yahveh."

"It brings me the greatest of joy to hear your words. I have prayed so long," Zura said in a shaky voice.

Jael hugged Zura. "Thank you for your perseverance through all the years when I couldn't see any benefits in following Yahveh. Now we can pray together for the rest of the family."

"It's much easier to persevere in prayer when there are two of us. I am seeing Yahveh answer prayer for Abida. Even Zipporah seems to have tiny sparks of life."

"It is interesting seeing the different responses," Jael said. "The children seem to lap up the stories and give perceptive comments."

"They don't have any barriers. Older people have barriers to belief and even more to trust."

"You mean belief and trusting in something aren't the same?" Jael asked. "What's the difference?"

Zura pursed her lips for a few moments. "You can believe Yahveh exists but still refuse to trust and follow him. Think of Pharaoh in Mosheh's time. He had no doubt that Yahveh existed. He even believed Yahveh was powerful and in total control. Yet time and time again, he rejected him."

"It's been seven days since you prayed for Hanok, and he hasn't had any more nightmares," Jael said.

"Since *we* began praying for him," Zura said. "Don't make the mistake of thinking my prayers are more powerful than yours. It is not the prayer that is important but the one we pray to. We could sincerely pray to the Canaanite gods and see no answers or timidly pray to Yahveh and he would answer."

Zura was able to explain the things of Yahveh so clearly.

"Do you think Hanok will have those nightmares again?" Jael asked.

"It's possible, but we'll just concentrate more prayers on him. I had many nightmares about my injury at the beginning. I still get an occasional nightmare if I'm overtired or anxious."

"I'm hoping he'll become less clingy and be able to start learning from his grandfather again."

One of the birds, insect in its beak, darted across in front of them and disappeared from sight.

"When Reuel returns, Hanok might find it difficult for a while."

"Do you think Reuel will return?" Jael wasn't sure if she was excited or nervous at the thought.

Zura nodded. "But it might be some time yet. It depends if he completes his full circuit. I have been praying that Yahveh will somehow make himself real to him."

"Reuel was always so scornful of all gods. He said that they only bind people into an endless cycle of sacrifices and make people miserable." And Jael had been happy to agree with him. "He might be angry that I want to follow Yahveh."

"He's never objected to me following Yahveh," Zura said.

"You're not married to him."

"That's true, but I've been praying the whole family will come to trust Yahveh."

"But look at how long you've been praying!"

Zura laughed. "It has been many years, but hard times are some of the best things to make us think. My accident and the despair I felt prepared me to listen. The same has happened with you and Abida. Let's ask Yahveh to do the same for Reuel."

Zura was so strong and confident. Would Jael become the same if she kept following Yahveh?

There was a burst of chatter from the rooftop where they'd left the family.

"We'd better pray before the boys want to eat," Zura said.

"I'll start," Jael said. She no longer felt embarrassed to pray in front of her sister or the rest of the family. It was getting easier for all of them. Even Hanok had prayed a short prayer last night, in a voice no one could hear, but it was progress.

Both ladies stood and raised their arms.

"Great God of heaven," Jael began. "Thank you for this new day and that Hanok has slept peacefully all night. Please take away his fears. Help him to grow in his trust of you. Help him to begin to play with the others and be willing to go to the workshop and work with Reba and his grandfather."

Beside Jael, Zura murmured her agreement.

"Yahveh, you know where Reuel is. Please meet him and teach him about yourself. Help him to meet others who truly know you, and keep him from making bad choices."

* * *

"Jael, it is too hot to work or even to be in the city," Abida said. "We are going to the only cool place we know."

Jael raised an eyebrow. "The stream?"

"And the shady tree. If we sit with our feet in the water, we'll feel cooler."

"I'll prepare some food and we'll take the goats," Jael said. Both their camels were with Reuel. The more she saw of life in the town, the less Jael wanted the settled life. The walls absorbed the heat and blocked the breeze. Everyone she knew was sleeping on their rooftops at night.

Preparations didn't take long. Soon they were all exiting the less-used back gate of the town. Several other family groups had had the same idea, but they easily found a large terebinth tree on the bank of the stream.

Abida and Jael tethered the goats in the long grass then went to sit with their feet in the water. Not that the water was cool, but it was considerably better than being at home. The goats munched behind them, trying to extract as much goodness from the dry grass as possible.

Today's story was about Yitzchak, Yaacov, and Esau. By now, they all expected a story when they gathered, so they'd placed Zura in the middle with Abida close by so he could hear better.

At the end of the story and after some general discussion, the boys asked permission to go and play.

Once they were out of hearing Abida said, "It seems to me that most of the family's problems were caused by Yitzchak and Rivkah."

Jael took a breath and tried not to look excited by the statement. If Abida could understand the problems he had caused between his sons, there might be hope for his relationship with Reuel.

"In what way?" Zipporah asked.

"The way they each championed one of the twins then worked against each other. Although it is completely normal to have favorites."

It might be normal, but it was harmful to show favoritism. *Yahveh, please help him see. Help Zura to have wisdom to know what to say.*

"Why might Yitzchak favor Esau and Rivkah favor Yaacov?" Zura asked.

"Yitzchak favored the elder," Zipporah said.

"Esau was only a little older. Could there have been other reasons?" Zura asked. "The story tells us at least one other reason."

"Esau and Yitzchak were more compatible. They both loved hunting and being outdoors, but Yaacov enjoyed being closer to home with his mother," Abida said.

"We often favor the person most like ourselves, but what was the impact of this favoritism in Yitzchak's family?" Zura asked.

"The two brothers were estranged for years," Jael said. Reuel had felt jealous and angry at Ephah.

Zipporah sighed. "Life became a competition for Yitzchak's love and blessing."

Had Zipporah basked in the favorite daughter-in-law status, or had she found it distressing? Jael couldn't ask her. Not now, not this soon after Ephah's death and all the changes that had brought.

"We know Yitzchak and Rivkah showed favoritism, but how could they have done things differently?" Zura asked.

Yahveh, help Abida see some of the harm he has caused with his actions and words. Reuel had been devastated when his father said he wished Reuel had died rather than Ephah.

"We can always do things differently," Zipporah said. "They could have chosen to treat their twin sons the same regardless of how they felt about them."

Jael's heart was drawn more to Hanok because he needed her more. Reba was already pushing to assert his independence. He no longer welcomed his mother's hugs as he once had, but Jael was determined to keep showing consistent love to both. *Yahveh, don't let Abida repeat his mistakes and favor Reba because he's older.*

"So it's a choice for the good of others?" Abida asked, looking thoughtful.

Zura nodded. "It's a choice. I notice that when I choose not to show favoritism, my heart soon gets in line with my choice."

Thank you, Yahveh, that Abida seems to understand. Help him to apply this story to Reuel.

Reba came racing back to the shade of the tree and flopped down next to Jael. "Ima, I'm so hot. Will it ever rain?"

Jael pushed back a sweaty lock of hair on Reba's forehead. "Do you remember what rain is like?"

"Not really, but Abba used to talk about how green the land once was. He told me about rain."

"Do you know why there is no rain and the land is parched?" Zura asked.

Reba shook his head.

Zura looked across at Jael. "Do you remember?"

Jael narrowed her eyes. "It's something to do with the Israelites failing to love Yahveh with all their hearts, and souls, and strength."

"That's right. If Yahveh's people would follow and obey him

then he will pour out blessing on the land and it will rain and the land will be green again."

"I'd like to see that," Reba said. "How many people have to follow Yahveh?"

Zura smiled. "As many as possible. But at the moment, not many people do."

"But we do, don't we?" Reba said.

"We're learning," Jael said. "But so many people around us worship Baal."

"But Baal is useless." Reba pointed to the brown land around them.

"Most people can't see that," Zura said.

"What can we do?" Abida asked.

Zura paused and then raised a finger. "First, we must follow Yahveh with all our heart and strength." She raised another finger. "Children, can you think of other things we can do?"

"We can pray that our neighbors start following Yahveh," Zipporah's eldest said.

Zura smiled. "That would be an excellent thing to do."

"As our lives change to the patterns pleasing to Yahveh, they can impact other people. Only yesterday when I went to the well to draw water, a woman asked me why I seemed so at peace even after what had happened in our family," Jael said.

"And what did you tell her?" Zura asked.

"I told her I'd been listening to stories about Yahveh and the more I heard, the more they helped me."

"The change starts with us. The more we obey Yahveh and honor him, the more opportunities we will have to tell others."

Hanok leaned against his aunt and whispered something. Zura hugged him. "Can I tell the others your question?"

Hanok nodded.

"Hanok asked, 'But what if they won't listen?'"

"Then we keep praying and we keep telling them," Reba said.

"Well said, Reba," Zura said. "It won't always be easy, and some people will laugh at us, but we mustn't give up. It's too important."

"And it's the only way to have rain again," Reba said, as though all Israel's problems were now sorted out. He turned to rush off to play again.

"Reba, before you go, let's pray for our town and these lands," Zura said.

"I'll pray," he said. "If others do too."

Jael's heart thrilled as the family prayed for their neighbors and the towns they often traveled through. There was something special about young and old praying together. Yahveh must love it too.

CHAPTER THIRTY-SEVEN

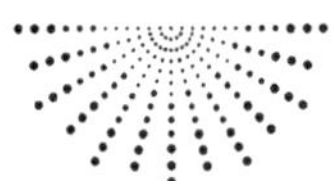

"Let's walk," Reuel said to Dedan as he laced the tent after their final day of work in the town. Tomorrow they'd move on, although he wasn't yet sure where they'd go.

"Just let me take the stew off the fire." Dedan leaned forward and lifted the pot and put it to one side.

"You've become quite the cook," Reuel said with a grin.

"You can thank Dinah for that."

"We have a lot to thank Dinah and Asher for."

Dedan grunted his assent as he covered the stew and put rocks around it to keep out any inquisitive animals.

Reuel glanced around the campsite to check it was secure, then pointed to the closest high point. There'd been a little rain overnight, and there should be a clear view from the top.

"Where were you planning to go next?" Dedan asked, as they set off.

"That was one of the things I wanted to discuss with you. Normally I'd continue south, but I'm hankering for home. I'm not sure if I will be welcome, but I want to see Jael and the boys." Tension gripped his chest as he remembered the fear written all over Hanok's face, the disappointment on Reba's, and the mix of both on Jael's.

"I've been praying for you and your family every day," Dedan said.

"Thanks," Reuel said. Asher and Dinah would be praying too. He probably should do the same, but he still wasn't sure of his welcome from the god of the Israelites. Yet Dedan hadn't been struck down for his presumption in following Yahveh.

The ground began to rise. Reuel took slow and steady strides, he still limped a little but he enjoyed using his leg muscles for a change.

"You do know you could pray too?" Dedan said with a quick glance across at Reuel.

"I'm still stuck at that point. I still can't grasp that Yahveh would welcome me to come to him. Someone who has rejected him all these years."

Dedan looked at Reuel. "I struggled with the same thing. I'd always thought of Yahveh as the Israelites' god." He shrugged. "I guess I saw the lack of welcome the Israelites gave us and thought that reflected Yahveh's attitude toward us."

Until Reuel had met Asher and Dinah, he'd always felt rejected by the Israelites. Sure, they were willing to buy his copper and bronze products and let him repair their metalwork, but there had never been any warmth. He had always been a mere coppersmith selling his wares.

Dedan continued, "Yahveh's promises to Avraham always included all peoples. Yahveh said, 'Those who bless you I will bless, and through you all the peoples of the earth will be blessed.'"

"I've been thinking about what Asher told us—that Yahveh didn't choose the Israelites because they were more numerous or intelligent or especially deserving." Reuel snorted. "Although they seem to think they are special. I just wish they'd been more obedient so we could have seen the blessings and wanted to know

Yahveh earlier." Shame curdled in his gut. Maybe knowing Yahveh earlier would have helped him. He needed to change but didn't seem to have the strength to actually do it.

"It all started when the Israelites didn't fully obey Yahveh in bringing Yahveh's judgment to these lands," Dedan said. "They allowed people to live, people who later enticed them away from worshiping Yahveh."

Reuel detoured around a large rock. He still found it hard to swallow that Yahveh had wanted Yehoshua to totally wipe out the peoples within the borders of Canaan. But he could see the results of not doing so all around him.

A stone shifted under Dedan's foot, but he quickly righted himself. "It is always going to be hard not to chase other gods. It is so much easier for people to worship what they can see and touch rather than a Creator they can't see."

"Why do you think Dinah and Asher had no statue or object to remind them of Yahveh?"

"Can't you think of a reason?" Dedan asked.

Sweat trickled between Reuel's shoulder blades. He stopped to take a breather and looked around. "I'm not sure that I can."

"What object could be used to represent Yahveh?" Dedan took a swig of water from the waterskin he was carrying.

Reuel looked around him. Even the tallest tree was not enough, nor the highest mountain.

"You see the difficulty," Dedan said. "Even the sun is not great enough to represent Yahveh, for he created it with a word from his mouth. There is no object great enough and no statue beautiful enough. Any object would only reduce Yahveh in our sight."

"So he commands his people not to have any such object."

"Exactly." Dedan turned to climb the last part of the hill. "Come on. We're nearly there."

Reuel struggled to keep up, his leg still a little stiff. "Asher mentioned Rahab from Jericho and the tricky Hivites. Have there been other non-Israelites who have followed Yahveh?"

"Do you remember the man who sells olives in the Ramoth market? He's a descendant of one of the Egyptians who accompanied Mosheh and the Israelites. He still has an Egyptian-sounding name, but he is a committed follower of Yahveh."

"You must introduce me one day," Reuel said.

Dedan stopped talking while they negotiated the last rocks of the hill. Reaching the top, Reuel paused, hands on knees. His breaths were ragged with the effort of the last section of the climb. Finally, he stood. Shielding his eyes with his hand, he looked across to where he knew the Jordan River must be. Ridge after ridge of hills glowed in the late afternoon sun.

"Despite the drought, this is a good land," Reuel said. "If the people of Israel would simply follow their god with their whole hearts, this land would be green and bountiful and oh, so very beautiful."

Dedan stared at the view. "It's easy to talk about them, but what about us?"

"What do you mean?" Reuel asked.

"The decision to follow Yahveh starts with one person, then it touches others. Like Asher and Dinah impacted me."

Dedan made it seem so easy.

"Mosheh invited our ancestor, Hobab, to follow Yahveh, but we have strayed from that choice." Dedan smoothed his beard. "All peoples are called to make that choice, and it is the best choice. A choice to return home."

"You are a good man." Reuel sighed. "I am too broken to turn to Yahveh."

"Is that the barrier preventing you from making this choice?" Dedan asked. "No person is anything but a broken vessel. I've seen you mending hundreds of pots and metal objects since we left Ramoth Gilead. When I see the pots come in, I don't see how they can be fixed, but each time you surprise me. You have the skill to mend anything."

"Not quite anything," Reuel said, thinking of his broken family.

"You see the potential and you mend it with new metal and heating and molding and beating. Whatever is needed. Then you polish it and make that joke about it lasting at least two hundred barley harvests and to bring it in again then." Dedan laughed. "If you can mend a broken bronze or copper vessel, don't you think the Creator can mend us? He's already mending me. You and I turned to strong drink to help us forget and fill our emptiness. It was laughable, like trying to fix one of your pots with woven cloth."

Reuel sighed. "I've been a failure as a husband and father."

"Not to minimize what you did," Dedan said, "but failure doesn't have to be forever."

"It's tempting to let your words soothe me, but I am a failure as a father and even worse as a husband. I gave the boys the scraps of my time. The moment they annoyed me, I handed them over to their mother and went back to work. Work has also been my strong drink."

"It seems we men often use work like that," Dedan said. He took a handful of water from his waterskin and splashed it over his head and beard.

Ever since their final meal, when Reuel had seen how Asher and Dinah related to each other, he'd been thinking about his relationship with Jael.

"I have never looked to Jael's needs. I've seen her as someone to serve me so I can achieve my ambitions. My mother always anticipated my needs before I asked, and I've demanded Jael do the same. I often let her know by critical words and frowns that I thought she had failed to serve me as well as my mother." Reuel shook his head, sorrow deep in his heart, remembering how the spark had faded from Jael during their first year of marriage. "I was proud that I didn't beat her like some husbands, but I've beaten her down with my demands just as surely as if I'd used my fist."

Dedan was silent.

"I haven't seen her as a person like me with her own needs, and I haven't bothered to find out what she wants. I have thought her too demanding when she asked me to spend time with the children. Maybe she was wanting my time, too, but she knew me well enough not to even bother asking."

Dedan looked thoughtful. "I have regrets too. If I'd known my wife would die so early, I like to think I would have treasured her more."

"Treasured…" Reuel said thoughtfully. "Yes, that's what I've failed to do. I have never told Jael what I appreciated about her. I could see the way my words made her hang her head, but I thought the failure was hers for being too sensitive."

"Asher never failed to thank Dinah for everything she did. He made her stand tall, and she adored him."

Jael had adored him before they were married, but Reuel had seen the disappointment in her eyes too often since. Every day he took her for granted or belittled her, she had shrunk a little, had become more shadow-like.

"I was not kind," Reuel said.

Dedan pointed to a nearby flower. "Asher said that kindness in a marriage is like watering a plant."

"I have not given her any water and Jael has shriveled. She is probably glad to be rid of me." Reuel stared at the ground ashamed.

The sun was sinking in the sky and staining the clouds with pink. They would have to go back to their tents soon. "I'm afraid to go home in case Jael asks me to leave again."

"But if you don't go, you'll never know if things have changed," Dedan said.

"But what if her attitude is still the same?"

"You have changed. Didn't you say that Jael's sister is a follower of Yahveh? Perhaps Yahveh has been changing Jael too."

"Perhaps, but Jael followed my lead and never paid much attention to Zura's beliefs."

"Well, we can pray for the situation. We must pray for your father as well."

Reuel swallowed. "I fear that is a lost cause."

"What did I just say? No one is a lost cause for Yahveh. What your family has been through and your being away might be the very thing that opens their hearts to Yahveh."

Dedan was a man full of hope. How had Yahveh changed him so quickly?

Dedan shifted his feet and squared his shoulders. "More importantly than Jael and your father, what is your response to Yahveh going to be?"

Reuel admired Dedan for having the courage to ask. It was almost a relief to answer. "If he'll welcome me, then I'll follow him."

Dedan stood and hauled Reuel to his feet and enthusiastically hugged him. "Good choice, brother. Good choice."

And all at once, Reuel knew it was. A weight rolled off him, a weight he hadn't known was so heavy. Yes, this was the best choice he'd made in his life. A choice that would impact everything else.

CHAPTER THIRTY-EIGHT

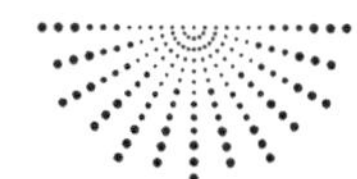

"*D*inah, Dinah, come quickly! The boys have returned," Asher yelled over his shoulder as he enfolded Reuel in a back-crunching hug. "We missed you."

"And we've missed you," Dedan said as he was hugged in turn. "We've decided to head back to Ramoth Gilead, but Reuel insisted we detour a little to see you again."

"We're both glad you did." Dinah arrived, out of breath and with flour up to her elbows. "Come in and sit down. I'll get something to drink. The bread will be ready soon. I knew I baked extra for a reason."

Reuel and Dedan followed Asher into the guest room. Soon after, Dinah brought refreshments.

"Tell us your news," Asher said once Dinah had seated herself.

"Most of it is just routine, mending and polishing copper and bronze," Reuel said. "And enduring Dedan's cooking."

Dedan punched Reuel's shoulder.

Reuel ducked and laughed. "Truthfully, his cooking is much improved, thanks to Dinah's instruction."

"Reuel's telling you the boring stuff. He didn't come all this way to talk about mending bronze," Dedan said.

Reuel swallowed. Asher and Dinah would be thrilled at his decision, but it was still so new that he didn't know quite how to start. Asher and Dinah were looking at him, obviously hoping for the very news he wanted to share. "I made my decision."

"The most important decision?" Asher asked.

Reuel nodded. "I've decided to entrust my life to Yahveh and follow him."

"That's wonderful," Asher said.

Dinah struggled to her knees and threw her arms around him. "Welcome to the family."

"That's what it feels like," Reuel said. "Like I've come home." He had never really felt at home before, but he was now recognizing the feeling as he was experiencing it. It was something he'd longed for all his life.

Dinah released him and they both sat down. She was smiling as if she'd never stop. If she'd been a little girl, she would have been bouncing in excitement.

Reuel continued. "I struggled to make the decision, but once it was made, I felt such peace."

"I think it's usually like that. Yahveh's great enemy doesn't want us to follow our Creator. He will throw everything in our path to prevent us making the right choice," Asher said. "My experience was the same, and so was Dinah's."

"And mine," Dedan said. "I was battling for days to choose Yahveh. It was such a relief and joy when I finally made the choice."

Dinah sniffed the air. "The bread smells ready. I'll be back as soon as I can with a celebration meal."

"Don't go to any trouble," Reuel said. "We want to see you more than we want to eat."

"That's good to hear, but you are young men. You need your food. It just so happens that we have cheese and olives."

She got to her feet and left the room.

"We'll have to wait for the rest of your story. Dinah won't want to miss anything," Asher said.

Dinah didn't take long. Soon she was passing around the still-warm bread with its unexpected accompaniments. Reuel didn't think he'd ever tasted anything so good, but maybe it was the company and the joy in his heart. Everything seemed renewed, even his taste buds.

It didn't take long for Reuel to finish his story. "Once Dedan assured me that Yahveh accepted broken people like me, I was willing."

"Yahveh specializes in accepting broken people," Asher said. "In fact, broken people are more likely to realize they need Yahveh."

Zura had said it was because she was blind that she'd considered Yahveh. Not that Reuel had ever let her speak much about her beliefs.

"Proud and self-reliant people find it easier to reject Yahveh," Asher said.

Dinah nodded. "We often pray that people will face tough times so they'll become aware of their need to follow Yahveh."

"Reuel hasn't completed his usual circuit. He feels he should go home to see his family," Dedan said.

Reuel laughed nervously. "I always rejected any gods, and my wife followed my lead. My change of heart may give her another reason to separate from me."

"Yahveh is a great and gracious God," Dinah said. "It wouldn't surprise me if you find he's already working in your wife's heart. He is always seeking us." She held out a bowl of olives. "You haven't eaten enough."

Reuel took the proffered olives and some more bread. "We've been talking too much, but the conversation is as sustaining as the bread."

"Have you been praying for your wife?" Dinah asked.

"Every day," Reuel said.

"And I've been praying daily for Reuel's family too," Dedan said.

"She's been well prayed for, then, because we've been praying for all of you every morning and evening," Asher said.

"Are we supposed to pray twice a day?" Reuel asked.

Asher finished his mouthful. "There are no rules about it. We like to pray morning and evening because it means our first and last thoughts are of Yahveh. It is too easy to forget him when there are so few other faithful followers around us to encourage us."

"But we often pray silently for those around us as we go about our day," Dinah said. "The more we pray, the more natural it becomes. Like breathing."

Reuel wondered if he could learn to pray for each of his customers as he made and repaired their metal goods.

Asher looked over at Reuel. "Are you praying for your father?"

Reuel shook his head. "I can't."

The memories of his father's rejection and his final words were still like a punch in the gut.

"He hurt you, didn't he?" Asher said gently.

Reuel clenched his jaw. "I might be able to pray for him if he were sorry for what he said and did."

Asher looked toward his wife. "Dinah, why don't you share what you've learned. You have had a lot more to forgive than I have."

Dinah took a big breath. "The two hardest people for me to forgive were my aunt and my first husband."

Reuel was not surprised she had struggled to forgive them, after all one had made her unwelcome and treated her like a slave. The other was a drunk who had beaten her.

"I remembered the story of Yosef and how he forgave his brothers. The first thing I learned to do was pray for them." Dinah laughed. "At the beginning I prayed through gritted teeth with the attitude, you-want-me-to-forgive-well-I'll-do-it-but-don't-bless-them."

"They didn't deserve anything good," Reuel said. And neither did his father.

"No, they didn't deserve it, but neither do we. We tend to compare ourselves with the wrong standard."

Reuel wrinkled his brow. "What do you mean?"

"I compared myself with my husband and aunt and thought I measured up well, but we need to compare ourselves with Yahveh. Compared with him, we're broken and impure, and we don't deserve any blessings."

Ouch. Dinah was right. He had been so focused on his father's failures that he quickly forgot how broken he was himself without Yahveh.

"Slowly my prayers progressed to asking Yahveh to change them, but I still didn't want them to have the blessing of being accepted by him." Dinah laughed. "But Yahveh never gave up on changing me. After a long, long time I was able to pray that Yahveh would rescue them, save them, but I still wasn't at the stage of forgiving them. Like you, I wanted them to be sorry before I was willing to forgive. I wanted them to admit they had wronged me and for them to beg me for forgiveness. Neither ever did."

"Did you ever forgive them?" Dedan asked.

"I did, but I didn't do it for them. I did it for me," Dinah said. "Failing to forgive made my stomach ache when I thought of them, and that wasn't healthy. So I prayed to Yahveh for strength to forgive and made the decision to live each day as if I had forgiven them. Gradually my attitude toward them changed."

"Did either of them ever know you forgave them?" Reuel asked.

"My aunt became really sick at the end of her life. I went to visit and told her I forgave her. She didn't say anything, but before I left, she squeezed my hand. I think she understood something. Maybe she was thanking me, even if she couldn't say the words." Dinah sighed. "I never got a chance to tell my husband I forgave him because he died well before I reached that stage."

Dinah and Asher knew Reuel's parents had played favorites. He'd told Dinah that even before he knew her name. But they didn't know about the words that had plunged into him like a dagger.

Reuel took a small piece of bread and soon found himself shredding it instead of eating it. Dedan looked at the bread and then looked at Reuel's face. "Dinah, could I help you by carrying things?"

She looked surprised but said, "I'd be glad for the help."

Had Dedan seen that Reuel wanted to speak but struggled to do so in front of three others? The moment Dinah and Dedan had left the room, Reuel spoke up. He must not waste the opportunity Dedan had given him. "You know my parents each had their favorite son. It destroyed any brotherly feeling between Ephah and myself, and it made me dread going home once my mother had died."

"I remember." Asher leaned forward.

"After my brother died, my father took it very hard. Before I left, he said, 'I wish you had died instead of your brother.'" Reuel took a shaky breath. "That hurt."

Asher reached across and placed his hand on Reuel's shoulder. "No father should ever say such a thing to their child," Asher said. "I see why it would be a struggle to forgive. Thank you for telling me, for it lets me know how to pray for you and your father."

"I will need your prayers, and there is no need to keep this to yourself. I don't mind if Dinah knows, but I couldn't talk about it in front of everyone."

"Hence Dedan's thoughtful exit."

"He has become a good friend. One of the many blessings Yahveh has sent to me, along with you and Dinah."

Reuel took a deep breath. Just speaking of these things was a relief. "Would you pray for me now? I'm afraid to go home. I didn't handle my brother's death well." He took another breath. Speaking of his failures was so hard. "I drank to forget and neglected my family. Eventually my wife asked me to leave because I beat my younger son very badly." Shame washed over him again as it did every time he thought of his last day at home.

"You do know Yahveh can forgive your past?" Asher asked.

Reuel nodded. "But I still feel the shame of it."

"Shame is hard to erase. Satan loves to accuse and remind us of our failures. But you're right. Praying is what we should do." Asher got to his feet and Reuel stood too. Asher laid his hands on Reuel's shoulders, their weight like a hug, heavy and comforting.

"Yahveh, Creator and sustainer of all, thank you for Reuel. Thank you that he has made the most important decision of all and now follows you. Thank you that knowing you changes everything."

Reuel was just beginning to grasp the effects of these changes.

"Yahveh, you know how Reuel's father has hurt him, especially with the unkind words he spoke after Ephah's death. You know why his father would say such a thing, but I expect he speaks out of a place of brokenness."

That was a new thought. Reuel had never heard anything about his father's background. Memories of Reuel's grandparents were shadowy as they'd died when he was very young.

"Help Reuel to rely on you, and give him the strength to forgive those he needs to forgive. Help him to come to you for forgiveness each day and to extend the forgiveness he receives to those around him. Not just because you command it, but also because forgiving others is the best way to live. It brings peace and joy to our hearts as we obey you."

Already he had seen evidence of what Yahveh meant to those who followed him.

"Bless Reuel's family. May his wife and family turn toward you too. Help his wife's sister to have a profound influence on the family so her faith becomes theirs. May not only Reuel's wife, but his sons and his father and his brother's family all come to know you. Bring your peace to their family. And as Yahveh blesses us in the Torah, 'May Yahveh bless and keep you, may he make his face to shine upon you and be gracious to you both, may Yahveh turn his face toward you and give you peace.'"

Yes, Yahveh, please help me to be part of the process of my family coming to know you. Help me to trust you.

Footsteps approached the room. Asher leaned forward to kiss Reuel on both cheeks. "Bless you, my son."

CHAPTER THIRTY-NINE

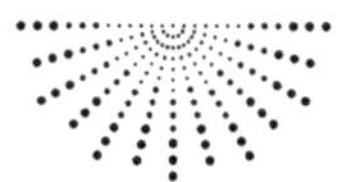

"*R*euel, there she is! Ramoth Gilead," Dedan said, pointing ahead.

Reuel slumped and a tightness encircled his chest. Would there be a welcome for him, or would Jael take one look at him and ask him to leave again?

Yahveh, may she give me another chance. Help me to show her that you are changing me. Give me the strength to love her as she deserves.

Dedan strode in front, leading his camel and the goat who'd caused them so much more trouble than its milk had been worth. Next time they'd simply buy milk.

Dedan glanced back over his shoulder and waited for Reuel to catch up. They could now walk next to each other as the track had petered out and broadened into a flat plain as they approached the town walls.

"You will always be welcome at my place, you know," Dedan said, "if things don't go as we hope."

Reuel gave a grateful smile. "Thank you. I've been praying constantly ever since we got close."

"Why don't you bring the camels and store your things at my place until everything is worked out?"

"Thanks so much, I will accept your kind offer.." It would be far more noticeable to curious neighbors if Reuel arrived home with his camels and baggage and then had to leave again.

On arriving at Dedan's house, the aunt he lived with was cautiously welcoming. She was probably relieved when Dedan had left and taken his drunkenness with him.

After unloading, feeding, and watering the animals, Reuel washed, changed his clothes, and trimmed his beard.

"Before you go, let's pray together again," Dedan said. "And I'll be praying until you come and tell me what's happened."

Yahveh had given him many gifts during his last trip, but Dedan, Asher, and Dinah were the best gifts of all.

* * *

The gateway into the courtyard was closed but opened at Reuel's touch. All was quiet inside. His breath caught in his throat. Had they moved elsewhere? No. There was fresh manure on the ground and clothes drying on a beam to one side.

He walked to the doorway of the home and called, "Anyone home?"

Total silence.

On the floor, toward the back, he saw a little copper sheep. He swallowed. He'd made that for Reba.

The outside gate creaked and Reuel whirled round. Disappointment. It was only the woman from next door.

"They've gone to the stream outside the back gate," she said.

He thanked her, closed the gate as he had found it, and set off for the stream. *Yahveh, calm me. Help Jael, Reba, and Hanok not to be afraid of me.*

It was that look of fear that continued to haunt him and make him worry about the future. A look he had deserved.

Reuel took a deep breath and continued walking through the streets of the town leading to the back gate. He greeted the gate-keepers then went out the gate and scanned along the line of the stream. There. They were near a large oak tree covered in bright green new growth. The two boys were half hidden in the branches. A lump clogged his throat.

Please, Yahveh, please.

His legs shook but Reuel slowly walked forward. His father was among the group, which meant not only was he alive but that at some point he'd left off staring at the wall.

No one had seen Reuel yet, for their backs were toward him. Reuel glanced over his shoulder back at the town. Someone waved from the town wall. Dedan. Dedan held his clasped hands above his head to let Reuel know he was praying. *Thank you, Yahveh, for a friend like Dedan.* It gave him courage to go forward. Forward to who knew what kind of welcome.

"Ima, there's Abba!" Reba's clear voice rang out. Everyone on the riverbank turned to look where Reba was pointing.

Reuel's face warmed. He didn't want to be the center of attention.

Reba scrambled down the tree, but Hanok stayed where he was, watching. As Reuel approached, he could only look at Jael. She was chewing her lip. She didn't rush forward, but neither did she turn away. Reba reached the bottom of the tree in a flurry of broken twigs and leaves and halted, indecision written all over his face. He looked at Jael. She held out her hand and drew him to her side.

Above them, Hanok was clinging to the tree, white-faced. "Ima," he wailed.

Reuel flinched. He had caused the fear on Hanok's face and the indecision on Jael's and Reba's. There was a sour taste in his mouth and shame filled his belly. *Yahveh, help!*

"I can't get down," Hanok wailed.

"Someone should help him," Reuel said to Jael. "Will he let me climb up to him?"

"I can't do it," Jael said, gesturing to her tunic. She looked up at Hanok. "Abba is going to climb up and help you."

"I want you," Hanok said, voice quavering.

"I can't climb the tree, but I'll be right here."

Yahveh, help Hanok not to be so afraid. Don't let him fall.

"Maybe I should come with you," Reba said. "I can help."

Reuel nodded. "Good idea, s—" He'd been about to say "son" but swallowed the word. It might not be welcomed.

"Thank you, Reuel," Zura said.

Zura's expression welcomed him, but she was the person Reuel was least concerned about. He couldn't read his father's expression.

Reuel boosted Reba into one side of the tree then pulled himself up onto the lowest branch. He climbed steadily, making sure Reba was keeping up. Above him, Hanok still clung to the tree trunk and watched him, eyes wide in his pale face.

"Hold on, Hanok. We're nearly there," Reuel said with the voice he used to calm the animals if they got spooked by something. It seemed to work, for Hanok's little arms relaxed and his face gained color.

"Reba, can you sit on the branch behind Hanok and give him a hug?"

Reba obeyed and gave his brother a good hug. Reuel would have liked to gather Hanok and Reba to his chest and never let go, but there was no telling what would happen if they resisted. He couldn't risk either of the boys falling.

He waited until Hanok had relaxed a little.

"Reba, if we go slowly, I think Hanok can get down on his own. Why don't you lead and show Hanok the way?"

Hanok swallowed and slowly, branch by branch allowed himself to be led down the tree. Reuel helped him several times, but each time he touched Hanok he felt the boy stiffen. It made Reuel's heart ache, but he couldn't blame Hanok. Reuel had caused these reactions by his own actions. It would take time to win Hanok's trust again, just as it would to win Jael's.

Help us.

At the base of the tree, Hanok ran into his mother's arms.

Reuel nodded at his father. "Good to see you outside."

"Zura and Jael have been a real blessing," his father said.

Blessing. That wasn't a word he'd heard his father use before, but it wasn't the time to talk further now. Jael went over to Zura, and they talked in an undertone. As Jael's back was toward him, Reuel had no idea what they were saying. His hands were clammy, but he reminded himself that Dedan had promised to keep praying. *Let me have time to speak with Jael.*

"Reba and Hanok, come with Grandpa and me. We can build a dam," Zura said.

"You can't see to build," Hanok said.

"That's why I need your help," Zura said. "If you take my hand, you can lead me into the stream, and I can feel to dig up some of the bigger rocks."

Zura squeezed Jael's hand and mouthed something at her. Jael pointed with her chin further along the riverbank. Aware of Reba's eyes on them both, Reuel followed Jael, his heart pounding in his ears. *Help us to be able to talk.*

Their feet crunched across the dry grass.

"Thank you for being willing to talk with me," Reuel said, feeling a fool but not knowing how to overcome the barriers between them.

"I am your wife." Jael didn't look at him.

That sounded like a good start, but was it? He didn't want a wife who simply did her duty but with no feeling of love toward him. Not that he'd ever cared much about her feelings before, but having seen the way Asher and Dinah related, he wanted what they had.

"Did you have a good trip?" Jael asked.

He hated this stilted exchange. "Business was good because we hadn't been there for a while. I sold all the mirrors I had made."

Jael paced slowly along, avoiding the rough edges of the stream. "They are beautiful work. I'm not surprised they sold."

Oh, this was hard.

"Many things happened on the way," Reuel said. "Life-changing things." *Help, Yahveh. I need courage. Don't let her hate me for my decision.* A decision he felt he needed to talk about now, not later.

"Oh?" Jael partly turned toward him and raised an eyebrow.

Reuel swallowed. "I met a couple, an older couple who spoke to me of many things and helped me to see them in new ways."

"Oh?" Jael said again.

She wasn't going to make this easy for him.

"They were Israelites. True followers of Yahveh."

Jael said "oh" again, but in a totally different tone than before. As though she suddenly perked up her ears.

Reuel squared his shoulders. "They told me many stories of Yahveh. What they said made sense."

She turned toward him then. "Are you saying you've become a follower of Yahveh?"

He couldn't tell by her tone if she thought this would be a good or bad thing. Sweat broke out along his brow. Following Yahveh was still so new, so wonderful. He wanted her to share his joy, but he had always scoffed at Yahveh before. He couldn't and wouldn't blame her if she was horrified. Was this to be the end of his marriage?

He took a deep breath. "Yes, I have recently become a follower of Yahveh."

"My brother, that is news indeed." Jael's voice quavered, and he was afraid to look at her.

He said the only thing that came into his head. "I'm your husband, not your brother."

"No, I think we are also like blood family."

He looked at her then, and she was smiling at him. A smile that warmed him deep inside. He wrinkled his forehead. "But we've been family for a long time."

"Now we're a new kind of family. Zura has also been telling us the stories of Yahveh."

His chest tightened and tears sprang into his eyes.

"All of you. Father and Reba and Hanok as well?"

She nodded. "And Zipporah."

His heart was pounding. "And are you all followers of Yahveh now?"

"I'm not sure about all of us, but we're all moving in that direction. We've been learning to pray and how to follow him."

Suddenly he couldn't contain himself. He grabbed her about the waist and lifted her off her feet.

"Put me down you oaf. You're squeezing me too tight," she gasped.

He put her down like she was a delicate flower. "I'm sorry. I was just so excited. I've been afraid about how you'd react to hearing I've decided to follow Yahveh."

The corner of her mouth quirked up. "Well, you don't need to be afraid any longer. I was afraid too. Afraid you'd be angry we were all listening to stories. I was worried how to tell you and whether this would be the end of us."

It hurt that she'd been so afraid of him, but he'd given her reason. "And Father?"

"Zura started telling him stories soon after you left, then took him for walks where she told him more. He's changed a lot."

A lot? Had he changed in his attitude toward Reuel?

"He's beginning to understand he has not been the best of fathers," Jael said. "But give him time. Yahveh doesn't change us all at once." She sat on a fallen log. "Perhaps too much change would be too much for us. He seems to do things at a different pace than ours, but I am grateful that Hanok is slowly losing his fears."

Shame swirled within him. "Caused by what I did?"

She nodded, looking sad. "He had terrible nightmares until we prayed together for him."

"I'm sorry, more sorry than you can know. Sorry for everything."

"Hanok has suffered badly."

She spoke with a new self-assurance that was so different from the timid woman he'd grown used to. She'd probably changed as much as he had. They'd need time to adjust.

Jael looked back over her shoulder toward the rest of the family. "We'd better get back. Hanok gets anxious if I'm away too long."

"And he might be afraid of how I'll treat you. I hope to prove to him that I've changed."

"He'll need you to go slowly," she said.

He suspected all of them would need to adjust slowly. "It's a bit like starting all over again."

"Exactly."

They started walking slowly back toward the others.

Jael flushed. "Do you have somewhere you can stay? It's been hot. We're all sleeping on the roof and there's not much room."

"I have been traveling with a new friend, Dedan, and he has room, but can I come to your story times?"

She nodded. "Bring your friend if he wants to come."

"Oh, he'll want to come. He'll love the chance to be with other believers. He made his choice before me and was the person who helped me to see things clearly."

"Then we'll want to meet him," she said.

They were now close to the others.

"Shall I tell them you'll come to the evening meal?" Jael asked.

He nodded. She turned and walked back toward the others. He

waved, and his father and Jael returned his wave. He began to walk back toward Ramoth Gilead.

Thank you, thank you, Yahveh. You couldn't have given me a better gift than a wife who also wants to follow you.

On the top of the wall, he could still see Dedan pacing one way and then the other. Reuel waved and hoped his wave communicated what was in his heart. *All is well. Yahveh has answered our prayers.*

Reuel broke into a run. There'd still be time to check the animals and unpack and spend some time in prayer before the meal. Perhaps Dedan would be willing to cook something for them to take.

He might not be able to stay at his father's home yet, but he'd pray they'd all be back on the road before long. Back on the road but following a different pattern from before. One in which he wasn't lord and master but rather a servant following Yahveh, Creator and ruler of all. He couldn't wait.

EPILOGUE

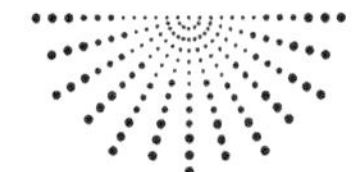

Two years later

"Oh, Jael, he kicked. Quick. Come and feel," Zura said.

Jael hurried to her sister's side and placed her hand on Zura's belly. She felt nothing until there was a sudden push under her hand. "I felt him. Or is it a her?"

"I don't mind which," Zura said with her hand on her bulging belly and a smile of shining joy on her face. "I never expected to be a mother. Not long to wait now."

None of them had expected Zura to marry, but Dedan had been interested in Zura from the first time they'd met. Reuel said Dedan had asked many questions about Zura even before they did meet. Having met Yahveh himself and suffered the loss of his entire family, Dedan wanted a wife who loved Yahveh more than she loved him. He'd seen beyond Zura's blindness and scarring to the beautiful person beneath.

"I am blessed beyond measure." Zura blushed. "Dedan is the most wonderful husband, and he will be an amazing father to our little one."

Jael leaned in and kissed her sister's brow.

"I am delighted for you. And your little one will have an almost-sibling with my daughter, as they'll be close in age. Reba and Hanok will be fighting over who gets to protect the two of them."

"Your boys are great older brothers," Zura said.

Jael laughed. "When they're not fighting between themselves or trying to prove who is the better coppersmith."

"Their skills are improving. I can feel the shape of their items as I polish. I can still tell whose is whose, but one day they will be as skilled as their father."

"We're hoping they might have Dedan's cooking skills," Jael said.

"We don't want them to imitate Reuel's," Zura said with a chuckle.

"You're right." After Reuel had made one or two attempts at cooking, Jael had asked if they could leave it to Dedan. He did most of the cooking for their households as they traveled, which left Jael with more time for the new baby.

The first six months of Reuel's return hadn't been easy, for there were many patterns in their marriage and parenting and the relationship with Abida to work on. With much prayer and patience, Yahveh had brought them through. Through to a place of peace and contentment and spurts of such joy that sometimes Jael couldn't stop praising Yahveh.

Three times a year, they would collect Asher and Dinah and go to Shiloh together to celebrate Pesach, Shavuot, and Sukkot. They were times of thankfulness and much laughter. Abida loved being with another couple his age, and he'd spent much time with Asher. After the first festival at Shiloh, he'd come to Reuel in tears and they'd become reconciled.

And Reuel? He was becoming the man she'd always dreamed of. Of course, he wasn't perfect, no more than she was, but the changes were increasingly noticeable. He still worked hard, and he still wanted to be the best coppersmith possible, but he also took plenty of time for his family. Even better, he spent time with her. He was thankful for all she did, and they were working as a true team, appreciating the other and being appreciated. Reuel had asked Asher how to show kindness and followed Asher's advice. Jael's face warmed. Things were good, very good, between them.

"Mama, come quickly," Hanok yelled. "Water is falling out of the sky!"

"Help me outside." Zura clutched at Jael's arm. "I want to smell the rain."

They hurried outside as the rain spattered on the roof. By the time they reached the courtyard, it was falling with giant plops onto the baked earth. The air was filled with the smell of dampness, a smell Jael had almost forgotten.

Zura pulled Jael's arm and stepped out into the rain.

"You'll get wet," Jael said.

"Who cares?" Zura tilted her head and allowed the drops to wet her face.

Jael laughed and joined her. Within moments, the children were all around them, jumping and trying to catch raindrops in their mouths.

"What's going on here?" Reuel said with laughter in his voice as he came out of the workshop.

"It's rain, Abba," Hanok said. "I love it."

Reuel ruffled his already sodden curls. "I do, too, son. Rain will make the grass and plants grow. It will make everyone happy."

Jael walked over to Reuel, and he put his arm around her. She put her head against his shoulder as he drew her close.

The green might not last long, for the people so easily forgot their vows to Yahveh and were ensnared again by the cruel gods of Canaan.

But for Jael and Reuel and Zura and Dedan, their households would follow Yahveh to the end of their days. And if Jael had anything to do with it, so would future generations.

ENJOYED BRONZE AND BROKENNESS?

A book can never have too many reviews. My first novel has now passed 1300 ratings and I appreciate every one.

This book is independently published which means the only way it will be discovered is if readers tell others. Online reviews are an easy way of doing this.

How to write a review — easy as 1—2—3

1. A few sentences about why you liked the book or what kind of readers might enjoy this book. Even one word turns a mere star rating into a review.
2. Upload your review — the same review can be copied and pasted to each site. Look on my website for the post, *Reviews the where and how,* for the priority sites.
3. If you loved the book please also share your review on social media or by word of mouth. Anywhere you can spread the word is helpful.

HISTORICAL NOTES

<u>Names of the characters</u>

It is not easy to find appropriate names for my characters because we only know a very limited number of Midianite names. Another challenge is that we know far more male than female names. For Zura's name I adapted the male name, Zur, mentioned in Numbers 25:15.

One of the difficulties about writing a story where many of the incidents are well known is figuring out how to make the story fresh. I decided to call the biblical characters by less familiar names to make us enter their world with new eyes. I consulted several places for how to better anglicize the Old Testament names.

<u>Names of God</u>

You might have noticed that I used both capitals and non-capitals when referring to God. If it is written as god (lower case) then the character is not a believer (yet).

I have tried to use the names that followers of God used in the days of the story. Hence names like "Yahveh" or the "Creator."

Many of you will know that Jewish folk today don't use the

name Yahveh as a mark of respect. However, this custom probably developed much later than the events in this novel.

Canaanite gods

There were many gods of the Canaanites. Some are mentioned in this book. Baal was a distinct god in his own right but the term could also be used as a plural to represent a collection of gods.

Copper/Bronze

Why did I make this a story about bronze/copper workers? Jael, of tent peg fame, and her husband Heber, are listed as descendants of Hobab, Moses' brother-in-law (Judges 4:11). They are also called Kenites and apparently the word likely means "coppersmith." It was interesting to research everything I could about copper and bronze in ancient times. Deuteronomy 8:9 tells us that the Promised Land would be a place where they could "dig copper out of the hills."

STORYTELLER FRIENDS

Becoming a **storyteller friend** (https://subscribe.storyteller-christine.com/) will ensure you don't miss out on new books, deals, and behind the scenes book news. Once you're signed up, check your junk mail or the promotions folder (for gmail addresses) for the confirmation email. This two-stage process ensures only true friends can join.

Facebook: As well as a public author page, I also have a VIP group (https://www.facebook.com/groups/242910632748639) which you need to ask permission to join. Those in this group pray for this book ministry. They also vote on covers, comment on book blurbs…and are free to ask questions.

BookBub - allows you to see my top book recommendations and be alerted to any new releases and special deals. It is free to join.

DISCUSSION QUESTIONS

- Who were your favorite characters? Why?
- What were significant steps in their spiritual journeys?
- What were significant barriers?
- Did you learn any new things about the ancient cultures?
- Did you learn any new things about the biblical stories?
- What were the original beliefs of Reuel and his family?
- Without written scriptures, it would have been easy to forget the Lord. How did believers remain in the Lord?
- Choose a character and trace their faith journey.
- Which faith journey do you most relate to? Why?
- How did this story encourage or inspire you?
- What might be some lessons or warnings for marriage?
- What did you learn from this story that you can apply to your life today?

Please feel free to write your own discussion questions. I would love to see them and am happy to include them for others if you give permission.

FICTION BY CHRISTINE DILLON

Prior to writing Biblical-era fiction, I wrote a six-book contemporary Australian set of novels.

I prefer you to buy the ebooks/audio directly from my online store (https://payhip.com/ChristineDillon). It uses PayPal or Stripe (Visa/Mastercard).

Book 1 is also available in Dutch (*Verborgen Grenade*).

Of course the books are available from a wide range of other stores.

The *Light of Nations* series will likely be more than twelve books. The best way to hear about upcoming books is to subscribe and become a storyteller friend.

ACKNOWLEDGMENTS

In Ephesians 6 we are warned that those who follow Jesus are in a daily, spiritual battle. This has been apparent in every book I've written. *Bronze and Brokenness* nearly broke me. The first draft took much longer to write than usual (six months) and my mother's death was in the tail end of that time. There were many times I nearly gave up and thought, "Why am I doing this to myself?" Two things kept me going: the prayers of supporters and the words, often via online reviews, of people who loved my books. Thank you.

Thank you to my nephew, Tim, for the title. It was set much earlier in the process than usual. The funny thing is that he hasn't read any of my novels. Maybe he'll read this one!

Thanks as ever to my team:

Joy Lankshear with the cover.

Laura Tharion for edits on story, character, flow, pacing.

Iola Goulton on copy editing.

The proofreading team (they pick up more than proofreading errors) — Serene L, Susie L, and Cathy L (first-timers), Stephanie M, Anne M, Suzanne R, Lizzie R, and Elizabeth W.

Thank you also to the many (often unknown by me) who pray these books into existence and then continue praying through the long process of research, writing, editing, proofreading, and into readers' hands. Your part is much bigger than we comprehend.

*1-2-1 Discipleship: Helping One Another Grow Spiritually
(Christian Focus, Ross-shire, Scotland, 2009).*

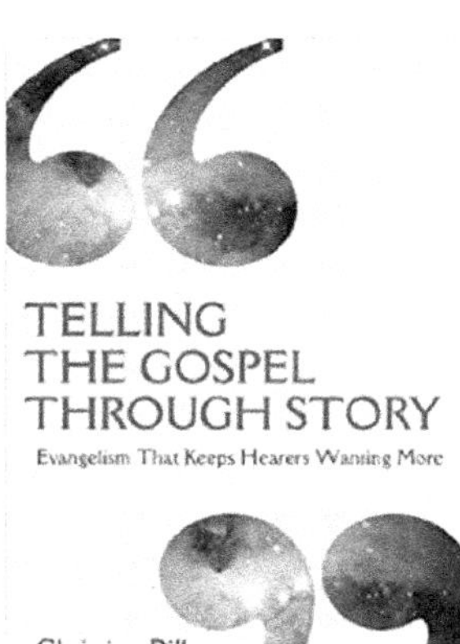

*Telling the Gospel Through Story: Evangelism That Keeps Hearers
Wanting More (IVP, Downer's Grove, Illinois, 2012).*

Stories Aren't Just For Kids: Busting 10 Myths About Bible Storytelling (2017).

This book is free for subscribers. It's a taster book and includes many testimonies to get you excited about the potential of Bible storying. These first three books have also been translated into Chinese.

Sword Fighting: Applying God's word to win the battle for our mind (July, 2020).

This book is also available in German under the title: *Siegreich Sein: mit Gottes Wort.*

ABOUT THE AUTHOR

Christine worked in Taiwan from 1999 to 2021 and still works with OMF International, but now based out of Australia.

It's best not to ask Christine, "Where are you from?" She's a missionary kid who isn't sure if she should say her passport country (Australia) or her Dad's country (New Zealand) or where she's spent most of her life (Taiwan, Malaysia, and the Philippines).

Christine used to be a physiotherapist, but now writes storyteller on airport forms. She spends most of her time either telling Bible stories or training others to do so.

Christine loves hiking, cycling, swimming, snorkeling, reading, and genealogical research.

facebook.com/storytellerchristine

pinterest.com/storytellerchristine

bookbub.com/authors/christine-dillon

www.ingramcontent.com/pod-product-compliance
Lightning Source LLC
Chambersburg PA
CBHW050439200726
48295CB00024B/734